REDEMPTION STREET

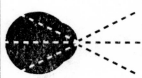

This Large Print Book carries the
Seal of Approval of N.A.V.H.

REDEMPTION STREET

REED FARREL COLEMAN

WHEELER PUBLISHING
A part of Gale, Cengage Learning

GALE
CENGAGE Learning

Detroit • New York • San Francisco • New Haven, Conn • Waterville, Maine • London

GALE
CENGAGE Learning

LIBRARY OF CONGRESS CATALOGING-IN-PUBLICATION DATA

Coleman, Reed Farrel.
  Redemption Street / by Reed Farrel Coleman.
    p. cm.
  "Wheeler Publishing Large Print Softcover"—T.p. verso.
  ISBN-13: 978-1-59722-836-7 (softcover : alk. paper)
  ISBN-10: 1-59722-836-2 (softcover : alk. paper)
  1. Prager, Moe (Fictitious character)—Fiction. 2. Private investigators—New York (State)—New York—Fiction. 3. Ex-police officers—Fiction. 4. New York (N.Y.)—Fiction. 5. Retirees—Fiction. 6. Large type books. I. Title.
  PS3553.O47445R43 2008
  813'.54—dc22   2008028199

Published in 2008 by arrangement with DHS Literary Agency.

Printed in the United States of America
1 2 3 4 5 6 7 12 11 10 09 08

FOREWORD
BY PETER SPIEGELMAN

I've been reading detective fiction for close to forty years, and more if you count Batman comics. While I'm catholic in my tastes (I draw the line at crime-busting vampires and talking cats), I've long been partial to the hardboiled private eye novel. I've had many conversations with writers and readers about the pleasures of these novels, and while I'm not sure I subscribe to all the theories I've heard about their appeal — the reassurance of seeing order brought from chaos, the vicarious experience of courage, brilliance, and moral surefootedness, the darker thrills of violence or vengeance by proxy, etc. — I do know that the best of the breed delivers what the best fiction of any sort does: a distinctive narrative voice, a palpable sense of place, and a compelling and fully realized protagonist. Which brings me to Reed Farrel Coleman and

Moe Prager.

It was plain from my first introduction to ex-cop, wine merchant, and sometimes PI Prager, in *Walking the Perfect Square,* that his creator, Reed Coleman, was steeped in the hardboiled tradition. And it was just as plain that he had his sights set on something more than merely rehashing it all. The Moe Prager novels, of which *Redemption Street* is the second, are affectionate and knowledgeable reappraisals of the genre, and Moe is a very different sort of PI.

That Moe is a singular animal is initially apparent in his voice. The Prager books are written in first-person, and their narrative voice — Moe's voice — is a surprisingly intimate one. It's self-deprecating and conversational in tone, pitched for a talk between two friends in a bar, or on a long car ride — and it makes Moe a remarkably accessible character. It reveals him as — in the best hardboiled tradition — smart, smart-alecky, dogged, cynical, philosophical, and brave, but also as anxious, guilt-ridden, and brooding. Moe is a thinking man who overthinks; a brave man who is keenly aware of his own fears and limitations; an honest man, who suspects that he too has a price; a devoted family man, who remains isolated in fundamental ways; a man who keeps secrets, even as those secrets threaten all he holds dear. Reed's is a warts-and-all depiction, and we embrace Moe not in spite of his flaws but in part because of them.

One of the things we quickly recognize about Moe is that he must have an affinity for Faulkner, and Faulkner's oft-quoted observation that "the past is never dead. It's not even past" could well serve as Moe's epitaph (though his fans hope his need for one is a long way off). The past — obsession with it, regret over it, denial of it — figures greatly in *Redemption Street* and in all the Prager books, as do the increasingly corrosive effects of secrets kept and truths denied. The setting of the novels, New York City in the closing decades of the 20th century, serves to illuminate these themes, as well as the more mournful aspects of Moe's character — even as Moe, our narrator, illuminates the city. This passage from *Redemption Street,* in which Moe ponders the decline of the Borscht Belt resorts, is a case in point.

Sometimes I think it was my fate to catch things gone to seed. Coney Island, the world's playground during my parents' generation, was a wretched ghost town by the time my friends and I were old enough to go there on our own. The Dodgers moved to L.A. the year my dad promised to take me to a World Series game. Brooklyn itself had taken a sour turn during my watch. By 1957, the Dodgers weren't the only ones fleeing the County of Kings. Why should the Catskills have been any different?

This is classic Moe: philosophical, melancholy, mourning the demise of a New York that he himself has never known — obsessed with the past and certain that ruin is inevitable. Like other fictional detectives, Moe carries a load of grief, but his is based not so much on a tragic past — the unsolved case, the accidental shooting — as on a dread of the future. Despite his warmth and sense of humor, Moe is a deeply pessimistic man. He knows that there's a rough beast slouching toward Bethlehem, and that the center will not hold. He knows that there's a bill coming due one day — and that knowledge, the sureness of it, alienates him from his present, and robs him of its joys.

It's a very human burden for a very human hero, and in *Redemption Street* Moe is struggling under its weight. Like the toughest of hardboiled PIs, he soldiers on.

Peter Spiegelman
Ridgefield, CT
October 2007

Peter Spiegelman is the Shamus Award-winning author of three John March private eye novels — *Black Maps, Death's Little Helpers, and Red Cat* — and the editor of the crime fiction anthology *Wall Street Noir.*

For Aunt Sylvia and Uncle Lenny

*and in memory of my late friends
Barry Feldman and John Murphy*

ACKNOWLEDGEMENTS

I would like to thank David and McKenna for being such dedicated fans of my work. It was their determination to see *Redemption Street* back in print that led to this becoming a reality. I'd like to thank Peter Spiegelman for his contribution to this new edition. Of course none of this would have been possible or worth it without Rosanne, Kaitlin, and Dylan.

Two elderly Jewish women are having lunch at a Catskills hotel. One says to the other, "My God, this food is terrible." The other woman looks at her plate, shaking her head in agreement. "Yes," she says, "and the portions are so small."

— Old Borscht Belt joke

Nobody forgets anything in this world. Because even if the mind forgets, the blood remembers.

— Domenic Stansberry,
The Last Days of Il Duce

CHAPTER ONE: NOVEMBER 23RD, 1980

I wasn't thinking much about anything, certainly not my past, as I dusted off several overpriced bottles of French Cabernet.

"Hey, boss." Klaus interrupted my dusting.

"What?"

"Some guy's up front looking for you," he said, rolling his eyes in disapproval. "He's a real loser, kinda seedy, and I suspect he took the shuttle bus up from Bellevue."

"You're dressed in a Dead Kennedys tee shirt, ripped jeans, and unmatched sneakers and you're callin' this guy seedy!"

"On me, boss, it's fashion. On him it's seedy."

"Whatever," I surrendered, handing him my duster. "Lead on, Macduff."

When I spotted the man worrying a rut in the floorboards around the cash register, I had to tip my cap to Klaus. His assessment was right on. "Loser" was the word that came immediately to mind. As a cop, I'd seen a million of them and escorted more than a few to the loony bin. That's official police jargon. You can look it up.

This guy was a classic: raggedy, all fidgets and tics, smoking the life out of a cigarette. Sometimes they were deathly still, catatonic, but mostly they were like this clown. Their clothes always ill-fitting, too loose or too tight. Their hair always messy — not dirty necessarily, just all over the place.

"How may I help you?" I asked politely. I had had to learn that line. It wasn't one that came easily to the lips of an ex-cop. "What the fuck's going on here?" was what I was more comfortable with.

When he pulled the poor defenseless cigarette away from his mouth and faced me, I got a funny feeling in the pit of my belly. Mr. Fidgets seemed vaguely familiar. Not like my long-lost Siamese twin or nothing. More like a face I'd seen on the subway every now and then, but years ago.

Fidgets laughed, showing me a perfect mouth of stained teeth. "You don't remember me."

"Should I?"

"I guess I didn't suppose you would remember," he said in a sturdy voice that was an odd contrast to his fragile appearance.

"Actually, there is something familiar about you. I'm not sure what it is exactly."

He wrinkled up his brow. "What's the line? We went to different high schools together. We both went to Lincoln, but I was a senior when you were a sophomore. You were in my little sister's grade." He waved the filter of his spent cigarette at me, shrugging his shoulders apologetically.

"Here," I said, offering my cupped hand as an ashtray. He dropped it in without a second's hesitation. I opened up the front door and, like any good New Yorker, flicked the butt at a passing yellow cab. Maybe, if the wine business didn't work out, I could get a gig at the Coney Island freak show: Mighty Moe, the Human Ashtray.

"Okay, now that we've shared that Kodak moment," I sneered, brushing my hands together impatiently, "what can I do for you?"

"I want to hire you."

"No offense, buddy, but let's get real here. Not to judge a book by its cover or anything, but my guess is you're not the president of a major liquor-store chain, and I already know the sales rep from Moët and Chandon."

19

Even he thought that was pretty funny. For a brief second, the tics stopped and the sun seemed to rise on his face. It quickly set. "No, no, you misunderstand. I want to hire you to find my sister."

I could feel my heart beat hard at the walls of my chest. "I think you've got me confused with somebody else. This is a wine shop, not the Bat Cave."

Without a word, he reached into the pocket of his shabby coat and produced a few sheets of badly folded glossy paper. They shook in his hand as he thrust them out at me. There was no need for me to look at them. I knew what they were, where they came from. To the uninitiated, they appeared to be pages from an old edition of *Gotham Magazine.* I knew better. They were, in fact, reminders of a ghost that would likely haunt me for the rest of my natural life. I dared not reach for the pages in Mr. Fidgets' fingers for fear my hand would tremble more than his.

LITTLE BOY LOST was what the bold black typeface read at the top of page 17. Just beneath the author's byline were two pictures. Both photos, though very different from each other, were of the same young man. His name was Patrick Michael Maloney, a handsome college student who'd come to Manhattan for a party on the night of December 7, 1977, and had vanished, never to be heard from or seen again. Well, that wasn't true. I'd found Patrick, alive if not exactly well, but let him slip through my fingers. Only four people on the planet knew I'd located Patrick. The author of the article, Conrad Beaman, wasn't one of them, so he couldn't be held responsible for omitting that fact from his otherwise scrupulously accurate piece.

What Beaman *did* know was that, during my investigation of the disappearance, I'd fallen in love with Katy Maloney, Patrick's older sister. Katy, now my wife, didn't know I'd found her brother or lost him again. I didn't have the balls to tell her after it happened. Now, over three years later, she could never know. I rationalized that it would have hurt her too much to lose Patrick twice, but it was just bullshit. My reasons were purely selfish. I was the one worried about losing a loved one. I couldn't risk Katy finding out I'd been complicit, even if innocently so, in Patrick's vanishing act.

"I can't help you," I said, waving away the crumpled sheets. With a pin stuck in his balloon, Fidgets' entire body seemed to cave in dejection. "But" — he puffed back up, unfolding the article — "you found that little girl. It says so right here on page nineteen." He held the page up to me and pointed.

He was right. There were two pictures on page 19 as well. One was of a little Puerto Rican girl. The other was of me in uniform. The text read:

On Easter Sunday 1972, Marina Conseco (above left) disappeared in the amusement park at Coney Island. The girl, the daughter of a New York City fireman, seemed to vanish without a trace. Even her brothers and sisters could not recall when they had seen her last. After four days of searching failed to produce any solid leads, a group of off-duty police and firefighters led by Moses Prager (above right) found the girl at the bottom of a rooftop water tank on Mermaid Avenue in Coney Island. Sexually assaulted and battered, she had been thrown in the disused tank by her attacker and left to die. Prager, credited by his fellow search-team members with the idea of checking rooftop tanks, refused comment. "He just sort of looked up and had a flash," said John Rafferty, one of the off-duty firemen.

"One more day up there and she'd'a been a goner. I don't know what made Moe think to look up there. It was like God zapped him or something. . . ."

So that was it. Nine years ago I'd gotten lucky and found Marina Conseco. Now Mr. Fidgets thought I had an in with the Almighty. I shouldn't have been surprised. My luck in finding Marina was what led the Maloneys to me. It was only a matter of time before someone else stumbled onto the myth of my mojo: Moses Prager, Finder of Lost Souls. *Give me a break!*

"I can't help you," I repeated.

"But you've got a license. I checked. And you used to be a cop." I could dispute neither point. I'd been on the job for ten years before a sheet of carbon paper and a freshly waxed linoleum floor had conspired to twist my knee in such a manner that not even Gumby could replicate. I had, in fact, gotten my investigator's license shortly after the whole Patrick business. But I'd gotten my marriage license at about the same time and hadn't ever taken my investigator's license out of my sock drawer. It was just a conceit, anyway, a lie I tried to tell myself, a hedge against the ifs in life. Unfortunately for Aqualung here, the wine business was working out, and there wasn't much he could do or say to inspire me to take the Endust to my license.

"Sorry, friend," I patronized. "Can't do it. The holidays are our busy season. Maybe if you come back in January we can discuss it. Okay?"

He deflated once again. "It'll be too late then."

"Sorry."

"But you haven't even asked my name, my sister's name. You went to school with her. Doesn't that count for something? Don't you even care?"

"I care about anybody who's missing." Impatience crept, not too subtly, into my voice. "If you read that goddamned article you keep wavin' in my face, you'd know I care. Now, like I said, I'm sorry, but the answer for now is no. So, if you don't mind —"

"Karen Rosen!" he hissed at me. "My sister's name is Karen Rosen."

Clearly, he meant her name to be a slap in the face, a jolt to snap me out of my stupor. But instead of hitting me like a bucket of ice water, her name rolled off my shoulder like a raindrop. I might've heard the name. Rosen is not exactly an uncommon name in Brooklyn. Maybe we did go to school together. Maybe not. There were eleven hundred kids in my graduating class. It wasn't like I was on a first-name basis with all of them.

I took a deep breath and repeated my new mantra: "Look, I'm sorry about your sister, but —"

"She's dead! Don't you even care that she's dead?"

"That's it! Out! Right now, get the fuck out!"

Fidgets thought about striking out at me. I could see it in his eyes, which, for the first time, seemed like crazy eyes. Finally, they matched the rest of his demeanor.

"Karen Rosen," he whispered her name like a plea. "Try to remember her. When I'm gone, someone has to remember."

Before I could say a word, he drifted out of the store. He did not look back, but I could not take my eyes off him. At last, he faded into the rest of the faceless crowd on Columbus Avenue.

"So what happened?" Klaus, the store yenta, was anxious to know.

"You were right. He was just some nut job."

"Good, I could use your help," Klaus confessed. "We're busy."

We were always busy. Business was booming. It had been from the moment my big brother, Aaron, and I had opened the shop on the Upper West Side of Manhattan. For Aaron's sake, mostly, I was pleased. Our success had, for the first time since we were kids, allowed Aaron to escape from beneath the shadow of our father's dreadful adventures in businessland. Neither Aaron nor my dad ever understood that it was the business, not my father, that had failed. Me, I was just along for the ride. If I hadn't blown out my knee, I'd still be on the job, patrolling the streets of the 60th Precinct instead of the French reds aisle.

Don't misunderstand. I kind of liked the wine business, and making real money had a major upside. I owned a home for the first time in my life and finally drove a car that didn't look like it belonged permanently attached to the ass end of a tow truck. Katy could afford to stay home with the baby and still do freelance design work out of her basement studio. My pension money was cream and went straight into a college fund for our little girl, Sarah. Yeah, it was all cake, but too much cake's a bore. I wasn't bored yet, not really — just restless, I think. There's only so many times you can explain the difference between champagne and *méthode champenoise* before you get itchy.

At least we did have a stimulating clientele: a mixed bag of actors in various states of employ, Juilliard students, TV producers, Columbia profs, black kids drifting down from Harlem, and tourists who, after too many hours at the American Museum of Natural History, needed a buttery Chardonnay with just the proper hint of oak. On Friday and Saturday evenings we did big volume with the under-twenty-five crowd from New Jersey and the boroughs. Though their selections tended to come with screw-off caps rather than corks, we still let them in the front door. Aaron and I never lost sight of the fact that, in spite of our fancy locale, we were just two schmucks from Brooklyn who'd made good.

I did get to meet a few famous people. I mean *really* famous people, not just this week's hot soap-opera star. John Lennon, for instance, bought a case of Perrier-Jouet for a friend's birthday gift. He was kind enough to take a picture with me. Emboldened by his generosity, I asked him if Paul McCartney was really the selfish, self-centered prick the press made him out to be.

"Nah," he said. "The real Paul's dead, you know. He was a great mate, a generous sort, but the sod actor we got to replace him is a genuine *shite*. We'd have gotten rid of him, too, but he was a better bass player than the real Paul. Not as good a songwriter, though. Do you suppose the Paul who wrote 'Yesterday' would write *roobbish* like 'Silly Love Songs'?" John winked at me, stuck out his tongue, and left.

I hadn't lied to Mr. Fidgets. This was our busy season. Yet, in spite of the huge influx of cash, there was something about the week leading up to Thanksgiving that made me blue. Was it that Mother Nature made sure to give us a nice kick in the ass to remind us that winter was just one calendar flip away? I used to think so. Now I'm not so sure. Maybe it's the inevitable onslaught of Christmas. All those holiday songs are great the first 3,411 times you hear them. . . . But it wasn't the music.

Christmas in America is an existential nightmare for Jews. We try to be both part of it and apart from it, and neither works. It was especially tough for Katy, unpracticed as she was at the ordeal. A Catholic all her life, she'd converted to Judaism of her own volition. I thought she was nuts for doing it, but . . . I had suggested we get a tree to sort of ease the transition, but Katy wouldn't hear of it. Maybe a tree would have made it harder for her. I was too embarrassed to admit the tree would have been as much for me as for her.

However, when things finally slowed down, I found I was not thinking of Christmas or even impending Thanksgiving. I found myself looking out into the darkness and into the clog of rush-hour traffic and wondering where Mr. Fidgets had got to. I was wondering about my past and trying to put a face to the name Karen Rosen. But no matter how much I tried, I could not remember her.

Katy seemed to be half listening to the story of Karen Rosen's brother over dinner. I wanted to think her lack of attentiveness was because Sarah was being fussy. It wasn't. It was about Patrick. Katy was always upbeat. It's one of the things I loved most about her. I couldn't help noticing, however, her mood crash whenever the increasingly rare lead about her little brother would come our way. Hope has an ugly dark side, and I was witness to it every single time some money-hungry idiot tried to pry a buck or two out of the reward fund Katy's dad had set up in '78. Whenever someone who looked like Patrick was spotted in Whitefish Bay or Bobo-Dioulasso, Katy and her mom would go into a tailspin. Then, when hope faded, some semblance of normalcy returned. The last thing Katy wanted to hear was another story of loss.

"Good night, honey." I kissed Sarah's forehead, but she was already well asleep, and, for the night at least, out of the dark reach of false hopes.

I watched Katy kiss our little redhead good night.

"Don't you remember her at all?" Katy whispered, pulling up the crib rail.

Her question caught me off guard. "What? Remember who?"

"Karen Rosen, the woman —"

"Oh," I whispered back, nodding my head for us to leave. "I didn't think you were listening at dinner. No, I don't remember her. I feel like I should, but I don't. It's buggin' me. Her name goes around in my head, but there's nothing there, no face attached to it. Christ, it's weird. I feel guilty about not remembering."

"What a shock." Katy giggled, closing Sarah's door behind her. "You feel guilty for the sinking of the *Andrea Doria* and the Dodgers moving out of Brooklyn."

"The *Andrea Doria* maybe, but I had nothing to do with the Dodgers. That was my Uncle Murray."

Katy folded herself into my arms, pressing herself into me. It was magic the way she

30

did that, blurring the borders between us. I think the first time she held me this way I knew I could not lose her, ever.

"I love you, Katy Maloney Prager."

"Look in your yearbook," she purred, her cheek to my chest.

"What?"

"For Karen Rosen, *yutz!*" Katy pushed me playfully away, wagging her finger at me. "Some detective! Put a face to her name. Maybe then there'll only be the two of us in bed tonight."

"I guess the conversion's taking. Your Yiddish is improving."

"And you can kiss my half-Celtic ass, mister. Now go find that yearbook. I've got a company logo and letterhead to design. Welcome to the exciting world of graphic arts. Oh, and, by the way," she said, turning back from the stairs, "I love you, too."

Quite a prodigious amount of dust had settled on my copy of the 1966 Abraham Lincoln High School edition of *Landmark*. That was the name of our yearbook. I don't know why, exactly. Maybe because the school paper was called the *Lincoln Log* and all the other good "L" words were taken. When I started thumbing through the yellowing pages, it struck me that *Losers* might have been a more apt name than *Landmark*.

Almost everybody looks like a loser in his or her high-school yearbook, even the beautiful people.

I think the only saving grace in '66 was the conservative nature of everyone's attire. The real social upheaval was just getting started, Vietnam was still far, far away from Ocean Parkway, and the Summer of Love was a year in the future. The girls' outfits were strictly proper, and the boys wore all-white shirts, thin ties, and skinny lapels. Boys still wore their hair short and parted. There were one or two Beatle haircuts. The girls . . . well, the girls featured lots of bangs and hair spray. Pages and pages of black-and-white photos of future Donna Reeds and Dr. Kildares. Today, I guess you'd say the boys looked like Elvis Costello clones. But Karen Rosen was nowhere to be seen.

Katy had been right to suggest I try and exorcise Karen's faceless ghost before going to bed. I went to bed all right, but not nearly to sleep. It was good that Katy was working late in the studio or I imagine I would have tossed and turned her to distraction. Admitting defeat, I snuck into the living room and took a few fingers' worth of Dewar's.

Sure, I owned a wine shop, but I wanted a real drink. The kind of stuff that didn't need to breathe or chill, that didn't have legs, a nose, or hints of pepper and berries. The kind of stuff that burned going down. I couldn't lay it all at Karen Rosen's dead feet. I suppose maybe I was a little more bored with our precious wine shop than I'd been willing to admit.

I stared at the phone like a nervous teenager. What was I going to say? To whom would I say it? Which one of my old friends was going to get the midnight call? It didn't really matter, because I had old friends in name only. Over time I'd seemed to shed friends as a snake does skins. They tell me it's natural. Things change. People change. They get married. They have kids. They get divorced. They stop smoking. They take up golf. Some die. I'd accelerated the shedding process by becoming a cop, not the most popular career choice for a college student in the late sixties. Though cops were no longer on the top of everyone's shit list, friendships are hard to rekindle. Both parties need to be up for the awkwardness of it all. More often than not, it was like a one-armed man trying to light a fire with two sticks.

I picked the phone up a few times, started to dial once or twice, imagining the conversation.

Hey, Bob, it's Moe, Moe Prager. . . . Sorry

*it's so late. Nothin's wrong. . . . Three kids,
huh? Yeah, I heard you owned a bread
route. . . . No, I'm off the job four years next
month. . . . I fucked up my knee. Listen,
anyway, what I was wondering was, do you
remember Karen Rosen from Lincoln? That
was Karen Bloom, Bob, and she swore to me
she was a virgin. Yeah, I know, she swore
that to everyone. . . . So do you remember —
No, huh? Yeah, sounds good. We'll have to
get together. Bye.*

The thought of a few conversations along
those lines rocked me right to sleep there in
the living room. That, and four more fingers
of scotch.

CHAPTER TWO:
NOVEMBER 25TH

The sun was up and bright and felt warmer on my face than it had any right to feel so late in the year. Katy and Sarah had already gone by the time I hit the street. They'd left early for the trip upstate to the Maloneys' house in Dutchess County. This way Sarah could have a long visit with her grandparents and Katy could help my mother-in-law prepare the holiday fixings. I'd head up myself after work. In the wine shop, the day before Thanksgiving is our second-busiest day of the year, so I decided to prepare for the inevitable onslaught by going to the gym to play at working out.

I felt pretty good, having last night abandoned Dr. Dewar's sleep remedy. Twenty-four hours' worth of perspective had let Karen Rosen recede back into the netherworld from which she had come. I figured I had enough of my own skeletons in the closet and didn't need to borrow anyone else's.

Maybe someday at a reunion or something her name would come up and my curiosity would be satisfied. Until then . . .

"Mr. Prager, sir," an unfamiliar male voice called my name as I pulled up the garage door.

It wasn't a threatening voice. It was stiffly formal. The voice knew who I was, but didn't want to advertise the fact.

"Yes." I turned, matching formality with formality. "What can I do for you?"

The deep voice belonged to a slight man. The first thing I noticed about him was his suit, a blue pin-striped business affair. Though not the most common attire in Sheepshead Bay, blue pinstripe usually didn't make passersby stop and stare. It was the cut of it, I think, that got my attention, so perfectly matched to the man who wore it that it seemed a second skin.

"Mr. Prager," he repeated.

"Yes."

"I'm sorry," he said. "My employer would like to see you."

The suit gestured with his arm. My gaze followed the tips of his thin fingers to the point where my hedges bent around to the sidewalk. The nose of a black Lincoln limo was clearly visible. During the spring or summer I wouldn't have been able to see

36

another inch of the car, but the rest of the landed whale was now quite visible through the leafless hedge.

"Tell him to look out the window. If he avoids the big branches, he should be able to see me just fine."

Blue Suit smiled. He had perfect teeth, too, and, apparently, appreciated my wit. "The car, Mr. Prager, please."

Unconsciously, I tapped the waistband of my pants to reassure myself. Yes, my .38 was there. Old cop habits die hard. I told myself I still carried the gun because of the wine shop, which was mostly true. I also think I carried it because I could. I didn't feel particularly threatened by the suit. It was just that the perfect tailoring, the perfect teeth, and the impeccable manners put me on edge. Perfection has that effect on me. It's so out of place in Brooklyn.

The movement of my hand did not escape the suit's eye. He smiled more broadly, showing off still more of his dentist's handiwork. "I assure you this is neither *Candid Camera* nor a pantomime of *The Godfather.* The car, please."

Blue Pinstripe opened the Lincoln's rear passenger door for me, but did not follow me into the black limo. Instead, he closed the door behind me and placed himself half a football field ahead of me, behind the steering wheel of the Lincoln. A thick pane of dark glass rose up, blocking my view of the suit. Turning, I noticed I was seated across from a man whose head was bathed in shadow. Though it was evident I was staring directly at him, he seemed in no rush to come into the light, where I could see him.

"Thank you," he said, still refusing to lean forward, "I appreciate you taking the time."

"Look, can you just say what you've got to say?" I asked impatiently. "I've got to go to the gym and watch other people work out."

He leaned forward slightly, but not quite enough to let me have a good clean look. He held his hand out to me, though not to shake. There was a picture in it. He didn't have to tell me to take it.

It was a faded color snap, a teenage girl in pink pajamas with a Siamese cat curled in her lap. She had a disarming smile, a crooked nose, and a poofy hairdo. There was a big stack of 45s at her feet, a portable record player — the kind with a bulky tone arm that you had to put loose quarters on to keep it from skipping — to her left, and a makeup table behind her.

When I'd taken what my host considered enough time, he said, "Karen Rosen."

I recognized her, finally, but now something else nagged me. I knew something about her. What was it? I wondered. What was it?

"Her brother came to see you the other day at your place of business," said the man in the shadow. "Arthur Rosen, a shabby fellow with —"

"My memory's fine," I said. "So now I know his name, but not yours."

"Carter, my name's R. B. Carter. Have you ever heard of me?" he asked with genuine curiosity, now extending his right hand to me for a shake.

"No," I answered, pulling his hand as I shook it, forcing him out into the light.

His face meant less to me than his name. It was a plain enough face. There were calm blue eyes, a straight but round-tipped nose, prominent lips, a too-pointy chin. His eyebrows were overly thick and probably required some cosmetic antitrust procedure to prevent them from merging. His ears were small and close to the skull. He had unremarkable brown hair, parted on the right. I guessed he was a little bit older than me. His palm was dry, his grip self-assured. And, like his errand boy up front, Carter wore a suit that probably cost more than the car. It didn't, however, fit him quite so

39

perfectly.

"I am in real estate," he let me know.

"My house isn't for sale."

He had an icy-cold smile. "I am in real real estate, Mr. Prager. Your house would be worth less than loose change to me. I own the buildings that Trump, Helmsley, and Tisch don't."

"Somebody's got to eat the crumbs, I guess."

He didn't like that, but resisted taking the bait. "I do not enjoy the spotlight. Having my name pop up in the *Post* increases neither my holdings nor my ego. Did you know, I own the building that houses City on the Vine?" Carter offered it as a boast, but it sounded like a threat. "That is your wine shop, if I am not mistaken."

"If you want to raise the rent, talk to my brother. And what has this got to do with Karen Rosen?"

He looked almost relieved. "You don't remember her, do you?"

"Now that I've seen this picture, I remember her face, yeah. But do I remember anything about her or her brother? No, I guess you're right, I don't."

"Perhaps," he suggested, "you would recall Andrea Cotter."

"Oh my God!" I was light-headed. "The fire."

Yes, the fire. When I closed my eyes I could still see the headlines of the Sunday papers:

SEVENTEEN DEAD IN CATSKILLS INFERNO

August of '65, I think, a Saturday night. Three girls from my high school were up waitressing at a run-down Borscht Belt hotel. Some drunken asshole fell asleep smoking a cigarette, and the workers' quarters went up like a Roman candle. The building was already collapsing by the time the volunteer fire departments arrived on the scene. There was nothing to be done but watch and help treat the people that got out alive. Unfortunately, most of the dead, the Lincoln girls included, got the worst and least accessible accommodations. It was a right of passage, I remembered the hotel manager saying. The new staff suffered their first year. For them there would be no better beds the second year. No second year at all. Nor would there be yearbook pictures. The dead girls were Karen Rosen and Andrea Cotter. I couldn't remember the third girl at all.

41

Suddenly, it was stiffling in the rear of that limo. "But what's this got to do with you?"

"Maybe I *should* let Arthur Rosen hire you," Carter sneered. "You seem not to be able to put two and two together."

"That's not a fuckin' answer."

"My sister Andrea died in that fire, too, Mr. Prager."

To label what I felt for Andrea Cotter a crush is both inadequate and inaccurate, but there is no single word to describe what my teenage heart went through. I was as much in awe of as in love with her. She was no goddess. Her hair was dirty-blond, straight. She was round-faced with unre-markable blue eyes. As I think back, Andrea did have a rich mouth. Her lips were lush and pillowy. That's it, though. You know how some people aren't beautiful to look at or anything, yet there's this energy, an aura about them. There was this magical way An-drea carried herself that drew people to her.

She was a little stocky, her legs were too thick, her shoulders too broad, but she moved gracefully as a tree in the wind. She danced, was a cheerleader, acted in the school play, sang. In spite of her effortless popularity, Andrea never lorded it over anyone. She was perfectly approachable, though I never dared. I guess I imagined she would be. What I think I was most awed by was her poetry. Her words seemed to bypass my eyes, seeping into my skin. Hers were the only words unaccompanied by music that moved me. Andrea Cotter did more for my understanding of poetry than any of my English teachers.

So moved by her, by her words, I wrote a poem. Editor of the school literary magazine, Andrea published my one foray into the world of verse. The poem was about her, of course. At least she inspired it. In my teenage formulations of the universe, I prayed she would recognize my longings for her in my words. On the other hand, I was panicked that she might indeed recognize those longings. I got my answer shortly after the magazine was published. I was sitting on the Coney Island boardwalk — the same boardwalk I would later patrol as a cop — watching the waves roll onto the beach.

"Excuse me." Andrea Cotter's voice was eerily tentative. "You're Moses Prager, aren't you? I love your poem. I wish I could inspire someone to write like that."

She took a copy of the magazine out of her bag and asked me to autograph my poem. When I finished, she just smiled and walked away. I think it was the last time I ever saw her.

"Carter . . . Cotter." I was incredulous, drifting back to the present. "You're Rudy Cotter!"

"Was," he corrected, "Mr. Prager, was. The name's R. B. Carter now."

"I had a terrible crush on your sister," I said, feeling immediately embarrassed. "She had me autograph her literary magazine."

He yawned with excitement.

"What's this all about?" I repeated. "The girls have been dead for fifteen years already."

"Sixteen, to be precise. They have been dead these many years, but the Rosens have never been able to accept it, especially that crazy Arthur. The parents, at least, are dead, but that lunatic is obsessed."

"Obsessed with what?" I wondered. "Dead is dead."

Carter threw up his hands. "Try telling that to Arthur Rosen. Apparently, the initial investigation into the fire was rather perfunctory and shoddy. There wasn't much to investigate, really. I mean, they went through the motions, held the necessary inquiries and panels. Believe me, I have since looked into it. But even in the mid-sixties, the Catskills were heading into the financial abyss. Let's just say the locals thought it best to get beyond the fire, to get back to business."

"But the Rosens weren't satisfied?"

"Christ, Prager, do you think my family were happy?" He let his real anger show for the first time. "What parent is satisfied with any explanation of their child's death? There isn't a satisfactory explanation in the universe. But we accepted it and tried getting beyond Andrea's dying that way. It took years for my mom not to imagine her only daughter burning up alive every time she shut her eyes. Can you imagine the torturous second-guessing my parents put themselves through? If they hadn't let her go. If they had forced her to go to a better hotel. If . . . If . . . If . . ."

"What about the Rosens?"

"No, they spent their life savings hiring and firing lawyers, detectives, anyone and everyone. They sued everybody you could sue and even some you could not."

"But what was the point? What were they looking for?"

Carter laughed bitterly. "Karen, I suppose. First they just could not believe she was really dead, so they sued the local cops, the fire department, the coroner's office, the DA, the dogcatcher. Then it was the hotel owner and his insurance company. Then, when the owner went into default and the

45

bank tried to sell the land, they sued the bank. But it really started getting ugly when they went after the families of the other kids caught in the fire. They —"

"They what?"

"You seem surprised, Mr. Prager. Don't be. You see, Karen wasn't a smoker, so her death had to be one of the other employees' fault. They sent private investigators to our homes. 'Did your daughter smoke?' 'Can you ever recall her falling to sleep with a lit cigarette?' They subpoenaed my parents. Eventually, we had the subpoena quashed and the case was thrown out, but can you understand the pain this caused? And it was always that Arthur pushing and pushing his parents. They quieted down for a few years. Then, about two, possibly three years ago, Arthur started up again. He was worse with his parents gone."

"Did you ever try to —"

"— reason with him?" he finished my question. "Of course. When I first began making real money, I offered him and the parents the moon, anything, for them to just leave it be, to let my folks rest. Then, when that nut started up again, I offered to pay a team of expert investigators go over the case from top to bottom. Not good enough. That paranoid schmuck just kept repeating,

46

'Something's wrong, something's wrong.' Something *was* wrong. Our sisters were dead, and nothing was going to fix that. Gone is gone, forever. He's certifiable, Arthur, a genuine manic-depressive. I thought he'd eventually let it go."

"I guess not."

Carter shook his head at me. "Obviously. If anything, Arthur got more obsessed. He began, let us say, to get more extreme."

"Look, you can't know how terrible I feel for you and your family, but I'm not an idiot. Arthur, as *meshugge* as he might be, has gotten somebody's ear, or we wouldn't be having this chat in the back of your limo. Otherwise, why would you care if he came to see me?"

"Maybe I should apologize for my earlier assessment of your capabilities." He bowed slightly. "Yes, he has gotten someone's ear, as you say. Some dipshit Catskill politician is trying to make a name for himself. He has decided to fight to reopen the case and hold a new inquiry, even a new coroner's inquest. He has been getting quite a bit of ink out of it. Ink to a politician is like blood in the water to a shark. So far, it's just talk. There really aren't any substantive grounds on which to reopen the case, but . . . I will not put my parents through this again." He

47

slammed his fist into the car door. "I won't!"

"But what's this got to do with —"

"— with you, Mr. Prager? I suppose, nothing. Arthur's been trying to hire investigators to go up to the Catskills and try and find something, anything to help push the politicos to reopen things. He knows that once the press gets bored with the story the ink will dry up and so will his hopes. The sharks will find a new carcass on which to feed."

"And you've been cleaning up after him, haven't you?" I smirked. "You've been paying off everyone he's gone to see. I'm just the most recent mess you've come to clean up. Christ, he must be scraping the bottom of the barrel if he came to me. How much it cost you so far?"

"Less than the pain it would cause my parents," he said, removing a leather-bound checkbook from his inside jacket pocket.

"So far, I've shielded them from this last go-around. They're too old for this. It took too many years for them to bury Andrea, and I won't let that nut rob her grave. Who should I make the check out to?"

"I don't want your money. I wouldn't've taken the job anyway." He didn't put the checkbook away. "Let's call it insurance, then."

"Let's not. Let's take my word for it. But if you wanna give me something, you can answer a question for me."

Carter stealthily slipped his checkbook away. "What is it?"

"Why the name change?"

That caught him off guard a little. "I've found it advantageous not to be pigeon-holed. I have financial interests outside the city. Don't fool yourself, Prager. Anti-Semitism didn't die in a bunker in 1945. The world's just as rotten as it's always been, worse maybe. The skin on the apple is shinier, but the worms have gotten better at eating from the inside out."

There must have been a signaling button somewhere, or maybe Blue Pinstripe was listening all along, but regardless of means the message was delivered. My door was being pulled back even as Carter was sharing the last syllables of his delightful world-view. There were no pleasant goodbyes, handshakes, or we'll-have-to-get-togethers. The business was taken care of and that was that. I didn't watch the Lincoln pull away. I was having a hard time reconciling the differences between that calculating son of a bitch and his sister, the girl I had loved from afar. But, then again, maybe losing Andrea the way he did would make a son of a bitch of anyone.

I went back inside and made a few calls. I'd have to pretend to work out some other day.

CHAPTER THREE: NOVEMBER 25TH (EVENING)

Klaus was just locking the front door when the phone rang. Aaron, already pissed off at me for, as he saw it, abandoning my family for Thanksgiving, picked up.

He waved the phone angrily in my direction. "For you."

"Who is it?"

My big brother ignored the question. Placing the phone on the register, he scolded: "Make it short. I've got your former family to get home to."

"Please, you sound like a grandma from one of those morose Yiddish films Mommy used to watch. *Oy vay iz mir*" — I clutched my heart — "the Cossacks are killing the cattle and you married a *shiksa!* Better I should be dead than the cows."

He waved his hand at me in disgust.

"Hello . . ."

It was a friend from the job, Jim Finney. It'd been Finn I'd called earlier after my chitchat with R. B. Carter.

Finney dispensed with the usual foreplay. "Got a pen handy?"

There was a lot about my tête-à-tête with R. B. Carter that bugged me, but mostly I didn't like the implication that I could have been bought off. Of course I could be bought off, everyone could. The truest of all Hollywood clichés is that everyone's got a price. It's just that no one likes getting his face rubbed in it. But I hadn't called Finn about Carter. No, for the moment anyway, I was more curious about Arthur Rosen.

"Yeah, Finn, I got a pen."

"He's a real nut job, this one."

"I know. I've had the dubious pleasure of making his acquaintance."

"Rosen, Arthur J.," Finney read matter-of-factly. "Born May 26, 1946, Madison Park Hospital, Brooklyn, blah, blah, blah. Six arrests for what you'd expect — three disorderlies, one for urinating in a public place, you know, that kinda crap. Been in and out of Bellevue and Kings County so many times they keep the porch light on for him."

"Address, Finn, what's his address?"

"Last known address . . ." His voice trailed off. "Last known address is . . . I don't see a recent one. Oh, wait . . . You ever hear of a place called Sunshine Manor?"

"Yeah, yeah, yeah. It's like a halfway house down in Alphabet City."

"Give the gimpy Heeb a cigar," Finney teased. "You want the number?"

"Nah, that's okay. Thanks. Enjoy your holiday."

"Happy Thanksgiving to you and yours."

Bearded and pale, the guy at the front desk looked like Rasputin after they fished him out of the river. It got worse. When the mad monk looked up from his book, I noticed he had a double dose of that lazy-eye thing going on, so that it was difficult to know if you were standing in his line of sight. Talk about the inmates running the asylum. If this guy was at the front desk, I couldn't wait to see what was behind door number two.

"I need to see one of your . . . an inma—" I stuttered.

"We call them clients or patients, if you prefer," Rasputin corrected, flashing an uneven but very friendly smile. He pointed to the clock on the wall behind me. "Unfortunately, it's well past visiting hours. Even then, we don't usually allow unscheduled visitation. It can have a very destabilizing effect on the —"

"— clients. I understand. But," I said, producing my old badge. "Can't you make an exception?" I didn't bother explaining about my being retired.

His friendly smile went the way of thirty-three-cent-a-gallon gasoline. "Have you got a warrant or probable cause?"

"Look, I'm not here to bust balls. Can I talk to somebody in charge?"

"You already are. I'm Dr. Prince."

"You always do desk duty, Doc?" I wondered, not sure I quite believed him.

"It's the holiday," he said, the smile creeping back. "We like to let as much of the staff as we can get an early start. This is tough work here. Rewarding, but very tough. I didn't catch your name, Officer, or is it Detective?"

I stuck out my hand. "Moe Prager. And it's neither. I'm not anything official anymore. I just find that the badge helps cuts through the bullshit sometimes."

He took a firm grip of my hand. "I wish it were that easy for me. I don't think you can conceive the amount of bullshit I have to cut through. Maybe you'll lend me that badge sometime, it might be worth the shot. So — who is it you'd like to see?"

"Arthur Rosen. Is he still —"

"Another private investigator, huh?" The

shrink let go of my hand. Given the look of disgust on his face, I'm surprised he didn't immediately go for the disinfectant. "You're not a stupid man, Mr. Prager. You must know that Mr. Rosen is not fully capable of making rational decisions. And I'm afraid your presence will only feed his ——"

I threw my hands up in surrender, explaining I had no intention of taking the case. I understood, I said, that Arthur Rosen wasn't exactly making lucid decisions when it came to the matter of his long-dead sister. I told the doctor about Rosen's showing up at the shop, about my having gone to school with his sister, about the article in *Gotham Magazine*.

"Look, Doc, I kinda kicked him outta my store the other day. I couldn't remember his sister, and then, when he told me she was dead . . . I mean, what was I supposed to think? I just want a few minutes to apologize. That's all."

Dr. Prince asked me to give him a minute while he found someone to cover the desk for him. He made a call or two. Eventually, a slender young black man came and took Rasputin's seat. A few whispered words passed between them.

Prince led the way up the stairs. He told me he wasn't Rosen's therapist, but as clinic director was fairly familiar with the file. He laid down some preconditions for my talk with Arthur. He, Dr. Prince, would enter the room first and make certain Rosen was willing to meet with me. Prince would remain in the room for the duration of the visit. I was not to raise my voice or have physical contact with Rosen beyond a handshake, and then only if Rosen initiated the contact. If Rosen became agitated, I was to leave immediately. I was to leave immediately if Dr. Prince, for whatever reason, indicated that I should.

"Do I have to sign away my firstborn?" I whispered as we stepped out into the hall.

He understood I was joking, and I understood it was his job to protect the patient.

Sunshine Manor was a converted four-story walk-up, so it did not feel institutional, per se. In appearance, it rather reminded me of my grandparents' old building on Avenue P and East 4th Street in Brooklyn. Their hallway was always fragrant with the sweetly sulfurous scent of frying onions and garlic, roasting chickens, and meats stewing on the stove. But any stirrings of romance over my past were murdered by the nostril-burning, lung-choking minty-pine scent of industrial cleaner. Hospitals, jails, courthouse washrooms — they all smelled this way. Looks can deceive, but not smells.

Dr. Prince, reading the expression on my face, explained that this was only a semi-secure facility. "This is, for lack of a better term, a halfway house. The people staying with us have been thoroughly evaluated and are not considered dangers to others or, for the most part, to themselves. Depending upon the situation, the clients are allowed a certain amount of unsupervised time outside the confines of the building. Many of them have jobs. As long as they take their meds and follow the rules, they have a lot of freedom. There are curfews and bed checks and small windows on the doors, but, with few exceptions, we don't lock people in. Here we are," he said, tilting his head at the door.

I bowed. "I know, you first. I'll wait right here."

He knocked, announced himself, hesitated a second or two, and pushed the door in. "Arthur, there's someone here to . . . Holy shit!"

I didn't wait for an engraved invitation.

I smelled death even as I crossed the threshold. Maybe I just imagined I did. Not all death smells the same. Ask any cop. There's old death, death where rigor has set in and let go. Death where flies have had time to lay their eggs. There's death that stinks of maggots and flesh rotting in the heat of a sealed black garbage bag beneath the noonday sun. This was not what I smelled as I ran into Arthur Rosen's room.

This was a fresher death. The stench of urine and feces hung in the air, not quite overwhelming the minty-pine atmosphere. Arthur Rosen's nude, soiled body was slumped in the corner. He'd hanged himself with his belt tied to the closet-door handle. They did it in Rikers this way sometimes, with a bedsheet. You have to really want to die to do it this way. It's not like kicking the stool out from beneath your feet. This way, all you have to do to save yourself is stand up. No, Arthur Rosen had been determined to die. He got his wish.

The cop in me knew he was gone at a glance, beyond resuscitation. I wanted to admonish Dr. Prince, warn him to touch nothing. I wanted to grab him by the shoulder, back him out of the room, and call 911. Instead, I pulled out my knife and cut the belt. Dr. Prince stretched the body out on the floor, removed the ligature from Rosen's neck, and began the exercise in futility that was CPR.

"Where's the phone?"

"Forget it," he said, abandoning his efforts. "He's cold. The blood's begun to settle."

"Okay, Doc, you go call this in. I'll secure the scene. Anyway, you're gonna have to deal with all the other patients' reactions. That's not gonna be easy."

He stood and left without comment. I closed the door behind him. No need for a curious passerby to wander on in. Word would spread soon enough. In institutions, bad word spread on the wind. And I wanted a private look around. Cops are trained to treat the scene of an apparent suicide no differently from how they would treat the scene of a homicide. My snooping was bound to screw up the forensics some, but that was just too damned bad. Both the doctor and myself had already gotten a good start by handling the body so much. What would it hurt if I handled it a little more?

I gently rolled Arthur Rosen onto his stomach. Other than the angry ligature marks around his throat and what looked to be an old burn scar on his left forearm, there was nothing remarkable about his body. He just seemed frail, and lighter than I expected. Though I didn't really know him, I suspected the years of smoking, torment, and medication had taken a heavy toll on him.

I checked his hands, his fingers. His nails were dirty, and he seemed to have some fresh cuts on the tips of both index fingers, but I couldn't be sure how fresh. Maybe he'd cut them days ago or had split the skin while rigging his belt. No matter how much uniformed cops may brag about it, they don't usually get up close and personal with stiffs. They know the smell of death, but they don't know the feel. They may touch a throat to check for a pulse. That's about it, though. Mostly it's hands off. The detectives and crime-scene guys have all the real fun.

I rolled him back over and tried replacing his arms as they had fallen after I cut him down. I'm not sure I got it right. I stood up, a little too fast, I think. The stink was getting to me for sure, and just maybe it crossed my mind that my refusal to take the case had been the last straw, that my words had been the last bit of motivation Arthur Rosen needed to stick his head in a noose and keep it there. I was pretty nauseous and grabbed the first solid thing I could get my hands on — the dresser. I steadied myself. I found myself looking into the mirror. I didn't like what I saw, and what the mirror saw didn't like me. The nauseousness was ebbing away when I spotted something other than my sorry face in the lower right-hand corner of the reflection.

I turned and walked quickly to the opposite wall, to the side of the bed. I pulled the nightstand away from the side of the bed. Several words were scrawled on the wall in crude block letters. **WRONG. HAMMERLING. FIRE. POEMS. JUDAS.** There was one more word, a name, my name. **PRAGER.** Only my name was different. It was smeared in reddish-brown lettering for which Arthur's veins had contributed the ink. Apparently, the cuts on Arthur's fingers were very fresh. Below the graffiti, and, until now, hidden beneath the night table, were a stack of yellowed newspapers. They were copies of some rag called the *Catskill Tribune.* I had begun to thumb through them when I heard footsteps coming down the hall. I rolled the papers up and tucked them under my jacket.

The footsteps out in the hall were coming in my direction. I scanned the room, looking for a suicide note. I didn't see one. There was a perfunctory knock at the door, and Dr. Prince stepped in. Prince gave me a perplexed stare as he reentered. And believe me when I tell you, with eyes like his, Dr. Prince's perplexed stare was unrivaled.

"There's no note," I blurted out guiltily.

"The cops will be here" — he was interrupted by sirens outside the window — "any minute. There they are now."

"I was the last straw," I said, pointing at my bloody name on the wall.

Dr. Prince understood without explanation.

"It's not that simple, Mr. Prager. Those words are not like the numbered dots on a paper place mat. The mind is curved just as space and time. It defies easy answers. Straight lines don't apply. The dots don't connect in sequence."

The cops came in. They didn't bother to knock.

I was purposefully vague with my former brothers in blue. And they weren't especially interested in me. If Rosen hadn't written my name on the wall in his own blood before hanging himself, they probably would have dismissed me without a second thought. As it was, the detective who caught the case accepted my explanation without question. I had known the deceased man's late sister in high school. He had looked me up, but I had been too busy to talk to him. I felt bad about not making time to talk to him and had therefore come to apologize. Why did I think he'd put my name on his wall? I didn't know why, I said. I didn't really know him, and he was crazy, after all, wasn't he?

I knew what I was doing. It isn't like on TV. Sherlock Holmes is strictly for the PBS crowd. Cops want easy, reasonable answers, not headaches. They want to close cases, have a few beers, and go back home to Massapequa. They don't eat their guts out over every stiff, especially losers like Arthur Rosen. It's sad but true that cops value some lives more than others. Hey, I'm not throwing stones here. I'm as guilty as anyone. I suspect we all are. When Marina Conseco went missing, it seemed like the whole city mobilized to try and find her. When something happens to the Arthur Rosens among us, the city sighs in relief, says good riddance, and sleeps better that night.

I wouldn't sleep better for some nights to come.

CHAPTER FOUR:
THANKSGIVING

Silence was neither golden nor unusual around the Maloneys' holiday table. Maybe before Patrick had disappeared, before Francis Jr. was shot down over Vietnam, things had been livelier. Somehow I doubted it. The icy presence of my father-in-law was enough to dampen any celebration. But I couldn't lay all the blame on his plate, not today, not after Arthur Rosen's suicide.

"You were awfully quiet at dinner," Katy whispered, snuggling up to me on the couch.

"Is Sarah asleep?"

Katy knelt forward and stared directly into my eyes. "You know she is. What is it? What's the matter?"

"Remember that nut who came into the store?"

"Karen Rosen's brother." She smiled. "The one who wanted you to find his dead sister."

"Last night, when I told you I was late getting up here because of an accident on the Tappan Zee Bridge . . . there was no accident," I confessed. "I went to see him. His name is — was — Arthur Rosen."

"Was?"

"He's dead. He hung himself. Or is it 'hanged himself'? Hanged, hung — whatever. I found him. Just in case I didn't feel quite shitty enough, he wrote my name on the bedroom wall in his own blood. I pushed him over the edge when I turned him down."

Katy knew better than to argue the point. If I was determined to feel responsible, nothing she was apt to say was going to change it.

She tried a different tack. "Did you ever find out about his sister?"

"Remember when we first started seeing each other I told you about the girls from my high school who were killed in the fire in the Catskills?"

"I remember. You mean she was one of the dead girls, Karen Rosen?"

"She was."

"There were three girls, weren't —"

I cut her off. "Technically, there were three girls, but one had graduated Lincoln several years before and was just working at that hotel as a matter of unhappy co-incidence. I don't even recall her name. There was Karen Rosen and —"

"— Andrea Cotter," she snapped. "You don't think I'd forget the girl you had such a big crush on, the girl who inspired you to write poetry, do you?"

I was taken aback by Katy's tone. "You almost sound jealous!"

"Maybe I am," she confessed, "a little. You know, I had an English-lit professor who used to say that no one would have remembered Romeo and Juliet if they got married and had three kids. Death made them eternal."

"This is the Catskills we're talkin' here, kiddo, not Verona."

"You're gonna do it, aren't you?"

I didn't bother playing dumb. "Yeah, I know it sounds crazy, but I feel like I owe it to him, to Arthur, to look. So I'll go up there for a few days and find out what the world already knows, that his sister and sixteen other unlucky people were killed in a fire."

"There's something else, isn't there? Something else is bothering you."

She stared at me coldly. She did that sometimes, like a boxer sizing up his opponent. She watched how I moved, my gestures. She waited to listen to my voice, my inflection. Did I mean what I was saying? It put me on edge, the way she did that, how she waited me out. It was the only part of her father I recognized in her. So I explained about my backseat visit with R. B. Carter and his attempt at checkbook diplomacy.

"So which is it, Moe?" Katy broke the silence. "Are you going up there because you feel guilty or because you're pissed off that someone thought they could buy you off cheap?"

"A little bit of both, I suppose. A little bit of both."

Katy pushed herself away from me and got to her feet. "I'm going to bed."

I was momentarily perplexed by the anger in her voice and the abruptness with which she pushed herself away. Then it came to me: Katy was frightened, even if she didn't quite realize it herself. Was she jealous? Yeah, maybe a tiny bit. There was, after all, a certain quixotic romance in the task I was about to take on. But mainly, I think, she was just scared.

I was no longer a cop when we'd met, and Katy hadn't had to deal with the silent fears every cop's wife faces every time her husband works his shift. And though I know for a fact that she thought my having an investigator's license was pretty cool, I guess it was cool just so long as it stayed in my sock drawer. Now I was actually taking on a case, crazy as it was, and leaving her and Sarah for the first time. I'd never thought it through before, because I didn't think anyone would actually come to me for help.

Explaining myself any further would just dig a deeper hole, so instead of talking I stood up and took her in my arms. I held her close, though she stood rigid in my embrace. It was Katy who had taught me that kind of physical reassurance. What my words could never say, my touch would. I loved her, and nothing, especially not some stupid high-school crush, could ever threaten that. I had already risked a lot more than a trip up to the Catskills to guarantee nothing would come between us. I had made a deal with the devil himself. I could feel the tension flow out of her, and we sat back down on the sofa. I guess we nodded off.

I woke up still on the couch, alone. Katy, who must have moved up to bed or to check on Sarah, was gone. Gradually, though, I became aware that I was not alone. I heard him breathing. Seated diagonally across the room from me on a wooly blue recliner was my father-in-law, Francis Maloney Sr. Regardless of what people say, when you marry a woman you marry her family. And it was times like these, these quiet moments alone with Francis Sr., that were the only aspect of my married life I dreaded.

When he noticed I was awake, he stopped swirling the glass of Bushmills whiskey he held in his right paw. His full attention was focused on me. It was his turn now to size up his prey, to survey my weaknesses, as his daughter had before him. But I mean it less metaphorically with Francis Sr. For, although he'd not spoken a word in protest against my marrying Katy, I always got the feeling he was toying with me the way a feral cat does with a grounded sparrow.

He took the opportunity, as he often did, to reinforce my uneasiness. My father-in-law smiled that cold, knowing smile at me and raised his glass in a mocking toast. Placing the whiskey upon his thigh, he continued to stare, continued to smile. That he despised me was fair enough. The feeling was more than mutual. It was only one of our silent secrets. What unnerved me was that he so enjoyed my discomfort. When we were alone like this, everything about him seemed to say: "Your day will come. You won't see it coming, but it will come." I think I understood what the grounded sparrow felt like.

We never discussed the biggest secrets, the roles each of us had played in Patrick's disappearance. He was one of the four people who knew about my having let Patrick slip away. I had tracked Patrick to his lover's apartment in the West Village, fully prepared to haul him back to his family by the scruff of his neck if necessary. But Jack, his lover and protector, convinced me that Patrick would go back voluntarily in a few days. They both gave me their word that Patrick wouldn't run, and, like a stupid-assed rookie, I believed them. No one had seen him since.

It was a secret, of course, that could ruin my marriage. A bomb the old man could drop in my lap at any time. I was pretty sure he wouldn't, though, because it was him who'd driven Patrick away in the first place. It'd been very ugly between them, very ugly. No, Francis Sr. had already lost both his sons. He wouldn't risk losing Katy, too. So, without ever discussing it, my father-in-law and I had created our own version of mutually assured destruction. But, just like it is with us and the Russians, I'm a lot more comfortable having my finger on the trigger than his.

The silence grew so steep that the only sound I could make out above my own breathing was the cracking of the ice as it melted in the whiskey glass. I would not speak. I would wait him out. A word, even a cough, would be a sign of weakness, and weakness was something I dared not show my father-in-law.

He transformed his cold smile into a cruel, joyless laugh. And, raising his glass to me a second time, grudgingly complimented: "A tough Jew, good. Good."

He was baiting me. I held my tongue.

Bored by my unwillingness to engage him, Francis Sr. worked his way out of the recliner and started toward the kitchen to freshen his whiskey. He stopped, as I knew he would, as he always did when we were alone, to turn back for a parting shot.

"Ghosts," he said. "Do Jews believe in ghosts?"

Ghosts again, always with the ghosts. I didn't get what his preoccupation was with ghosts, and he never seemed inclined to enlighten me. Though tonight, given the job I was about to take on, the subject of ghosts seemed oddly appropriate.

Katy was asleep when I got upstairs. I was exhausted, but almost too tired to sleep, so I took my first blind steps into the world

Arthur Rosen had left behind. And "blind steps" was just the right term, for I wasn't even sure what I was trying to find. Karen and Andrea were dead. The inquiries and inquests, no matter how shoddily performed, were sixteen years finished. Chances were the scene of the fire had been bulldozed, filled in, built over, sold and resold. All I had to work with were some disconnected words scrawled on a crazy man's walls, some old newspapers, and a dead man's paranoia. I was certain other detectives had worked with less. I just couldn't think of their names at the moment.

CHAPTER FIVE:
NOVEMBER 27TH

Katy's resistance to my Catskills adventure was a stroll in the park compared with Aaron's reaction. Unlike Katy, though, my big brother couldn't have cared less that I had taken a dead man's case. It mattered not to him whether my client was President Reagan or the Ghost of Christmas Past. To Aaron, there was no good reason to miss work short of open-heart surgery. And then only with a signed note from the doctor. We went round and round like a two-headed dog chasing its tail.

Dizzy from the chase, I put an end to it. "Look, Aaron, I haven't taken a vacation day or a personal day since Sarah was born. I got four weeks coming to me, so I'm takin' one of them. What's the big deal? It's not like I'm takin' Christmas-and-New Year's week."

"And for that I'm supposed to be grateful?"

"No, you're just supposed to understand. It was part of the agreement when we went into this business. I have the right to work cases."

"I have the right to wear a bra and panties and run through Times Square," he chided, "but it doesn't mean I'm going to do it."

"That's an image I don't want to think about."

We both laughed. Aaron surrendered.

He slapped my face playfully. "Get back soon or I'll start wearing sensible pumps and a handbag into work. Go already."

I gave Aaron my buddy Kosta's phone number and suggested he call him if things in the store got out of hand. Kosta was initially Katy's friend, but we'd grown pretty close. He managed a few punk and new wave bands. Yet even in punk's heyday, he was only slightly less successful at rock-and-roll management than the captain of the *Titanic* was at iceberg avoidance. Kosta was heading down the homestretch toward the poverty line.

"Don't worry." I cut Aaron off before he could object. "Kosta knows wine."

"Be safe, little brother," he said. "Be safe."

November was through teasing. It had definitely decided to pack up the denim jackets and stick them in the attic next to the plastic garbage bag marked "Indian Summer." Time had come to haul out the parkas and boots. And if there were any lingering questions about November's intentions, the mean shade of gray hanging in the air outside my windshield answered most of them. The remaining questions were answered by my throbbing knee. "Snow," it said in its unique kind of Morse code. "Snow." Just what I needed for my drive upstate.

Us denizens of the five boroughs referred to the Catskills as "upstate," but that was just another manifestation of our warped view of the universe. What do you expect? There are still a sizable number of lower-Manhattanites who consider Chelsea a northern suburb, Brooklyn another country, and Yonkers a distant planet. What they thought of the rest of the world, who can say? Potsdam, up on the Canadian border — now, that's upstate. Buffalo and Rochester to the northwest, they're upstate. In truth, the Catskills, a low mountain range only an hour or two north of the city, was actually downstate.

During the thirties, forties, and fifties, the Catskills had flourished as a summer-vacation spot for New York City's lower-

and middle-class populations. With its rich green valleys, numerous lakes, waterfalls, and scenic vistas, the Catskills offered a nearby escape from the sweltering city streets. The Catskills also offered something else: a place for individual ethnic groups to get relief from the pressures of the melting pot and associate in peace with their own. The Irish and Italians had their own enclaves in the mountains, but the Catskills would always be most closely associated with the Jews.

The Borscht Belt was a series of hotels that had sprung up in the Catskills over the years to service a vibrant Jewish clientele. The Concord, Grossinger's, Kutshers, Brown's were the big-name places that every Jewish kid knew. Unlimited quantities of bland kosher food, shuffleboard, goofy rituals like cross-dressing mock weddings, endless sessions of Simon Says, amateur talent shows, dance contests, and a house band with a trumpet player that shtupped every lonely skirt in residence — these were just some of the goodies you got for your money. But above all else, what defined the Catskills were the comedians who played the hotel ballrooms: Myron Cohen, Milton Berle, Jerry Lewis, Henny Youngman, Don Rickles, Stiller and Meara, Totie Fields, Joan

Rivers, David Brenner. All had cut their teeth doing the rounds.

Now don't get me wrong, the Catskills, like any other resort area had a pecking order. Not every hotel was so grand and gaudy. There were second- and third-rung hotels with second-and third-rung comedians. The food was a little blander, the portions smaller, the trumpet player a little less frisky. Never mind the bottom feeders like the motels, boarding houses, and bungalow colonies.

As a kid, I'd spent a few weeks during a few summers in the Catskills. Only once had we ever stayed at a top-notch hotel. I think I was seven or eight. Miriam, my baby sister, was just that, a baby sister. My dad, a supervisor for a big supermarket chain, had won a week at the Concord as a bonus for surpassing his quarterly projections. It was all right, I guess. There were other kids my age to play with, a pool, and lots of crappy food. Aaron, Miriam, and I were too young to see the shows, but my mom finished third in a beautiful-legs contest, and my parents won a cha-cha dance-off. I inherited that dance trophy. Katy put it up in the living room when we bought our house. What I remember most about that week in the mountains was that my parents were happy.

It was perhaps the only full week in my life when my parents seemed weightless.

We returned sporadically to the scene of the crime, but it was never the same. And with each return, the quality of the accommodations dropped a rung. My dad changed jobs; once, twice. Then he bought his own store. There was less money. There wasn't enough money. There was none. Then we stopped coming. Happiness was no longer part of the equation, and weightlessness was beyond my parents' escape velocity. Eventually, they were ground into dust by the tonnage of their own failures and other unseen forces of the universe.

But it was more than just my parents' balance sheet that had changed. The Catskills themselves had started to slide into the pit. Two things doomed the Borscht Belt: fast, reliable air travel and dependable, affordable air-conditioning. Who wanted to play seven days of shuffleboard when you could fly to Vegas for a week for the same money? Who needed to pack a hot car full of kids and in-laws to feel cool mountain air when cool air was available at the flip of a switch? And the dynamics had changed. Baby boomers were less ethnic, less traditional, more restless. By the mid-seventies, some of the big hotels had gone the way of Yiddish theater. Some hung on, but the clientele was much older, the lavish shows with first-rate talent were no more.

Sometimes I think it was my fate to catch things gone to seed. Coney Island, the world's playground during my parents' generation, was a wretched ghost town by the time my friends and I were old enough to go there on our own. The Dodgers moved to L.A. the year my dad promised to take me to a World Series game. Brooklyn itself had taken a sour turn during my watch. By 1957, the Dodgers weren't the only ones fleeing the County of Kings. Why should the Catskills have been any different?

But in the mid-sixties, though the seeds of its ruin had been sewn, the Catskills was still the place a lot of city kids went to gain some work experience while getting away. Even Aaron had done it for a summer — working as a waiter at a second-rate Borscht Belt hotel. That's what Karen and Andrea were doing that fateful summer, working at the eminently forgettable Fir Grove Hotel in the little burg of Old Rotterdam, New York.

Though it wasn't quite slavery, it wasn't exactly fair pay for a fair day's work either. You did receive a nominal weekly paycheck, but anything resembling real money came from tips. Your meals and room and board were free. That the food was leftovers from the paying guests' meals was a given. Oh, and that free room and board . . . True, the barracks at Auschwitz were worse. And not all the hotels housed their summer staffs in cramped, overcrowded firetraps like the one in which the girls had perished. No, some were more substandard. I guess if you survived it, like Aaron had, you could look back at the experience with a smile.

I wasn't smiling when I pulled up to Old Rotterdam Town Hall. My knee had been annoyingly correct about the snow, and the drive up along old Route 17 had been a slip-sliding adventure. Downstate New Yorkers, myself included, are great drivers until you introduce any of the various incarnations of wet weather into the mix.

Old Rotterdam, according to my AAA guide, had been established in 1698 as a fur-trading outpost. Baruch Rotterdam had immigrated first from Poland to Holland and then to the New World. Though his original surname was now an irretrievable artifact of history, it was widely held that he had taken on the name Rotterdam to honor his adopted country.

Town Hall was a hideous, nearly window-less concrete pillbox that looked like the prison from a Bauhaus acid trip. The place was as inviting as a sarcophagus. The thing of it was, it probably cost a fortune, whereas almost every house and business I passed on my way through town seemed weather-beaten and dirty even beneath the lie of whitest snow. I just knew its guts were going to be all hunks of prefab cement and acoustic tile.

What I was still trying to divine, however, as I hobbled in from out of the snow, was what I was doing here. It was silly, really. In New York City, the last place you'd start looking for anything or anyone would be City Hall. You might start at the morgue, the local precinct, the hospital, but never City Hall. Christ, on seven out of ten days, you wouldn't even find the mayor there. I suppose there was a part of me, in spite of lots of experience to the contrary, that wanted to believe that America outside of the Big Apple was *Leave It to Beaver*-land. Though my depressing drive through town had pretty much shot that fantasy all to hell.

In the end, I figured, I was here because it was someplace to start. With Marina Conseco and later with Patrick, there were obvious starting lines. Marina had vanished in Coney Island, Patrick at Pooty's Bar in TriBeCa. But even if I'd known exactly where to start, I still didn't know *what* I was starting. At least with Marina and Patrick, it was clear what — or, rather, for whom — I was looking.

"I want to hire you to find my sister," is what Arthur Rosen had said. Yeah, well, maybe in my next life. Maybe he had meant it figuratively. You know, he wanted me to track down people who had gone to school with her or worked with her that last summer, people who had survived the fire. Could he have wanted me to find her in their memories? I believed that for about ten seconds. It simply didn't jibe with the strange man's demeanor. He hadn't spent a decade and a half hiring lawyers, detectives, butchers, and bakers just to create a happy-family scrapbook.

Obviously Arthur felt something was wrong, but what exactly? What had produced such hopelessness in Arthur Rosen that he had chosen Thanksgiving Eve 1981 to end his life? He had had fifteen, sixteen years of hopeless nights from which to choose. Guilty as I felt for turning him down, not even I believed my rejection was the sole determining factor in his death.

Figuring Arthur Rosen hadn't kept old copies of the *Catskill Tribune* to line the bottom of a birdcage delusion, I had hoped to find a starting point in the pages of one of the editions I'd "borrowed" from his room the night he'd hanged himself. Nothing doing. As far as I could tell, the only thing that tied the papers together was the masthead. In fact, I was more confused after reading through them than when I'd started. The papers were from different days, different months, different years. No two stories carried over from one paper to another. I could find no common theme. Even the reporters seemed to change from month to month. I guessed that was pretty common with small-town papers.

As it turned out, Town Hall wasn't such a bad place to begin. Inside the predictably sterile lobby were the usual flags, plaques, and glass cases featuring displays of local elementary-school art. But all was not lost. There was this huge wooden signboard up on one wall listing all the current elected officials of Old Rotterdam and the surrounding county. You had to love politicians and their egos. The smaller the politician, the larger the sign. The damn signboard was bigger than the scoreboard at Shea. I wondered if it lit up when a local high-school kid hit a homer. I'm not complaining, mind you, because up there on the big board was a name I recognized from the wall in

Arthur's room.

Councilman at Large
RICHARD T. HAMMERLING

The logical thing to have done, I didn't do, not immediately anyway. I didn't rush up to the information desk to find the location of Councilman Hammerling's office. I stood there instead, trying to formulate an approach to take with Hammerling. Somehow I didn't think my presence would be well received if I barged into his office proclaiming I was the part owner of a Manhattan wine shop looking for a long-dead girl because her recently dead brother had said there was something wrong with a sixteen-year-old investigation. I guess I'm just funny that way. Yet, no matter how I tried to spin the words in my head, they always came out sounding rather ridiculous. I decided to take a more subtle approach and not divulge exactly what I was doing there.

"Oh, I'm sorry," the heavy woman at the information table apologized. "Dick — I mean Councilman Hammerling — is out of town for the weekend. I think he's in Vermont skiing. You up from the city?"

"My Brooklyn accent's showing, huh?

84

Twenty years of diction lessons all to no avail."

She stared at me, blankly and unsure. Sarcasm isn't a universal language. That's a thing most New Yorkers forget when they venture beyond the city limits. Most Americans don't spend 80 percent of their waking hours constructing witty comebacks and snide remarks. Not everyone acts as if they're onstage at the Improv or trying to outwit Groucho Marx or George Bernard Shaw. Most people say what needs to be said and shut up.

"I'm sorry," I said, "just joking. Will Mr. Hammerling be back on Monday?"

"Sure will, Mr. . . ."

"Prager, Moe Prager."

"I can leave him a message if —"

"That won't be necessary," I assured her. "I'll just come back Monday morning."

She smiled sweetly. She had a pretty face that even all her added weight couldn't disguise. She had sincere brown eyes, high cheekbones, plush lips, and a never-say-die smile.

"Okay, then," she said, "enjoy your weekend. I hope you had a pleasant Thanksgiving."

I thanked her, began walking out, and turned back. "Listen, I used to stay in a

place up here when I was a kid. I think I
might like to spend the night there for old
times' sake. The . . ." I snapped my fingers
for effect. "The . . . the Fir Grove Hotel.
That's it!"

The smile ran away from her face. I could
see she was struggling to find the words to
tell me what I already knew.

"Fir Grove burnt down maybe sixteen,
seventeen years ago." She shook her head
sadly. "Lotta folks died in the fire, teenagers
mostly. Of course, I was just a kid back
then, but I remember the fire."

"I'm sorry to hear that. They didn't
rebuild, huh? Are there any other of the old-
style hotels up there, by where the Fir Grove
used to be?"

"On the other side of town, yeah, plenty."
She perked up, grabbing at a stack of
brochures. "But up where the old Fir Grove
was, no, nothing. No one up there now but
the hayseeds and the Hasids."

"Hayseeds and Hasids?" I repeated.

"You know, Hasids: the funny-dressed
Jews in black clothes and beards. The
women shave their heads and —" She cut
herself off. Clamping a hand over her
mouth, she clenched her entire body. She
blushed red as a cherry cough drop, her eyes
darting dizzyingly from side to side. "Oh, I

didn't mean to offend you." Her voice cracked as she whispered through her meaty fingers. "That was a stupid thing to say. It's just a local sort of joke — the hayseeds-and-Hasids thing. I forget myself sometimes. Oh God, I'm so embarrassed."

"Relax. Relax. It's okay. No offense taken. If I gave myself a nickel every time an embarrassing thing came out of my mouth, I'd'a made myself a rich man by now. Forget it. Look, I'm the one who should be ashamed," I confessed. "I knew about the fire at the Fir Grove. I'm up here doing research on the demise of the Borscht Belt and I thought you might let something interesting slip."

That did the trick. Her body unclenched.

"Take me for a drink later and I'll let something interesting slip."

I held up my left hand and wriggled my ring finger. "Sorry, terminally married."

"Hey, Moe, I've seen last call too many times to fret details like wedding bands. Besides, maybe I could really help you with the research. Sitting in this chair, I know everything about everything in this town."

I winked. "Maybe you can help, but first you gotta pass a little test."

She was intrigued. "What kind of test?"

"Remember when I asked about a hotel

87

to stay in?"

"Yeah," she purred.

"Which one of the hotels on the other side of town would still have some old-timers on the staff. You know, people who've worked up here since you were a —"

"The Swan Song Hotel and Resort," she stopped me. "Here." She dealt me a brochure out of the handful she had originally pulled out of the rack.

"Did I hear you right, the Swan Song?" I asked, even as I read the name. "That's an odd name."

"It is?" she wondered, that blank stare returning.

"Never mind. Listen, I'm sorry, but what's your name?"

"Molly," she said, "Molly Treat."

I winked again. "You certainly are. I'll hold you to that drink."

"I'll be here."

I didn't doubt it.

The place was exactly what I expected. Just like all the other buildings in Old Rotterdam, excepting, of course, hideous Town Hall, the buildings that made up the Swan Song Hotel and Resort were well on their way to disintegration. The chill and mask of snow only seemed to heighten the sense of despair. Huge icicles hung off neglected fascia boards. Soffits were missing everywhere, and windows throughout the campus were covered by plastic sheets and plywood. Although the top layer of snow presented the eye with the illusion that the long, twisty driveway up to the main house was paved smooth as an airport runway, my tires and shock absorbers told a different tale.

The main house, a beast of building, had probably once been a beautiful study in Victorian asymmetry. But, like many of the structures of that era, it had had its turrets and porches, its intricate spindles and fish-scale shingles stripped away and replaced with an incongruent hodgepodge of stucco, aluminum siding, and fake brick. One vestige of the original building remained: a curvy porch extended from one side of the front entrance around the right side of the big house. Even in the dying light I could see it was sagging terribly. The numerous missing spindles from its rails gave it the look of a jack-o'-lantern's mouth. Before getting out of the car, I popped the dome light on and studied the brochure Molly Treat had given me. Clearly, the pictures for the brochure had been taken a very long time ago. A very long time indeed.

A bent little man patrolled the front desk,

his bald head and crooked back barely visible above the mahogany counter. There was a big old-fashioned bell atop the counter, but, like the rest of the room, the bell hadn't been polished in recent history.

"You Prager?" the gnome asked as I approached. "Molly gave a call from the town, said you might be coming. I'm Sam Gutterman, the proprietor of this lovely establishment. The brochure says Swan Song Hotel and Resort. Considering the age and health of our guests, it's more like the Swan Song Hospice and Last Resort."

I was laughing by the time I shook Gutterman's hand. It felt good to laugh again. His grip was surprisingly firm. In spite of his sparkly blue eyes and white smile, I figured him for his mid-seventies.

"I'm Prager. And you should have been a comedian."

"Anybody ever tell you you got a flare for the self-evident?" Gutterman wagged his finger at me. "What, you think I owned this palace my whole life? I used to be Sudden Sam Gutterman, Blue Boy of the Borscht Belt. You shouldn't know from it! I used more four-letter words than Webster's Unabridged! You know what one wise-guy critic once wrote?"

"What?"

" 'Sudden Sam Guttermouth is . . .' Wait," he said, rubbing his chin, "I vanna get this right. 'Sudden Sam Guttermouth is perhaps the only man alive — if you call what he does living — who could make Belle Barth sound like Oscar Wilde.' You know Belle Barth?"

"My folks had her records," I said. "I used to listen to them when I stayed home sick from school. My favorite joke of hers was about the famous Yiddish actor Boris Tomashevsky."

"If you want bread, go bang a baker," he recited the punch line without missing a beat.

"That's the one."

He glowed. "We're gonna get along, you and me. You're a good audience." Sam turned behind him to the maze of little mailboxes, recited eenie-meenie-minie-moe, and picked a key. "This is where you would expect me to say that I'm giving you our best room. But since we don't have even a good room, this one will have to do." He handed me the key.

"Two twenty-one," I said, reading the number off the tag.

"I could lie to you and say I gave you that room so you wouldn't have trouble carrying your bag upstairs. You can guess already the elevator hasn't worked since the last time I got laid. And you wouldn't want to insult an old man by guessing how long ago that was."

"I didn't know they had elevators during the Civil War."

"Don't be such a wiseass." He wagged his finger again. "You're supposed to be the straight man. Got it?"

"Got it."

"Like I was saying, it's not about how far you gotta carry your bag. It's about how far you'd fall when the fucking building collapses."

I feigned dismay. "Maybe I'd like a room on the upper floors. This way I'd fall on top of the rubble instead of it falling on me."

"It's your funeral, *bubeleh,* but the heat don't work up there."

I shook Sam's hand good night and asked if I could have breakfast with him. In spite of his protestations, he accepted my invitation. When I reached for my bag, the former Blue Boy of the Borscht Belt ordered me to stop.

"I gotta ring the bell for the hop," he explained. "It's tradition."

"Let me guess, you haven't had a bellhop since the last time you got laid."

"Since the first time I got laid." Sam

laughed. "George Washington was in the next bed."

The room was actually clean and quite a bit more pleasant than the rest of the Swan Song. The furnishings were old, but neat. They dated back to the late fifties or early sixties, all very retro, very *Jetsons*. There were lots of big square cushions covered in thick orange wool. The lamps sort of looked like B-movie rocket ships. The Bakelite phone on the bedside table was a real relic. You didn't quite need a crane to lift up the receiver. I buzzed Sam and asked for an outside line.

"Would you believe me if I told you all the outside lines were busy?" he wondered.

"No."

"Good. I'll patch you through."

I dialed the Maloneys' number. Katy answered. The sound of her voice made my heart sink. I was suddenly very lonely. My cells, I think, were remembering just how empty my life had been before I met her. She asked me how things were going. I told her about Sam. She thought he sounded like fun. Katy held the phone up to Sarah, who talked at me some. Katy said Sarah smiled when she heard my voice. I promised to call the next day, said I loved them both probably one too many times, and hung up.

When I turned the TV on, I decided to downgrade my assessment of the room. There was more snow on the screen than on the collapsing roof.

CHAPTER SIX:
NOVEMBER 28TH

The phone was ringing louder than I'd heard a phone ring in quite some time. Given what Sam had said about the average age of his clientele, loud was probably good. Still groggy, I reached for the receiver and promptly dropped it on my forehead. Believe me, with how much the thing weighed, dropping it on your head was either going to snap you completely awake or plunge you into a persistent vegetative state. I escaped with only a mild concussion.

It was dark when I trundled down to meet Sam in the kitchen. I wasn't thrilled about the hour, but I had asked him to breakfast, and it seemed we were going to do it on his terms. I told myself that this was a good thing, that I'd get an early start. What I was getting an early start with had yet to be established. Hammerling wasn't going to be back till Monday morning. I hoped Sam might have some insight. Maybe he could point a blind detective in the right direction.

I still had trouble thinking of myself as a detective. Not because I'd never officially worked a case since getting my license. It had more to do with my never getting a gold shield while I was on the job. I'd spent my whole ten years in the bag, in uniform. My buddies thought finding Marina Conseco would have earned me my shield. It got me a medal instead. I had almost convinced myself that I didn't want to make detective because of dumb luck or on the back of a little girl's suffering. Sometimes I still believe that.

Something smelled delicious but completely out of place in the Swan Song's allegedly kosher kitchen: frying bacon, God's quintessential torment. With bacon you were fucked either way. Even if you were an observant Jew and disdained pork products, there was no prohibition against breathing. And one sniff, one breath that contained that sweetly smoky aroma, could torture the most devout rabbi. If, on the other hand, you were, like myself, a bad Jew, or someone unconstrained by five-thousand-year-old dietary laws, you were still screwed. Bacon was cholesterol's perfect delivery system. Bacon-egg-and-cheese sandwiches had killed more cops than all the cheap hand-guns ever made.

"Tsk, tsk, Sam." I shook my head in mock disapproval. "This is gonna cost you a dozen mitzvahs. If there was a hell . . ."

"What'd'ya mean, if? This *is* hell! Sit down, Mr. Wise Guy, and eat. The bacon's from my own private stock. Once the natives stir, we're all of a sudden kosher again."

"Can't they smell it?" I asked.

"Most of my guests are beyond breathing, let alone smelling." Sam waved, shoving a mouthful of eggs, potato, and bacon into his trap. "And if they do smell it, they forget before they complain."

I did as the man said and sat across from Sam at a two-top table set up in the back of the kitchen. We could make out the first rays of daylight through a big window that gave new meaning to the term "stained glass." The windows were so thick with accumulated grease that the world appeared in sepia tones. You could see the hole in the ground that used to be the pool, and many of the other buildings from our vantage point. Sam didn't waste his time looking. Eventually, I stopped playing the wide-eyed newcomer and got down to eating. The food was good, but the coffee tasted like the brown water at the bottom of what used to be the pool. Sam noticed the look on my face.

"Stinks, doesn't it? It's this freeze-dried crap we mix with hot water. Then we put it in the urns to give the impression that it's brewed. I'm always afraid to look at the percentage of real coffee in the packages," he admitted.

"Smart thing," I said, trying to wash the taste out of my mouth with something that was supposed to be orange juice. "They probably measure the percentage of real coffee in parts per million."

"Probably," Sam agreed. "Listen, if you don't mind me asking, what the fuck are you doing here? It's not that I'm not flattered you chose my establishment, but your being on the premises brings the average age around here down from ninety-eight to ninety-seven and eleven months and twenty-nine days."

"Research," I snapped back without hesitation. "I'm doing research on the demise of the Cat—"

"Bullshit! Pardon my French, Mr. Moe, but you can't bullshit an old bullshitter like me. You might be able to feed the Molly Treats of the world that line of crap, but not old Sam. So . . ."

"Were you around when the workers'

quarters at the Fir Grove burned down?"

Sam changed. I can't say how, exactly. His expression remained constant. The corners of his mouth didn't suddenly turn down, nor did he furrow his brow. He did not avert his sparkly blue eyes. He did not cough or hem and haw. Yet something was different, as if the gases in his exhalation had turned sour.

"I was around. I was around the fucking corner. I was the entertainment director of the Fir Grove back then. I did two shows a night, emceed, ran the dance contest, bussed the tables, and cleaned the toilets if I had to. It was a real topnotch job, just below child molester and just above cancer-study participant. Why you wanna know, *boychik?*"

"That's what I'm here researching." And for the very first time since I received it, I showed someone my license. That I kept it in the same case as my old cop badge was completely calculated. Like I'd told Dr. Prince, badges help cut through the crap.

"Sixteen years after the fact." The old comedian beamed. "Now, that's what I call a late start."

"What can you tell me about it?"

"What's to tell? Some putz was smoking in bed, and — poof! — teenagers well done.

You working for Hammerling, that publicity-seeking missile?"

"No."

"For who, then? Who would be interested so long after it happened?"

"Sorry, Sam, I can't tell you that. But I bet you knew that?"

"Sure, Sudden Sam knows all, sees all, says nothing." He rolled his hands and fingers at me like Svengali putting his victim into a trance. "You hypnotized yet? My fingers are gettin' stiff already."

"Anything left of the old place" — I was curious — "the Fir Grove, I mean?"

Sam shrugged. "Maybe some stuff. They bulldozed a lot of it. This I know for sure. I don't get over there much. Only the hayseeds —"

"— and the Hasids. Yeah, I know. Molly told me."

"Yeah, well, I like to think of 'em as the rebels and the rabbis myself. See for yourself. Take a ride over, but leave your chai in your room," he suggested, placing his hand on my forearm.

"Why?"

He patted my arm. "You'll see when you get there."

Before I could ask him about his odd warning, a chubby Hispanic man in chef's pants and hat approached Sam. He bowed to me slightly. *"Jefe,"* he addressed Sam, "the old people, they comeeng."

Sam got up without a word of goodbye and marched into the dining room right past the cook. The cook smirked, shrugged his shoulders in puzzlement, and headed back to his kitchen station. I waited a moment or two before heading through the dining room. I was curious to see if my fellow guests were really as close to meeting their Maker as Sam made them out to be.

It was still early, but there were several fully seated tables. Most of the breakfast diners were old ladies. Most were closer to Sam's age than Methusehah's. I spotted a cane here and there, two walkers, and one wheelchair. It wasn't quite the hospice Sudden Sam had made it out to be. As I walked through the dining room, I felt a tug on my arm. An elderly gent, rather elegantly dressed for this hour of the morning, had latched on to me.

"Friend of Gutterman's?" he asked.

"A guest just like yourself," I said, smiling down at the man, who vaguely reminded me of my dad.

"A guest, maybe, but not like me." He let go of me and threw his arms in the air. "You must be a special guest for Sam to share his bacon with you."

"Nothing special about me. Sam says no one knows about the bacon."

"Sam says a lot of things. Sam's a —"

"Sam's gonna burn your cane for firewood, Mr. Roth." The old comedian appeared out of thin air. He introduced me formally to Mr. Roth. Mr. Roth didn't seem much in the mood to chat anymore and went back to the task of forcing down his breakfast.

"Here," Sam said, handing me a piece of paper as he ushered me out of the dining room. "These are directions from here to where the old Fir Grove was. Listen, I wasn't kidding before about leaving your jewelry behind. You still carry?"

"My off-duty piece, yeah."

"Good. There's some real *meshuggenehs* around there. Serious people. Watch yourself. I can't afford to lose a full-price customer." He winked.

The sky was cloudy, but not threatening. Some of the snow had melted, and the roads, though winding, were less of a challenge than they'd been the previous day. As I approached the vicinity of what had once been the Fir Grove, I saw one half of the cast for the favorite local joke. Crowds of bearded men in long black robes or coats, fur and black felt hats trudged along the roadside, followed by groups of younger boys in yarmulkes, with curls extending down their cheeks along their ears. Behind the men and boys were a few women and girls. Their skirts, revealed beneath their coats when the wind came up, were uniformly long. It was Saturday, Shabbas, the Jewish Sabbath. Unfamiliar with the area, I couldn't know whether they were coming from or going to temple. I could see the look of condescension and disdain on the men's faces as I slowed to pass. "Bad Jew!" their eyes accused. The women did not look at all.

On the streets of Crown Heights, Williamsburg, or Borough Park, I would have barely noticed the Hasidim. I was used to them in their Brooklyn enclaves, their self-imposed ghettos. It was just that they seemed so out of place here in the snow, among the tall pines and country roads. But, no, that's a lie. I always noticed and was never comfortable with them. The sight of them evoked two powerful and wildly opposite responses in me. I both envied their faith and was horribly embarrassed by them. Their faith allowed them a kind of freedom I could never have. So sure were they in their knowledge of God that they could ignore the real world. They could even thumb their noses at the rest of us by wearing their curls and beards and black coats. "Look. Look at us!" they seemed to say. "We know the truth."

I left my discomfort in the rearview mirror. A few miles up the road I noticed two carved-granite pine trees standing silent vigil at the entrance to what had been the driveway up to the Fir Grove Hotel. They weren't quite in the same class as Cleopatra's Needles, but they were impressive nonetheless. Astride the stone trees were three-foot-by-three-foot rough-hewn hunks of rock to which, I imagined, were once affixed brass plaques reading "FIR GROVE HOTEL." You could still make out the holes where the bolts had fitted, holding the plaques in place. These days, however, in lieu of brass were two plywood placards held to the rock with duct tape. Their message was simple: "KEEP OUT."

I did not.

Just like the driveway at the Swan Song, the pavement was chewed up and neglected. The approach was a steep uphill climb, and the entire driveway was an impressive semicircle around what would have been the great lawn. I stopped my car at the stone-and-concrete footing where the main house of the old Fir Grove had once stood. I tried imagining it in its mid-century splendor, but since I'd never actually seen the old place, all I could picture in my mind's eye was the dilapidated main house of the Swan Song. I wondered where the workers' quarters had been and realized I was probably going about this all wrong. I should have gone to the library first and done a little research. But should-haves are like ifs, they're both tremendous wastes of time.

I drove a little farther on down the driveway, until I spotted a left turnoff. Ahead of me, the snow marked out a huge, slightly sunken rectangle. The guest parking lot, I suspected. I continued to the very back edge of the lot, which was marked by wildly overgrown hedges. Now out of my car, I stepped through the tangle of hedges, its branches slapping my cheeks as I went. On the other side of the thicket, I finally got my first glimpse of what had become of the old place.

I was atop a hill. Several feet ahead of me were concrete steps leading down to where the pool had been. A moot fiberglass slide and a set of rusty metal bars that had once held the diving board helped delineate opposite ends of the pool. To the right of the pool, rising out of the snow, stood two ten-foot-high poles. A half-moon backboard dangled off the top of one of the poles, swinging in the wind like the blade of the executioner's ax. These days, my surgical knee ached at even the thought of playing hoops. No one had played ball here in a very long time. Looking out at the impotent equipment, I found myself thinking of Coney Island. Once the world's playground, it, too, had been abandoned, the frames of its disused rides rising out of the earth like metal and wooden bones of vanquished dinosaurs. But it was neither the pool area nor Coney Island that currently captured my attention.

I managed to descend the steps without breaking my neck. No small feat, given the state of the wrought-iron guardrail. About half a football field beyond the pool area I saw smoke rising above yet another hedge-row. As I approached I could smell it. It smelled of pine resin and bacon. And, perhaps for the first time in sixteen years, I imagined the horror of the night the work-ers' quarters burned to the ground, the panic and terror. I'd seen the ugly things fire did to people. But it was the smells of fire that stayed with you, particularly the smell of burnt human hair. I thought of the flames licking at Andrea and shuddered.

Stepping through the second hedge, I was still preoccupied with the image of Andrea's charred body. So I was unprepared for the thud of heavy paws against my chest that sent me sprawling in the snow. Scrambling to stand and reaching for my .38, I slipped back down. As I continued to fumble for my gun, I caught sight of the thick-chested Rottweiler that had put me down in the first place. He came at me again, a string of white saliva dripping from his blunted snout. As I raised my pistol into the best shooting position I could manage there on my ass in the snow, two things convinced me to lower my weapon. One was the rattle of the heavy chain which I noticed would prevent the dog from actually getting to me. The other, and by far more convincing, reason was the unmistakable *chiching* of a round being chambered into a pump-action shotgun. In fact, I did more than just lower my weapon. I tossed it into the snow and raised my hands way, way up.

"On your feet, asshole!" the man with the shotgun ordered. "This is private property. What are you doin' here?"

He was a tall man in his thirties. He sported a stocking cap and long underwear.

In fact, he would have looked quite ridiculous if it weren't for the shotgun aimed at my chest. He was standing on the wooden steps of a double-wide trailer, which itself was set on cinder blocks. Two flags flew behind him, on either side of the front door: the good old Confederate flag over his right shoulder and a Nazi flag over his left. The red-and-black Nazi flag wasn't the typical swastika flag but, rather, one that bore a black cross. It was the Maltese Cross, a favorite with motorcycle gangs.

Earlier, I had seen one half of the favorite local joke: the Hasids. Now it was my turn to meet the hayseeds. This was where the other half lived. No wonder Sam warned me to leave my jewelry at home. I somehow got the feeling no one was going to invite me in for a little chopped liver on matzoh.

"I'm a cop!" I lied. "I got my badge in my pocket." I nodded my chin at my chest.

"Let's see. Slow."

I waved my badge at him, but he didn't put the gun down. Cops, apparently, weren't the rage around here either. There were several other trailers in the little compound, and Mr. Pump Action and I were beginning to attract a crowd. Doors were opening and people, including women and children, in various states of dress, were sticking their heads out to have a look-see. It did not escape the attention of my friend with the shotgun that we were no longer alone. He eased up a bit now that we had an audience.

"That's not a local badge!" he shouted for everyone to hear.

"New York City," I answered.

"Jew Yorker, huh? Okay, you can put your arms down and go pick up your piece."

As I knelt to pick up my .38, I took a look around. Along with the double-wides were a few ratty car-trailers, sheds, even a shack or two. There were cars in various states of disrepair strewn about the place, some with flat tires, some on milk crates. Not every residence flew racist flags. But there were dogs, lots of dogs, though most of them were a lot scrawnier than my pal the Rottweiler.

I also noticed that no one, not even the guy with the shotgun, was willing to approach me. Everybody seemed to be waiting, but for what or whom was unclear. It didn't remain unclear for very long. The front door of the double-wide immediately to the right of Mr. Pump Action's swung open. All heads, including mine, swung that way, and the crowd held its collective breath. Through the door came a little man so thin he was nearly two-dimensional. Only in the movies do Nazi types look like blue-eyed, blond-haired supermen. In real life they usually look like the kids no one wants to play with. This clown was no exception.

He stood about five foot seven on tippy-toes and was, I guessed, in his mid-twenties. He looked like a cat sneeze could snap his femur. He wore his hair slicked back, but the natural wave of his dark-brown hair defeated the look of authority he was going for. Having tried to tame my own hair in this manner and to the same end, I almost felt sorry for him. He had a rather too-long face, plain brown eyes, and a skinny nose that had caught too many unblocked left hooks.

"Cops are unwelcome here," he squeaked at me.

"Yeah," I said, "I got that."

"What's your business?"

"Sightseeing."

Everyone had a good laugh at that one. Skinny came down from his perch and approached me, making sure Mr. Pump Action kept his weapon on me. He strode right up into my face.

"We don't get many sightseers around here," he prodded, playing to the crowd.

"I don't see why not. With this kinda

hospitality, I'm surprised they don't come by the busload."

"Okay, everybody," he said, turning, "go back to what you're doing. We're not gonna have any trouble. Are we?" he whispered to me out the side of his mouth.

"Not from me."

He waited until the crowd broke up before addressing me again. He also motioned for the man with the shotgun to come join us.

"My name is Anton Harder," Skinny declared without offering me his hand. His smile, I noticed, had vanished along with the onlookers. "Who are you and what are you doing here?"

I figured to let him choke on the truth — my version of it, anyway. "My name is Prager. I'm up from the city on an investigation. We got an arsonist in lockup confessed to starting the Fir Grove fire all those years ago. Maybe he's fulla shit. Maybe he's not. Personally, I think he's one of those guys who confesses to any unsolved crimes."

"The Fir Grove fire was an accident!" Harder snapped through clenched teeth. "Some bitch or nigger was smoking in bed."

"Hey, I'm with you, but I go where the brass sends me."

"I saw your badge through the window," he said, pushing me gently to start walking.

111

"It didn't look like a detective's shield."

So Anton Harder wasn't an idiot. He knew what was what.

"I never said I was a detective. Sometimes on task forces plainclothes cops do some of the legwork. So — where's the workers' quarters — I mean, where were they?"

"That's where we're going, Officer Prager."

The three of us took a short stroll over another hill and down into a little glen. At the crest of the hill I could make out the foundation of a building that was no longer standing. It was partially obscured by the snow, but not completely. So this was where the workers' quarters had been. As we moved down toward its location, a horrid stench came up the hill to greet me. It was two parts Fountain Avenue dump mixed with three parts Knapp Street sewage plant. My tour guides seemed to take no notice of the foul odor. When we got up close, the smell was so overwhelming I had to cover my nose and mouth with a gloved hand.

Harder made a sweeping gesture. "This is what you came to see."

In the woods beyond the old foundation were piles and piles of garbage left to sit and putrefy in the open air.

"Cesspool's right under your feet," Mr.

Pump Action wanted me to know. "Be careful where you step, now. We wouldn't want you to drown in shit after coming all this way."

Harder snickered. Then there was silence. And now that I was here, I wasn't sure why I'd bothered to come. I guess I had had a need to see the place for myself, the place where they had died. Their bones and souls were long gone from here, as was any hint of the fire. Maybe I had wanted to come and add one more name to the list of fatalities. Arthur Rosen's name needed to be uttered here, so I said it aloud.

"What was that?" Harder pounced.

"Nothing," I said. "Just some dead guy's name. That's all."

Then Harder said something very odd. "Fitting tribute."

"What is?" I wondered aloud. "To whom?"

"The cesspool and garbage, to the trash that died here. Fitting, isn't it?"

I could easily have twisted his head off his twiglike neck before Mr. Pump Action could even have raised his weapon, but I wasn't here to play out a scene from *Gentlemen's Agreement* or to preach on the brotherhood of man. I had just wanted to see the place.

"All right," I said, turning in the direction of the hill, "I've seen enough."

"No," Harder protested, "don't go yet. There's something else I want you to see. This way, Officer Prager, please."

We strolled a further thirty yards on away from the garbage and the cess. And here was a most incongruous sight: a lovely and perfectly trimmed thicket. The thicket was rectangular in shape, measuring a good twenty by twenty feet, with the hedges a good seven feet in height. We walked around the bushes and passed through an archlike opening in the shrubbery. A single gray granite cross stood at the head of what appeared to be a grave. The name Missy Higgins was etched into the horizontal bar of the granite cross. At the foot of the grave was a stone bench. Fresh red roses lay at the base of the cross. The flowers looked especially bloody set against the pure snow.

I stared intently at Harder, but he did not return my gaze. He was focused on the cross. I opened my mouth to speak, and though Harder could not have seen this, he anticipated my question.

"They weren't all kikes and niggers, you know."

"No one's really buried there," I said rather feebly.

"No," he agreed. "She'd still be alive if she'd stuck to her own kind." He turned.

114

"You can go now, Officer. And don't come back around here without a warrant next time. We wouldn't want to mistake you for a deer or a trespasser. Peter, show Officer Prager off the land, will you?"

Peter Pump Action nodded that he would and gave me a shove with the butt end of his shotgun. We took a more direct line toward where the old pool area was as Harder faded away over the crest of the hill. I couldn't help watching the little man fade out of sight. I tried engaging Peter in a conversation, but he wasn't much of a conversationalist without an audience. He left me by the swimming-pool slide without so much as a ta-ta.

Climbing the steps to the guest parking lot wasn't any easier than it had been getting down. When I finally got to my car, I saw that I'd been rewarded for my efforts with a brick thrown into my rear windshield. And, as if that wasn't enough, the word **JEW** was spray-painted across the hood in a particularly bright yellow paint. The brick, at least, had not penetrated the glass, managing only to pit it. Spidery cracks spread across the glass. I camouflaged the spray paint with some slush and snow, leaving behind the Fir Grove grounds and the angry white men who now lived there.

115

The snow and slush worked for about two minutes. The wind and the heat of my engine conspired to expose the yellow paint. Deciding to give the snow-and-slush routine another shot, I steered up onto the shoulder near a bend in the road. I regretted my decision almost immediately, for at the precise moment I shut the door behind me a group of Hasidic men turned the bend.

I was taken aback by my sense of nakedness. I wanted to throw my coat over the hood and run and apologize and explain all at once. I said nothing. There was nothing to be said. Instead, I stood as still as the granite cross. Only my eyes moved, watching their eyes, watching their faces watch me. But the accusal that burned in me was absent from their faces. What I did see were almost imperceptible smiles, subtle nods, a raised eyebrow. Once past, they never slowed their pace. They did not look back. They moved on. Their silence cut through me like shrapnel. I dispensed with the camouflage until I reached the very edge of town.

There's just something about men and hardware stores. I am by no means a handy sort. The tool I use best is the telephone, to call the superintendent. It's to civilization's benefit that it was never dependent upon my dexterity to move from one stage of development to the next, or we'd still be without fire, stone tools, and the wheel. Having said that, I could spend endless hours strolling the aisles of nuts and bolts, plungers and pipes, paints and pry bars. Even the scent of a hardware store was like a siren's song. *Quick, lash me to the mast!*

Making a selection was no easy task. I debated whether to go for basic flat black paint to get good coverage until I got the hood properly repainted, or to try and match the red of my car as closely as possible. I went for the black. I waited my turn on line listening to the local chatter.

As the line shortened, my eye caught sight of a ghostly figure passing by the big plate-glass window. I don't mean Halloween ghostly either. Maybe ghoulish is a better word. He was a tall man with very close-cropped hair. His shoulders were stooped as if he were bearing Atlas' load, but without the requisite strength. His skin was pale, drawn tightly against the skull and high cheekbones. He was skeletally thin. Because I could not see the lower half of his body, he seemed almost to float. His faded wool coat was three loose threads away from the rag pile. I don't know why I found him so fascinating. Maybe because there was something about the way he carried himself that made him seem so out of place.

"Will that be all, sir?"

"Huh?"

"The spray paint, will that be all?" the hardware store clerk asked, pointing at the can.

I paid the clerk, and by the time I got outside, my ghost had gone. Safely off Main Street and out of town, I toweled off the hood and got busy spraying. It was a pretty neat job and would do for now. Yet, as I drove back to the Swan Song, I could not help staring at the hood. Though I knew it was impossible, I swear I could see the raised letters **JEW** beneath the top coat of black. I guess I wasn't going to feel better about things until a sanding wheel was taken to the hood.

From all appearances, the remainder of my journey back to the hotel went without incident. No one insulted or threatened me or vandalized my car. No one hurled bricks or snowballs or epithets in my direction. But my guts were churning. All of a sudden, the idea of introducing a new customer to the power and dry complexity of a fine French Cabernet seemed very appealing. I was out of my element. I'd lost my chops for the job. I'd grown soft and happy and comfortable. Even when I was on the job I was never as tough as I made myself out to be, and now it was worse.

Eventually, I stopped trying to convince myself of that lie. Keeping the truth about Patrick away from Katy, and the silent collusion between my father-in-law and myself, had taught me a painful lesson: to be an accomplished liar, I had to be brutally honest with myself. Over the last few years, I had honed the skill to a fine art, and was superb at lying to people as close to me as my own shadow. No, I was now so intimately familiar with the mechanics of lying that I understood my current unease had nothing to do with my having grown fat and happy, or with my lack of toughness — perceived or otherwise. The truth was, Old Rotterdam was getting to me.

For all its considerable decrepitude, the Swan Song was looking pretty good to me as I pulled up its long driveway. I'd spent fewer than twenty-four hours as a guest here, yet it felt suspiciously like home. Given my day to that point, a discarded refrigerator box might have felt like home. I also felt suddenly very tired. I pulled into a parking spot, killed the engine, and just sat there with my eyes closed.

Then something hit the glass next to my head. I startled. I must have looked a fool, jumping out of my skin there in the front seat, trying to yank up my coat to get at my gun. When I saw it was Mr. Roth, the old guy from breakfast, tapping the driver's-side window with his cane, I decided shooting him would have been a bit of an over-reaction.

"You all right in there, mister?" he shouted through the glass.

I rolled the window down. "Fine. I was just resting my eyes a little, Mr. Roth."

"You remember my name!" He was delighted. "I was worried that you'd fall asleep with the motor running or something."

"I guess I did doze off for a second there, but the car was off. Thanks anyway."

"I didn't notice. I was just worried," he repeated.

"Thanks again."

He sort of hesitated. His body language suggested he had more to say but needed me to cue him.

"Listen . . ." I said just to say something, my head still a little foggy.

He smiled. "Would you like to come up to my room later on, or maybe tomorrow, to have a drink? Word around the hotel is you're here doing research on the golden age of the Mountains." No one from the city called the Catskills "the Catskills." It was "the Mountains," as if the phrase could refer only to one place on earth. What were the Himalayas, foothills? "Boy, I could tell you stories. . . ."

"Sure, Mr. Roth, I'd like that very much. Later today or tomorrow."

We shook hands on it. Strolling away from the car, Roth didn't seem to need the cane. He didn't click his heels or anything, but his walk was definitely happy. Who knows, maybe Mr. Roth knew something about the Fir Grove fire that I didn't. Besides, with his receding gray hair, pencil mustache, and sad eyes, he reminded me of my dad. Passing a few hours with him yakking about the good old days might do us both some good. I missed my dad a lot, more now that Aaron and I had achieved a level of success which always eluded him. Come to think of it, I realized I'd better call my big brother. Katy and Sarah, too.

The store was still standing, so said Aaron. Friday had been so busy, he'd done as I suggested and called my buddy Kosta. Aaron approved. Kosta, as I had promised, knew his shit.

"Maybe I should have gone into business with him," Aaron joked.

I wasn't laughing. It had been Aaron who for years stubbornly refused to include anyone from outside the family in the ownership of the business. Several of my cop friends had offered up big chunks of change for a chance to get into the business with us. Cops and firemen are always looking ahead at what to do after retirement. There were these legends floating around the department about groups of cops who had invested in McDonald's or Kentucky Fried Chicken. Now they were multi-multi-millionaires, so the legend went.

Yeah, sure. Somehow, no names were ever attached to these stories, but they served their purpose, I guess. Apocryphal though they may have been, they made you think about your future. Most retired cops I run across go into security. It's what they know. Some open up bars. Like I said, it's what they know.

Katy didn't answer at home. I thought she and Sarah might have stayed an extra day at her parents' place. The thought of calling there again and having her father pick up was less than appealing to me, but I tried it anyway. I got my mother-in-law instead.

"Sorry, Moe. They're not here. I think Katy mentioned visiting your sister-in-law Cindy and the kids. I think Miriam was gonna meet them there."

"Okay, Mom, thanks."

Even at my bravest, I thought twice about dealing with Katy, Cindy, and my sister, Miriam, all at once. I wasn't up for listening to Cindy and Miriam lecture me on abandoning Katy and Sarah during the Thanksgiving vacation.

I was about to go find Sam and have a little showdown with my new friend about his cryptic warnings concerning the occupants of the former Fir Grove. He found me first. Stepping into my room, he surveyed it as if this were the first time he was seeing it. He was impressed.

"Nice room for such a shithole, you think?" He wasn't really asking.

"The television reception's awful."

"It's all the tall buildings, *boychik* — what can I do?"

"We're in the mountains, Sam."

"Mountains, buildings . . . Doesn't matter, they're tall and they're solid, right?"

"Forgive my attention to detail," I begged sarcastically.

Sam winked. "I'll think about it. So — how's my friend, the little hateful bastard? What's he calling himself this week, Anton Hard-on?"

"You know him?"

I was stunned. I figured Sam knew about the little shantytown on the grounds of the old Fir Grove, but I hadn't counted on his being on a first-name basis with any of its occupants.

"Know him!" Sam chortled, holding his right hand to his mid-thigh. "Since he was a little *pisher* this high. His mother worked as a chambermaid at the Fir Grove for years. She died in the fire. Why, did he neglect to tell you? He's a harmless putz. Just ignore him."

"I'd love to, but he had a brick thrown into my back windshield and the word **JEW** spray-painted across the hood of my car."

"You want I should go over there and wash his mouth out with soap?"

"Talk about the pot calling the kettle black," I chided. "Who's gonna wash out your mouth?"

"They don't make bars of soap that big."

"His mother died in the fire, huh?" That mock grave suddenly made some sense to me. "The mother," I wondered, "was her name Missy?"

"You're a smart one," Sam complimented. "I gotta watch out for you. Yeah, Missy, that was her name. Nice girl. Not too bright. Big tits." Sam held his hands a foot away from his chest. "The kid's name was Robby

Higgins. The father was a real *shikker.* You know what means a *shikker?*"

"A drunk," I said.

"Very good. Yeah, the father was a drunk, you shouldn't know from it. When the parents split up, our *shikker* moved down to Pennsylvania someplace. The owners of the Fir Grove were real soft touches. They let Missy and the kid move into the workers' quarters. He was a sweet kid until the breakup, used to help me around the place with errands and stuff. I'd throw him a coupla bucks here and there. But after the mom gave Dad the heave-ho, Robby went a little . . ." Sam waved his hand. ". . . a *bissel meshugge.* He blamed Missy, I guess. After the fire he moved to Pennsylvania with the drunk."

My mind went into overdrive, so much so that I barely took notice of Sam. Sam, a performer through and through, lost interest in me as soon as he lost me as an audience. It must be a scary thing to depend so much upon the approval of an audience, but I had neither the time nor the inclination to contemplate the performer's dilemma at the moment. Anton Harder or Robby Higgins was foremost on my mind.

He had obviously escaped the fire. And if what Sam had told me was true about the anger and instability of the young Robby Higgins, I thought the fog I'd been operating in might quickly burn off. Was Higgins angry enough with his mom to strike out at her? Had his parents' split knocked him so off balance that he could do something incredibly stupid and dangerous? I remembered my lack of judgment as a kid and had my answer to that question. Maybe it hadn't been some idiot smoking in bed after all. God, it all seemed to fit so perfectly: the displacement of anger and guilt, the transmutation of those raw emotions into blind hatred, the cesspits, the shrine to his mother. It was neat. It fit. It was easy. The perfect formula for an ex-cop. I wondered why someone hadn't put the obvious components of tragedy together before this. Maybe someone had, someone named Arthur Rosen.

I had Sam give me an outside line and called down to the city.

"Intelligence Division," a distracted voice picked up, "Detective Gigante."

"Is Larry Mac around?"

Detective Lawrence McDonald and I had worked together for a few years in Coney Island. Larry, Rico Tripoli, and I were known as the Three Stooges: Moe, Larry, and Curly. It would have been more accurate to call us Moe, Larry, and Wavy. Rico, who had a remarkable resemblance to the young Tony Bennett, had thick, wavy black hair. Both Larry and Rico had gone on to get their gold shields. Larry earned his. Rico sold his soul and our friendship for his, but that's another story.

"Hold on," Gigante said.

"Detective McDonald speaking."

"Larry Mac, how the fuck are you?"

"Moe, you tough Jew prick, how's the wine business? Christ, it's good to hear your voice."

"The wine business is good, ya shanty Irishman. You know it wouldn't kill you to come uptown and stop by the store one day. Ah, but maybe not, I don't think we have enough inventory."

"Shut up, fuck-o. What's up?"

I more or less explained what I was working on and asked him to do a little digging into the men of the Higgins family, formerly of Old Rotterdam, New York. I also asked for a picture of Arthur Rosen, even if it was only a mug shot or an autopsy photo. I spent a minute explaining just who Arthur Rosen had been. Larry said he'd see what he could do, which meant he'd have it nailed within forty-eight hours.

"You hear, Rico got his shield?" Larry asked.

"I heard."

"What's with you and Curly, anyway? You used to be like —"

"Used to be, Larry, used to be. He paid a big price for a few those few ounces of gold plating and blue enamel. I hope it was worth it."

"Yeah, Moe," Larry said suspiciously, but knew better than to ask, "whatever you say."

I gave him my phone number at the Swan Song.

"They got a fax machine there?" he wondered.

I wondered what he was talking about. "What the fuck is a fax?"

"They're like Xerox machines attached to the phone. You know, like those old gizmos that spun around we used to send pictures over to other departments with, but these are much faster. You can get two or three pages a minute."

"The next Edsel," I predicted. "I'll check and get back to you."

At least Sam knew what a fax machine was. He didn't have one, but said that the stationery store in town had one. He got me the number and I passed it on to Larry Mac.

"When your stuff comes in, they'll call, and I'll have somebody pick it up for you," Sam offered generously. "I got to offer something special to my only full-paying guest."

Now there really was nothing to do until I could arrange a meeting with Hammerling or until the info came in from the city. I considered Mr. Roth's invitation to share a drink and some stories of the good old days, but I wasn't up for it. I watched the snowfall on my TV for an hour or so. I think there was a college football game going on underneath it. The announcers said there was, so I suppose I had to believe them. I slept for a few hours, forced down the enormous amount of bad food on the plate the Swan Song served up for my dinner, and walked the grounds to try and burn some of it off.

Back from my constitutional, I found Sam and asked him if he knew how I could get in touch with Molly Treat. He asked if I'd ever heard of this thing called a phone book, but suggested I just go down to Hanrahan's Pub in town. Molly was always there on Saturday night, he pronounced with great authority. So I was off to Hanrahan's. I invited the old comedian along. He politely declined. It was the only polite thing the man had done in two days.

Located at the corners of Monticello Avenue and Loch Sheldrake Street, Hanrahan's was as predictable as another losing season for the Jets. The pub occupied the first floor of a two-story red clapboard walkup. Even if I hadn't gotten directions, I would have been able to spot it by the cigarette smoke pouring out its front doors. When I got within earshot, I could hear the jukebox blasting the Four Seasons. I'm talking Frankie Valli here, not Vivaldi. Big girls, Frankie explained, don't cry. I'd have to ask Molly Treat about that.

And that wouldn't be hard to do, for, as Sam Gutterman predicted, Molly was seated right square in front of the beer pulls. A cigarette dangled perilously off her bottom lip as she exchanged a few words with the girl behind the bar. Both the barmaid and Molly turned their eyes to ogle a burly twenty-something in a flannel shirt playing eight ball at the table near the juke. Maybe he was worth their attention. Frankly, it was hard to see through the tar-and-nicotine fog. After my first ten breaths in that place, I felt confident I was well on my way to emphysema.

"Hey, Molly." I took her by surprise, appearing out of the smoky darkness. "Remember me?"

"Mr. Prager."

"Moe, that's right. What are you drinking?"

"Bud," she said.

"Give the lady a Bud." I winked at the barmaid, an old cop habit, and laid a twenty on the bar. "I'll have a double Dewar's rocks, and buy yourself something on me."

The barmaid winked back, much to Molly's dismay. "Don't mind if I do," she said, putting a beer, my scotch, and her shot of Jack Daniel's on the bar top.

"To new friends," I toasted. We clinked glasses. Molly took half the mug in one swig, I sipped, and the barmaid slammed hers back. I whispered in Molly's ear: "Don't sweat it. She's not my type. I always hated women who could outdrink me. If I were in the market, you'd be first on the list around here."

It was shamelessly flirty of me and completely untrue, but other than that it seemed like a good thing to say at the moment. Whether Molly believed it or not was a completely separate issue.

"How do you drink that stuff?" Molly asked, trying to compose herself. "To me it tastes like expensive Listerine."

"It tastes like Listerine to me, too, but I like Listerine."

She raised her glass to me.

We went on like that for a little bit, the way you do at a bar with people you barely know — saying a lot and revealing almost nothing. I even smoked a cigarette, just to show Molly what a party animal I could be. Besides, with the amount of ambient smoke in that place, having a cigarette was like a drowning man drinking a glass of water. After another round with the barmaid and Molly, I suggested Molly and I retreat to a booth. She was happy to do so. I asked the barmaid to wait a few minutes and send over round three.

When we got settled in, I slid my badge and license across the table to her, making a show of keeping it just between the two of us. Molly was impressed all right. Now she started to look around to make sure we weren't being watched. The only thing that could have heightened Molly's sense of adventure would have been the James Bond theme coming out of the jukebox. We had to settle for "Piano Man." Well, it was nine o'clock on a Saturday.

"Molly, I need your help." I was earnest as hell, staring straight into her eyes. "I'm sorry I couldn't be more straight with you yesterday, but I needed to get the lay of the land. If you know what I mean."

"I think I understand. You didn't know anybody."

"See, I knew you'd understand. Look, I need to ask you some questions about the locals, okay?"

"Shoot."

I asked in a whisper: "Do you know Anton Harder?"

"His name wasn't Anton Harder when I knew him," she confided.

"He was Robby Higgins then."

Molly was impressed. "You knew that? Yup, I knew Robby when we were kids, before —"

"— the fire," I completed her sentence. "Before he moved to Pennsylvania with his dad."

"Well, if you know all this, why are you asking me?" she wondered, now more pissed off than impressed.

I waved at the barmaid for our drinks. "I'm sorry, Molly. Tell me about him. I'll just sit here and listen, cross my heart and hope to die."

Molly pretty much confirmed everything Sam had earlier told me about the young Robby Higgins. She did add an interesting detail or two. Apparently, Robby had been an okay student. He was quiet and didn't take teasing very well — "And he was teased a lot because of his size and all," Molly said — but got along pretty well with everyone but the class bullies. He had some friends. Molly even made out with him once.

"He was cuter back then, and I didn't outweigh him by quite so much."

I cringed when she said that. I hoped she hadn't noticed. People rightly despised pity.

The thing Molly remembered most was how much Robby changed when his parents split up. He started fighting in school, no longer willing to let taunts go unchallenged. He lost most of the fights, and his grades went south.

"He got suspended for fighting, and eventually got kicked outta school for setting off a cherry bomb in the teachers' lounge," Molly recounted, shaking her head. "He was really hurting and —"

I could scarcely believe my ears. This was too good to be true. "He got suspended for what?"

I tried to hide my smile as Molly repeated what she had said about Robby Higgins' first venture into arson. I was liking Anton Harder's younger incarnation more and more for the Fir Grove fire.

Molly began rambling a bit — she was already working on her fourth beer since my arrival — about other kids she had known in school and what had become of them. I took the opportunity to slow my own alcohol intake and try to refocus. No matter how appealing a suspect Robby Higgins might appear to be, I had to guard against latching on too hard. An old detective I knew at the 60th had warned me not to fall too deeply in love with any one suspect. "Love blinds you in both eyes," he said. "And pressure to make a case dulls a cop's vision enough to begin with."

Eventually, I steered Molly's ramblings around to the subject of Councilman Richard Hammerling. If the tipsy Molly was even half accurate, the Hammerling she described sounded like a cartoon cutout of a small-town politico. He was a publicity hound, fighting hard to get as much media attention as he could. It seemed he was a believer in that old adage about there being no such thing as bad publicity. To hear Molly tell it, old Dick Hammerling was never afraid to look silly as long as they spelled his name right.

"You know that stupid groundhog they have in Pennsylvania every year?" Molly slurred.

"Sure."

"Well, Dick came up with Beaver Day. Beaver's the state animal, you know?"

"No," I confessed. "In Brooklyn you sorta grow up assuming pigeons are the state animal."

"Anyhows, Dick is always the guy who yanks Old Rotterdam Rodney the beaver out of his hutch or den or whatever beavers live in, and shows him his shadow. It drew a lot of coverage for a few years, but just lately only the *Catskill Trib* and the local radio station send reporters."

"But Hammerling shows up nonetheless, huh?"

"Yessiree. Hey, Moe, how do you know if a beaver sees his shadow?"

"How?"

"You ask him!"

Molly thought this hysterically funny and laughed so hard she began choking. Sam Gutterman she wasn't. When Molly got done catching her breath and drying her eyes, she continued detailing Hammerling's career. Not only was he a publicity whore, but apparently he was power-hungry as well, always trying to wrangle the chairmanship on as many committees as he could get appointed to.

"I think he wants to be governor someday," Molly opined. "He does a bad job of hiding that."

He had a lot of other egomaniacs on line

ahead of him. When I expressed a version of this sentiment to Molly she disagreed.

"I guess Dick's got his faults like everyone else, but his trying to reopen the Fir Grove business ain't winning him too many friends in these parts."

"It's gotten him a lot of press, hasn't it?"

"Maybe so," she granted, "but it cuts against the grain around here. The fire's the worst thing ever happened in this town. The whole place went to hell in a handbasket after that. People don't like it being dragged up again. It's a part of the past I think we'd all prefer stay buried."

As she had earlier, Molly started off on a tangent. This time I was treated to the details of Richard Hammerling's other foibles. Unfortunately, none of this stuff was either pertinent or particularly interesting. I passed the time watching a baldheaded guy playing darts in the corner. I think maybe his hairline reminded me of the strange guy I'd seen pass by the front window of the hardware store earlier in the day. In any case, I decided to interrupt Molly's version of the life and times of Richard Hammerling before I began to twitch.

"Molly, let me ask you ask you a strange question."

"How strange?"

I described the man in the threadbare coat and waited for Molly to delve into the vast minutiae of his life, including his birth weight. However, for the first time all evening, Molly was speechless. She excused herself to go to the ladies' room. When she got back, she went to the bar to buy a pack of smokes. Then she bummed a few bucks off me and took the better part of a fortnight selecting tunes on the box that had already been played five times. Clearly, Molly was as anxious to discuss this subject as she was to undergo a full course of chemotherapy.

"Okay, Molly," I said, "you're stalling. I was only a little curious before. Now one of us ain't gettin' outta here alive unless I find out about that guy at the hardware store."

She actually looked frightened. I remembered about sarcasm not being a universal language and apologized. Not effusively, mind you. I wanted to know.

"You're not gonna get insulted or anything, are you?" She really was nervous.

"I promise."

"I don't know the man you described personally, but I think he belongs to a . . . to a . . . I guess you'd call it a cult. We call 'em the Yellow Stars. They're up in the same neck of the woods as Robby — I mean, Anton Harder's people. They keep to themselves mostly. Hardly ever come into town."

"The Yellow Stars?"

"They wear a big yellow patch on their coats that has the word —"

"J-U-D-E-N," I spelled out loud.

"That's it," Molly said. "It means —"

"Jew."

"You said you weren't gonna get insulted or anything. I remember how touchy you got the other day when this sorta thing came up."

"It's okay, Molly. I'm not insulted or anything."

"Not even a little?"

"Not even a little, but I am still pretty damned curious."

Molly told me what she knew, which wasn't very much. The Yellow Stars owned what used to be Koppelman's Bungalow Colony, about five miles north of the Fir Grove. They kept to themselves and rarely came into town. When they did, it was to see the doctor, usually, or to file papers with the town. They didn't sell roses or anything one had come to expect from a "cult." She was unsure of their agenda, or if they even had an agenda at all.

"The other Jews," she said, "the Hasids, they hate 'em."

Suddenly, I was less interested and pretty

fucking angry. Having grown up with several children of concentration-camp survivors, I found the notion of people playing at this sort of thing repulsive. The whole victimization thing made me want to puke. Didn't they know, everyone was a victim?

Oh God! Molly had played "Piano Man" again. It was no longer nine o'clock and it was getting perilously close to being Sunday. Time to go, but I feared making a graceful exit wasn't going to be easy. Molly had grown a little touchy-feely. There had been a time not too many years ago when I would have gone home with her. She was likable enough, cute in her way, and she sure liked me, but even before I met Katy I'd given up on one-night stands. The sex, good or bad, was never at issue. No one should ever mistake me for a knight of the Round Table. It was just that the lack of intimacy had begun to suck the life out of me.

"I gotta go, Molly."

She took my hand in a death grip. I admired people who didn't give up without a fight; however, I preferred admiring them from outside the ring. I took the offensive, knelt forward, and kissed Molly long, but softly on the cheek. Pulling away, I brushed my hand across her cheek and mouthed the words "Thank you." She let go of my hand.

The battle was won. No one seemed scarred for life. Then why did I feel like such a shit?

Fresh air had never smelled so sweet as it did when I stepped out of Hanrahan's. Another hour in there and I'd be coughing up a lung. As it was, I considered burning my clothes instead of having them cleaned. It's almost impossible to fully get out the smell of smoke. Apparently, the smoke from the old Fir Grove fire still hung over Old Rotterdam like a permanent cloud. I thought I could almost smell it myself. The vision of Andrea's charred body popped back into my head.

The street was awfully quiet. That's the thing about the city: it's never quiet, not like this. The quiet made me uncomfortable. A lot about this place made me uncomfortable.

CHAPTER SEVEN: NOVEMBER 29TH

I woke up missing Katy and Sarah. My evening with Molly had been a painful reminder of where my life had been headed before Patrick M. Maloney fell off the face of the earth. Most of the time, I could hold down the panic associated with the thought of my father-in-law's ratting me out. This was not one of those times. Panic was all around me. I had come close to confessing to Katy on several occasions, but the words weren't in me, nor was the courage to speak them if they had been.

I got out of my room as fast as I could. Bad food was apparently a remedy for panic. The coffee alone was enough to put a man back on the straight and narrow. And once I bit into my bagel with lox and cream cheese, the only thing I was panicked by was the onset of food poisoning. Admittedly, I was never much of a lox eater, but this stuff was rancid. The old folks around me didn't seem to mind too much.

When I spotted Mr. Roth, again splendidly dressed, entering the dining hall, I waved for him to come sit with me. He was only too pleased to join me as long as I was still willing to share a drink with him later in the day. I told him I wouldn't have it any other way.

"I see you're not enjoying your lox," he observed after placing his order for bran cereal and a banana. "Terrible stuff. I wouldn't feed it to a pig."

"Nice sentiment."

We had a laugh over that. I asked Mr. Roth where he came from.

"Boca Raton via Brooklyn via Auschwitz," he said, rolling up his sleeve to reveal a five-digit tattoo on his forearm. "And my name is Izzy, so you don't have to call me Mr. Roth, Mr. Prager."

"That's Moe, or Moses, Mr. Roth."

"*Oy gevalt,* they had less trouble figuring out the shape of the negotiating table for the Vietnam War, for Chrissakes! Call me whatever you want."

"You, too, Mr. Roth."

When his cereal came, I let him get some of it down before starting the conversation again. I asked him why he bothered coming to a place like the Swan Song if he knew it was a dump. He gestured at the other people in the room.

"Most of us live in the same retirement community. We have very little family left, the majority of us. So we get a big discount and come up to the mountains twice a year. We come at Thanksgiving, and in the summer for a week. Fewer of us come each year, but the mountains are a place we all have such happy memories of. Mister, I could tell you stories. . . ."

I smiled. "I hope you will."

"Later." He waved. "Later."

"Why the Swan Song?" I asked.

"They give the biggest discount, and we remember Sam from the old times. He was pretty famous almost, once. Would you believe it? I don't know. Where else would we go? Old people don't like change much. We haven't got the time to deal with it, so we put up with the bad coffee and the mystery lox and we remember sunnier days. Hold on to those days tightly, Mr. Moe, like an eagle holds its prey." Mr. Roth's lips turned down at the corners.

I changed the subject. "So what did you do for a living?"

"I owned a fine men's-clothing store on Flatbush Avenue for thirty years. House of Roth, you ever hear of it? The Dodgers used to shop there all the time. I got pictures. Let me tell you, I got pictures. Me fitting Gil Hodges, Pee Wee Reese, the Duke. But I liked the colored players the best: Jackie Robinson, and Junior Gilliam, and the crippled one, the catcher —"

"Campanella."

"That's him, Campy. Such a pity, a man like that. But the colored players, we understood each other," he said. "We understood what it was to struggle. We appreciated the little things."

I didn't doubt it. I excused myself. I found I really needed to hear Katy's voice.

"Later?" he almost pleaded.

"Later."

This time I got her at home. The wonderful thing about it was that she sounded even happier, even more relieved to hear from me than I was to hear the sound of her voice. Mr. Roth's words about appreciating the little things rang in my ears. She filled me in on what I had missed at my in-laws'. Nothing. It had been a quiet stay. Her father had mentioned taking a trip down to Coney Island in the spring to spend a day with Sarah on the rides. Those words rang in my head, too, but flat and out of tune.

Katy, Miriam, and Cindy had gotten

drunk together and spent the better part of the evening sharing bad blind-date stories. I thought about asking for more details and quickly changed my mind. I could have dealt with some of Katy's stories, but I didn't want to think about my little sister or my three-times-a-mother sister-in-law out on dates. Call me old-fashioned. Katy and Sarah had spent the night at Aaron and Cindy's. Sarah was still there being fawned over by her big cousins.

"It's good to get some time alone," Katy admitted, "but I'd rather spend it alone with you."

We got around to talking about the case. When I tried to explain, I realized the only tangible thing I had was a cracked windshield and a new paint job on the hood of my car. I carefully omitted those details. There was no need to worry Katy. What I did tell her was that I had a hunch, but, I cautioned, every broken-down horse-player I ever met had a hunch. Some had sure things. The only sure thing was that most hunches don't pan out.

"You had a hunch about me," she said.

"I said most hunches don't pan out, not all."

"Good thing for you some do."

Feeling better for having spoken to Katy,

and with nothing on my plate until later, I decided to go and do some souvenir shopping, or maybe even take a ride up to the Hall of Fame at Cooperstown.

Mr. Roth's room wasn't so different from mine. His TV worked a little better. Instead of snow on the screen there were wavy negative images. Everything looked like the special effects from *The Outer Limits.* "We will control the horizontal. We will control the vertical. . . ."

"In Boca, we got cable. Perfect reception all the time. Too bad there's only *dreck* to watch, but it's crystal-clear *dreck!* Sometimes I watch the soap operas, with their crazy plots, in the afternoons. I think more people get amnesia than the common cold on those things. And resurrection! They bring more people back from the dead than Jesus Christ. You got cable in Brooklyn yet?"

"The politicians haven't been sufficiently paid off," I said. "We'll get it just in time for them to invent something new, and then my grandchildren will wait for that."

He clicked off the set. "Vodka or scotch?"

"Scotch." He disappeared into the bathroom and quickly emerged with two hotel glasses in hand. He said something in a Slavic tongue I didn't recognize, clinked my

147

glass, and made his vodka vanish in one swallow. He didn't make a show of it: no grunting or throat clearing, no head shaking, no "Oh, that's good." I liked that about the man. There's something refreshing about a lack of pretense. Maybe that comes with age.

"Another?" he asked.

"Not just now, thanks, but you go ahead."

He made another trip into the bathroom and came out carrying both the scotch and vodka bottles.

"Too much exercise," he said. "I already make too many trips to the bathroom."

He helped himself to half a glassful and sat down on the edge of the bed, sipping his vodka this time. I took the desk chair over by the window.

"So you're a cop," he said matter-of-factly.

This was getting ridiculous. Too bad I didn't have my old uniform with me. It would save people the trouble of guessing.

"Who told —"

"No one had to tell me. You carry yourself like a cop. When you're a haberdasher for your life, you learn how people carry themselves. It's no different than in the jungle or in the camps. An animal survives by being able to see who carries himself like a predator or like prey." Mr. Roth looked down at his drink. When he picked his head up he was smiling. "Sorry, I didn't mean to go on that way. It's just that, when old people are together, we talk a lot but we never say anything. It's like you're suddenly aware that God is really listening and you better watch your mouth. You're gonna be seeing Him soon enough."

"You believe?"

"There was a French philosopher, I think, who once said something like if you can't prove God doesn't exist, you better act like He does. You know, Mr. Moe, it doesn't matter if I believe in Him or not. What matters is if He believes in me." He held up the bottle of scotch. "Another?"

I liked listening to Mr. Roth, but if he was going to plumb the depths of metaphysics I needed more than one scotch. I held up my empty glass for a refill.

"So . . ." he said.

"You wanna know what I'm really doing up here?"

He winked at me. "All I said was 'So . . .' "

Mr. Roth sat patiently as I introduced him to the cast of characters. Surprisingly, he seemed unperturbed by the Yellow Stars.

"Life is life," he said, "and dress-up is just dress-up. What does it matter to me?" He did remember the fire, but couldn't add any detail. "I was here with Hannah — my wife was still alive then. She'd spend the whole summer, and I'd come up on Saturday night to Tuesday every week. I couldn't leave the store for too long. That summer we were at Grossinger's with friends. When we got up that Sunday morning, the dining room was buzzing with the news. What was bad was that it was mostly kids. We all had kids who'd worked up here in the summers. That hurt. You know sometimes when you hear terrible stories on the news about a typhoon or volcano killing thousands of people, you can ignore it because when was the last typhoon in Brooklyn? But when it could have been you or your kids . . ."

I tried asking him about his kids, but he just deflected the questions. Eventually, I got the hint and moved on. We had one more drink and finally got around to talking about the good old days. I told him about my one week of glory at the Concord.

"The Concord, huh, Mr. Fancy Moe? Maybe I should call you Your Highness. From what I hear, only royalty and the rich stay at the Concord."

I held out my hand. "Kiss the ring and maybe I'll let you call me Moe."

He liked that. When he finished his drink, he sang me a song: "We're gonna hitchhike up to the Catskills. . . ."

"We lived for the summers, to come up here and be amongst ourselves," he said unashamedly. "You don't know the pressures of coming from another place, a different culture. We could speak Yiddish or Polish without the guy on the subway next to you giving you the eye. We could be ourselves again for a little while. Oh, the silly things we used to do."

"Like . . ."

"Will you respect me in the morning if I tell you?"

"Mr. Roth, I get the sense I'd respect you no matter what."

His mood turned suddenly dark: "Don't be so sure."

"Okay, but what about the silly things?"

He brightened up again. "Sometimes we'd plan and rehearse all week for a wedding, but not just any wedding. They called it a mock wedding. The men would dress up like women and the women like men. And we made up funny ceremonies. You know, like what we imagined the *goyim* did in their churches. And maybe there was a little drinking and a little fooling around. It was like a big party and play and a little revenge all at once. But it was fun like I can't tell you. It would seem so stupid now, but I miss it."

"Why don't you get your friends together here and —"

"Forget it! It's not like on the soap operas. You can't bring back the past."

"I didn't mean to get you —"

"You didn't upset me, Moe. I'm maybe just a little tired and a little drunk, you know?"

"Okay, Mr. Roth. I understand. Why don't you get a *bissel* sleep."

"Sounds good," he said, stretching back on the bed, yawning. "Sounds good."

I shook his hand and rolled the comforter over him, but when I got to the door, he called after me.

"What is it, Mr. Roth?"

"Remember what I said before about not respecting me?"

"I remember, yeah."

"I like you very much, so I'm gonna give you some advice. Be careful of the people you like. Unlike in the jungle, humans can learn to carry themselves like prey when sometimes they're the hunters."

"Are you talking about yourself?" I asked.

"Not this time, Mr. Moe. Just you watch yourself. A glad hand and a joke may not be what they seem. Go in good health."

Jesus, another cryptic warning. It didn't take a rocket scientist to figure out Mr. Roth was speaking about Sam, but exactly what he was saying was unclear. Was Sam Gutterman the Antichrist, or was he going to pad my hotel bill?

CHAPTER EIGHT: NOVEMBER 30TH

I ate breakfast out, escaping the sage advice and cryptic warnings of my new friends and mentors. A man can stand only so much imparted wisdom. Today I had to focus. Richard Hammerling, Councilman at Large, was batting in the lead-off spot, and I needed to be sharp. Silly songs about the Catskills and fanciful tales of mock weddings were fun but beside the point. Even before I woke up, the vision of Arthur Rosen's lifeless body weighed heavily on me. The stink of his room was in the air I breathed. I barely noticed the black paint on the hood of my car. The same could not be said about my rear windshield.

Old Rotterdam Town Hall hadn't improved with age. And with the warmer temperatures and thaw, the surrounding mud served only to enhance its ugliness. It looked even more out of place without the camouflage of snow. I wondered if Hammerling had had anything to do with selecting this neo-Sing Sing design. When I walked in, I checked the big sign to see if it listed the Sunday football scores. It did not, but the little politicos' names were all still up there for the world to see.

Molly Treat was at her station, faithfully guarding the information table. I tried sneaking up on her, to no avail. Molly, true to her word, knew everything about the place, including, apparently, the sounds in the hallways. Without raising her head away from the papers spread out before her, she pointed up at the big Seth Thomas clock across from her desk.

"I've been expecting you. Dick's set some time aside, but you better get in there. You're a little late. Room 112."

I laid down on Molly's desk the rose I'd bought from a Moonie on Ellenville Road and a cup of coffee. She finally looked up. She was meticulously made up and dressed quite a bit more lavishly than the job required. In any case, she was better dressed than the last time she sat at this desk, or at Hanrahan's Pub. Though she'd no doubt deny it, I suspected this fashion statement had more than a teeny bit to do with the anticipation of my presence.

"You look lovely."

155

"I had fun the other night." She licked her lips. "But you left too soon."

"No, I left just in time or I'd be feeling pretty guilty today."

"Guilty pleasures are the spice of life."

"And the cause of nine out of ten divorce proceedings. I didn't know how you liked your coffee, so I got it with a little half-and-half. I figured you had some sugar or whatever in your desk."

She pulled two packets of sugar out of a drawer and shook them at me. "Now you know for next time."

"Till then." I winked. "That was Room 112, right?"

"One twelve. Go to the end of the hall and make a left."

Room 112 was actually two rooms. There was a drab, uninviting room full of metal desks, filing cabinets, and phone banks for secretarial and administrative staff that was currently occupied by the invisible. I figured it must not have been an election year. During an election year, staffers work round the clock to make sure that every cat is rescued from every tree and that every media outlet in the Free World knows about it.

Richard Hammerling's office was another story altogether. The walls, what little I could see of them behind the photographs of Richard Hammerling with the famous, semifamous, infamous, and notorious, were painted a pale yellow. The carpet was a happy shade of green and deeper than the rough at a U.S. Open. There were groupings of oversized flags in every corner, ranging from the Stars and Stripes, the largest of the large, to that of the local high-school football team, the Old Rotterdam Fighting Beavers. I wondered if Old Rotterdam Rodney was their mascot. The man himself was seated behind a mission-style desk not quite half the size of the flight deck of the USS *Enterprise*. I checked for incoming F-14 Tomcats before taking a seat.

Before I could sit, Hammerling popped up out of his brown leather chair and threw a hand at me. I shook it in self-defense. He was a roughly handsome man with a grip firm enough to impress a local Teamster but light enough not to intimidate the librarian. Taller than me by an inch or two, with nice broad shoulders and a thin waistline, he was, I figured, about my age, in his mid-thirties. Clean-cut and shaven, he smelled grassy and sweet, like he'd used a bit too much Polo after shaving that morning. His blue suit, light-blue shirt, and yellow silk tie were more Sears than Brooks Brothers, but they fit him well.

"Where'd'ya play ball?" I asked, trying to throw him a curve.

"I was recruited by a lot of schools, even a few ACC schools like Wake Forest and Virginia, but I wound up at Cobleskill Community College. Then I screwed up my knee and that was that."

Translation: I was good, but my grades sucked. I got bored with school, hurt my knee, and came back home to work in my dad's business.

"I figure you for a small forward," I said.

"Shooting guard, but that's good. You play ball in school?"

"I'm from Brooklyn, Mr. Hammerling. I wasn't good enough to make water boy."

He liked that. "But I bet you play."

"Up until a few years ago, yeah. But I fucked up my knee on the job."

He winced at that, as if reliving the pain he'd suffered. In spite of myself, I found that I liked him. He sat down and gestured for me to do the same.

"We could spend hours telling war stories, you and I. I played a lot of ball with guys from the city. With them it was always more than just a game. But Molly tells me that's not why you're here, Mr. Prager."

"Did you know Arthur Rosen?"

He didn't answer immediately, rubbing

158

his hand over his face as he stared at me. "You're here about my attempts to reopen the Fir Grove boards of inquiry."

"That's not what I asked."

"And this isn't Brooklyn and you're not on the job anymore and you're in the office of a duly elected official," Hammerling admonished.

"Point taken. Sorry, that was out of line. But did you know Arthur Rosen?"

"I know Arthur, yes. But let me assure you, Mr. Prager, my desire to reopen this rather odorous can of worms goes well beyond the rantings of one disturbed man. I —"

"He's dead."

"Oh my God. How?"

"Suicide. Arthur hanged himself with a belt tied to a door handle in his room."

I backtracked a bit, letting the councilman in on how I'd gotten involved with Arthur Rosen in the first place. I told him how Arthur had written the name Hammerling on the wall of his room. That's about all I gave him, though. Sure, I liked him well enough, and he seemed genuinely shocked by Arthur's suicide, but I wasn't going to give out any information unless it was absolutely necessary. I still needed a scorecard to tell the players around here. I wasn't about to

159

reveal anything to anyone who probably knew the players better than I did.

"I wouldn't eat my heart out with guilt," Hammerling consoled me. "Mr. Rosen could be very lucid at times and was obviously an intelligent man, but he was very unstable. In some ways, though I would never have wished this on him, he was more a hindrance than a help. It doesn't exactly help a politician's credibility to have his biggest backer for a very unpopular cause be an out-of-town lunatic. If you get my meaning. My opponents used Arthur against me every chance they could."

"Then why bother if this is so unpopular a cause?"

"Because it's a just cause. It's the right thing to do, Mr. Prager." He pointed at a picture on the wall that featured himself holding Old Rotterdam Rodney, the celebrity beaver. "So much of what a local politician does is horse crap. Sometimes I think the meaning of life is fund-raising and publicity seeking. That's not what I got into this for. I want to help the people of this area thrive. I want us to get out from under the black cloud that's hung over this community for the past sixteen years."

He sounded earnest enough, but I half expected red, white, and blue balloons to fall from the ceiling and "America the Beautiful" to start playing in the background as he accepted his party's nomination for governor of the Empire State. I let him get it out of his system.

"But are you making any headway? Are you gonna get any of the inquiries reopened?"

The air went right out of him. "It's always two steps forward, one step back. Just when I think I've cobbled together the votes, things always seem to fall apart. I'm good at building a consensus, at putting together coalitions. With this thing, though . . ." He pointed to his forehead. "See this flat spot here? It's from banging my head against the wall. Sometimes it's like I'm fighting an unseen enemy."

I nearly bit through my tongue. I was pretty sure his unseen enemy had a name, drove around in a big black car driven by a svelte man in a perfect blue suit. But, like I said before, I wasn't here to give out information, just collect it. Maybe, when I got to the bottom of whatever there was to get to the bottom of, I'd make an anonymous call to Hammerling's office and let him know who he was fighting and how deep his enemy's pockets were.

"Don't you ever get discouraged?" I

asked. "I mean, you've probably gotten all the mileage you're gonna get out of this, right?"

"I get discouraged all the time," Hammerling confessed. "But I'm not giving up."

"Good for you," I said, and meant it. "Good for you." I looked at my watch and thanked him for his time. I was about to go when it occurred to me to ask him a few more questions about Arthur Rosen. "Just one more thing about Arthur Rosen, if that's okay?"

"Sure, it's the least I could do."

"You said he could be pretty lucid, but really unstable."

"I did say that, Mr. Prager, yes."

"When he was at his most unstable, what sorts of things did he say?"

"Sometimes it was the type of thing you'd expect." The councilman shook his head as he spoke. "You know, about the fire and the investigations being part of a big conspiracy and a cover-up aimed solely at his family. But sometimes he'd say really wild things, like that he knew someone who was killed in the fire was still alive, stuff like that."

That got my attention. "Did he ever say who?"

"He wouldn't tell me. He said he was afraid for me, that if I knew they'd come after me."

"No doubt he didn't tell you who 'they' were either."

"No doubt. But, like I said, Arthur was a profoundly disturbed man."

"How long ago did he start this particular craziness?" I wanted to know.

"I didn't keep a record of it." Hammerling was getting a little impatient.

"Take a guess, please."

"Two, maybe three years ago. He moved up here for a while, a couple of months, I think, before going back home. Now, will that be all?"

I thanked him again, wished him well, and left his office far more impressed than when I'd walked in.

Molly had the rose in a glass of water at the corner of her desk. Flowers, even one flower, could light up any room. I remembered the blood roses, white snow, the gray cross, and found myself wondering how long it would take Larry Mac to get me that info on the Higginses. Patience was a virtue, but not mine. None of us Pragers were much good at waiting. If we had a family motto, it would have been: "Bad news is better than no news at all." Catchy, huh? I asked Molly if I could use her phone to make a local call.

"Take me to lunch and I'll let you call Zagreb."

I should have known. "Sorry, madame, I made my weekly call to Yugoslavia yesterday. But don't you think a rose and a cup of coffee is worth a local call?"

"Yes, but you can't blame a girl for trying."

"I wouldn't have it any other way."

Sam said I hadn't gotten a call from the city, nor had the stationery store in town called to say the fax was in. I asked Molly where the library was. She answered with only a weak attempt at extortion. Hope may spring eternal, but, like Molly had said, she'd seen last call too many times not to factor reality into the equation. I promised to see her again before I left. "Promise," I assured her, wasn't a word I used lightly, so she could count on it.

The library was a diamond in the rough, a red brick building two blocks south of Town Hall. Unlike many of the other buildings in town, the library had not had its original Victorian spirit messed with. There wasn't a piece of aluminum siding to be seen. Wearing asymmetry like a crown, its dirty brick turrets and bay windows were still intact. It was kind of reminiscent of the Jefferson Market Library in Greenwich Village.

With the kids back in school after the holiday, the old library was abuzz with inactivity. If you listened hard enough, you could probably have heard a dust mite sneeze as it dined on the pages of *Moby-Dick.* I inquired as to the location of the reference area. The librarian, an older man in a sweater and bifocals, asked me if I had anything particular in mind.

"The fire."

He screwed up his face as if I'd just kicked him in the nuts with a steel-toed boot. He didn't have to ask that I be more specific. He knew which fire. Was there another? But he was a trooper — did his duty and did it well, too fucking well. There were volumes of old newspapers to go through, forget any of the other source material, like the inquiry transcripts or the coroner's reports. But the ratio of print generated versus useful information was ridiculous. Official conclusion: *Some putz was smoking in bed.*

There was one dissenting voice. He was among the first wave of volunteer firemen who responded to the initial alarm. His name was Gustavo Hammerling, a local potato farmer who thought the fire spread just too fast to have been caused by a careless smoker. I guess my brother, Aaron, wasn't the only man alive who carried the weight of his father's legacy on his shoulders. My respect for Richard Hammerling was growing, and there was little doubt in my mind that I would find a way to let him know R. B. Carter was the unseen force sabotaging his efforts.

I found Gustavo's obit from April 19, 1975:

FARMER, VOLUNTEER FIREMAN COMMITS SUICIDE

Monticello, NY — After receiving calls from his family, who had been unable to reach him, local police today found the body of Gustavo Hammerling in the woods behind his hunting lodge. Though the coroner refused to declare an official cause of death pending an autopsy and toxicology reports, preliminary indications are that Mr. Hammerling's death was the result of self-inflicted gunshot wounds. A shotgun was found in close proximity to the body. Gustavo Hammerling had gained some notoriety in the mid-1960s, when, as a witness appearing before the board of inquiry investigating the tragic Fir Grove Hotel fire in which 17 people perished, he raised the only dissenting voice disputing the theory that the fire was caused by a careless smoker. His son, freshman councilman from Old Rotterdam and former all-county basketball player, Richard Hammerling, said that his father never got over the fire. "It haunted him for the rest of his life. It broke him. He . . ."

I wrote down a few names, dates, a quote here and there, but from everything I read it sounded as if Gustavo Hammerling had killed himself over nothing. I was no fire investigator, believe me, yet all indications pointed to a careless smoker. What was fairly evident was that there had been a major push to get the investigations, boards of inquiry, etc., done quickly. All you had to do was count forward from the first news story to the last to see that the full-court press was on to rush things through. Old Rotterdam had seemingly adopted the Warren Commission philosophy. Too bad Arlen Specter wasn't available to be the lead investigator, or he might've invented the "Magic Cigarette" Theory.

It's funny how one event can so consume a period in history. But in my skimming the old back issues of the *Catskill Tribune,* I saw that life went on. Babies were born at the very same time Andrea and Karen were dying. Old people were dying, too. Kids were breaking windows, and Ferris wheels at the county fair spun round and round. There was even another big story that, except for the fire, might have dominated the news. It had, in fact, dominated the news for several weeks leading up to the fire. It seemed there had been a rash of well-planned burglaries at local hotels. It was petty stuff compared with what went on in the city, but in an area dependent upon tourism, it was major. Then, the day before the fire, things had turned violent. A guest at the Fleur-de-Lis had, according to the cops, stumbled upon the burglars at work and was beaten unconscious.

Yes, life went on before, during, and after the fire, but you wouldn't know it from the way folks acted around here. I went back over the papers, looking for another story about the burglaries. I wondered what had become of the beaten man — had he recovered from his injuries? Yet, after the fire, there seemed to be no other news worth reporting. I gave up. My eyes ached, and I had to limit my curiosity to one family's unresolved tragedy.

I went to talk to the local GP. Though I knew about as much about small-town life as I knew about quantum physics, I figured the local doctor always knew what was really going on in his town. According to Hollywood, the local doctor always knows the real scoop, right? He did in *Peyton Place.* Doc on *Gunsmoke* always knew the score. Dr. "He's Dead, Jim" McCoy was always a keen observer of the human and Vulcan heart. With my luck, the doctor was probably from Lahore, Pakistan, and had never heard of the Fir Grove or seen *Star Trek.*

The shingle outside the office read: ROBERT J. PEPPER, M.D. Good, I thought, I wouldn't need my Urdu phrase book. Pepper's waiting room was empty, and, I'm embarrassed to say, it looked like a movie set of a small-town doctor's waiting room. Norman Rockwell prints were prominently featured on each of the walnut-paneled walls. The furniture was colonial in style and probably in age. The magazines on the table were *Boys' Life, Life, National Geographic,* and *Trout Fisherman.* The receptionist, dressed in full nurse's whites, was a pleasant-looking woman of sixty.

When I introduced myself, lying to her about having a sore throat, she said there was a lot of that going around. What was, I wondered to myself, lying or sore throats? Probably both. She showed me right in without once inquiring as to my insurance or ability to pay. She took my temperature and blood pressure, and noted my knee surgery and lack of allergies to medication.

"My husband will be right with you, Mr. Prager," she said as she put my chart up on the door. "I'm sure you'll be fine."

Pepper was a wiry old bird with wild gray hair and posture like the letter "C." He wore green corduroy pants, house slippers with white socks, a brown button-down cardigan, and a stethoscope for a necktie. This guy was right out of central casting. The only missing prop was a pipe. He studied the chart his wife had started on me, moving his eyes back and forth from the paper to me.

"Says here you're complaining of a sore throat. Let's have a gander. Say ahhh," he ordered, shoving the tongue depressor just far enough down my throat to stimulate my gag response. "Throat looks fine. Eyes look pretty red, though."

Why I hadn't just asked his wife if I could speak to the doctor without the pretense of illness was now a moot issue.

"Were you around during the Fir Grove —"

"Yes, sir, I sure was. Terrible thing, that fire. Why do you ask?"

170

I showed him my license. "I've been hired by one of the victims' families to have a fresh look into the case."

He chuckled. "Find anything fresh? No, I expect not, after so many years. But it's good to have somebody besides poor Dick Hammerling looking into it. You don't really have a sore throat, do you, Mr. Prager?"

I confessed and told him how stupid I felt about not being upfront with him. In my defense, I said, the townsfolk hadn't exactly gushed forth at the mention of the fire.

"Nope, that fire was like our death knell. More than those poor kids died that day, let me tell you. Where you from in the city, son?"

"Brooklyn."

"For us, it was kinda like the day the Dodgers moved out. Now, I don't mean to disrespect the dead, mind you, by making such a comparison, but it was like we all had our hearts ripped right out of our chests that day. It never has been the same. The town — the whole area, for that matter — went right down the tubes, so you can understand the reticence of the people around here."

"But just before you seemed glad I was —"

"I was. I am glad! You see, I was sort of

drafted by John Crotty —"

"The county coroner back then," I interjected. I remembered his name from the papers.

"You've done your homework, good." He smiled broadly. "I'd done plenty of autopsies in my ten years in the army and done some forensics at Walter Reed before getting out in '64. Set up practice here in this very office with my missus a year later. I helped old Crotty with the bodies. In some cases there wasn't much to work with, a few teeth, X rays of old broken bones, that sort of thing. But the politicians were breathing down old Crotty's neck to wrap things up stat, so we did. It was just wrong to rush us like that. I'm almost certain there were still some bits of human remains bulldozed and carted away to be dumped unceremoniously in some landfill somewhere."

"Disrespectful," I offered.

"To both the victims and to science. You know, I've read some articles recently about DNA testing. You know about DNA, do you?"

"It was discovered by Abbott and Costello, right? No, sorry, Watson and Crick."

"A smart-aleck detective." He shook his head disapprovingly. "Next thing you know, you'll be making Dr. Pepper jokes like every

172

eight-year-old comes through that door."

"It hadn't occurred to me until you mentioned it."

"So, as I was saying, they say they'll be able to identify bodies beyond any question with only cellular amounts of tissue. Isn't that amazing?"

Yeah, I thought, and they'll send the results over fax machines. I remembered all the stupid promises for the future they made at the '64 World's Fair. The last time I checked, my turbine-powered, self-guided rocket car hadn't yet arrived. I'd just have to use my wireless videophone later to check in with my car dealer on Moon Colony Alpha. Oh, I forgot, he wouldn't be in today. He was being fitted for his nuclear-powered mechanical heart.

"Amazing," I seconded.

We parted ways, with him wishing me good luck. Though I tried to pay his wife, she wouldn't take my money. Maybe I wasn't that wrong about the rest of the world.

It was well past lunchtime, but I thought I'd go back to Town Hall and see what Molly was up to. She'd already eaten and, she said, in spite of how quiet it seemed, she really had a lot of work to do. Naturally, she warned me that this spontaneous visit didn't relieve me of my duty to see her before leaving town. She was only half serious. That half was serious enough.

I stopped by the stationery store to see if my documents were in. "They were," said the distracted woman behind the counter. "Sam came in himself and picked 'em up a few hours ago. Sorry." She went back to reading the *Enquirer* before I could thank her or ask if I owed her any money. I looked at the cover of the rag she was reading and immediately understood her rapture. It wasn't every day that a nine-year-old dying of old age was impregnated by the ghost of Elvis.

Sam was waiting for me, folder in hand, when I walked through the main entrance of the Swan Song. He was quick to tell me he had picked up the material himself. I wondered why. The stuff was important to me, but wasn't exactly gold dust.

"I couldn't get any of the local kids to do it. All back in school. And none of the *alter kockers*," he lamented, pointing at the old folks in the lobby, "were going into town today."

"Thanks, Sam. What do I owe you?"

"Nothing."

"Don't be silly."

"I'm not silly. I added it to your bill plus

174

twenty percent. So, *boychik*," he whispered, putting his arm around my shoulder, "how did it go with Molly the other night? We didn't get to speak yesterday."

"She was right where you said she'd be."

"So — did you *shtup* her?"

"I'm married, Sam."

"You're married, not dead."

"I'm in love with my wife."

"That's different, Moshe." He patted my face affectionately. "Why didn't you say so in the first place? I hope it lasts. Too bad about Molly. I like fat girls. More bang for the buck, if you take my meaning."

"With so few bullets left in the chamber, I guess that would be important."

He wagged his finger. "Sticks and stones may break my bones . . ."

"At your age, Sam, a strong wind could break your bones."

"This is way too much discussion of my bones. Get upstairs before I give you a *zetz*."

Upstairs, I spread out across the bed the papers Larry Mac had sent me, but regardless of how I tried to look away, my eyes were drawn to the mug shots and autopsy photos of Arthur Rosen. One look into his eyes and anyone could see there was nothing fun or funny about mental infirmity. Even in death he didn't seem completely free of the pain. Maybe that was my job, to free him of the pain at last. Was that what he wanted from me? I don't know. I must have stared at his pictures for twenty minutes. I had no answers.

The Higgins boys, on the other hand, provided answers to any number of questions. Not only was the father, as Sam had said, a serious drunk, but he was a petty thief, a low-life mutt working his way up the ranks to skell when his liver gave out. He died in some godforsaken local jail in some county in Pennsylvania I'd never heard of. I think I'd rather die in the street in the freezing rain than die alone in jail. I bet you no one paid for roses to be placed at the foot of his grave.

After Higgins the Elder woke up on the wrong side of the dirt, Robby bounced around from one foster home to the next, eventually taking leave of the system without bothering to ask anyone's permission. I doubt the system sweated the details. He'd been an angry handful from the day his dad's "career" forced Robby into the machinery of the state. His sad adventures might've interested Charles Dickens, but I was more concerned with the details of his less-than-extensive criminal record.

Robby Higgins had engaged in the sorts

of activities one might expect from a bright, angry, wounded teenage boy. Many a storefront window and mailbox had met their fate at his hands. There were the requisite graffiti arrests, the usual shoplifting of a six-pack at the local convenience store. Only two of his arrests were of particular interest to me. He was caught making a small pipe bomb, with which, as he confessed as part of a deal for reduced time in a county facility, he intended to put a scare into a foster father who had taken a belt to him. The other arrest, the one as an adult for arson, was the one that really caught my attention.

In 1972, at about the same time the firemen and I were pulling the battered but breathing Marina Conseco out of the water tank in Coney Island, Adolph X aka Robert John Higgins was burning a cross into the lawn of the Beth David Synagogue of King's Landing, Pennsylvania. Unfortunately for all those involved, Adolph used a wee bit too much accelerant, and the fire spread to a utility shed. It also spread to his pants leg, which is how the cops tracked him down. They arrested him at a local emergency room.

I should have been thrilled to read this information. I wasn't. Though this was the sort of thing a detective or a prosecutor

177

might look at to establish a pattern of behavior, I just didn't see it that way. For me it cut in the opposite direction, against Robby Higgins' being responsible for the Fir Grove fire. As for the cherry-bomb incident Molly told me about, so what? Me and every kid in my neighborhood had set off more fireworks than I could begin to count. My friend Ralphy was particularly fond of blowing up mounds of dog shit with M80s. The results were very Jackson Pollock. I set off a stink bomb in assembly once, so I guess the only difference between Robby Higgins and me was that he got caught.

What can I say about the pipe bomb? I don't know. My dad cracked me with his belt once or twice, and the second time he did it I was mad enough to kill him. At least I thought I was, or I remember it that way. He was in one of his I'm-a-failure-the-world's-against-me moods, and I said the wrong thing or looked at him the wrong way or didn't do anything at all. But someone was going to pay a price for his bad day, and Aaron wasn't around. He never hit Miriam, not because she was his baby girl, but because she could see through his cowardice and he knew it. It took me years to see it. Aaron didn't see it then and never will. So

Robby Higgins was going to put a scare into a man, not his father, who'd beaten him. From what I could glean from the material Larry Mac had sent me, Higgins hadn't really meant to do the man physical harm.

The cross-burning said something very different to me. What it said to me was that Robby Higgins had found a target for his rage instead of himself. Well, I think it would be more accurate to say someone else found the target for him and cultivated his anger. His name change told me as much. Disaffection and rage are the fuels that feed hate groups. I can't say who or what he had latched on to or who or what had latched on to him. Maybe he fell in with a group of skinheads. Maybe he picked up a copy of *Mein Kampf* or *The Protocols.* I can't say, and it's irrelevant in any case.

Regardless of how detestable I found the Adolph X's or Anton Harders of the world, I would always understand Robby Higgins. There were a lot of Robbys in the public-housing projects at the deep end of Coney Island. Rage was as available in the projects as nickel bags, but it cost less and did more damage. And though I was working backward with only hearsay, arrests records, and social workers' reports to go on, I just couldn't see Robby Higgins as the torch of the Fir Grove. That didn't mean that he didn't do it or that I'd scratch him off the list. It meant only that I wasn't prepared to march into anyone's office and offer him up as a scapegoat.

I'd hit a wall. History, as life in general, defies easy answers. Without Anton Harder to serve up as the answer to Old Rotterdam's sixteen-year-long nightmare, I had nowhere to go. Never any good at chess, I had trouble seeing my next move, or even if I had a next move. What I had were some new acquaintances, hotel bills, a paint job in waiting, and the stink of other people's cigarettes on my dirty clothes. I also had the stink of their fire in my nostrils. I cursed the day Arthur Rosen set foot in my store.

I picked up the phone to call Katy, but my mood was so foul I wasn't going to inflict myself upon her. A long time before I knew Katy existed, I promised myself that my father's penchant for striking out at those closest to him would die with him. Sometimes his rage leaked out of me, but only in words, never in deeds. I didn't beat myself up for it. A lot of his good leaked out of me, too. I miss him sometimes. I miss him a lot.

I was thinking of him in his coffin when there was a knock at my door. I hoped it was Mr. Roth. It was Sam. Maybe it was better that it was Sam. Sam didn't much remind me of my dad. As before, the old comedian made himself quickly at home, walking right on in without a hint of an invitation. He saw the papers spread out on the bed, but didn't ask about them.

"It's late, Sam."

"For who, your great-grandma?" He looked at his watch. "I'd be in the middle of my first show at this time. At midnight I'd be out onstage again. At three I'd begin unwinding, and when the sun came up I went to sleep. Come on, let's go down to Hanrahan's and have a drink."

"I don't know."

"What kinda bullshit is this?" he chided. "You don't even have to invite fat Molly. Just me and you, *kindeleh*. Come, make an old man happy."

"I'm tired, Sam, and I'm not in a very good mood."

"So! Look at me. I was born in a shitty mood. How's this, I get you to laugh, we go have a drink. Doesn't even have to be Hanrahan's. Deal?"

"Deal."

"Now, don't interrupt me, understand?"

"I understand."

"So — there's a priest, a minister, and a

rabbi," Sam said, giving the setup for a million old jokes, all of which I knew by heart. "And the three men of the cloth are discussing how to divide up the collection money between charitable causes and their salaries. The priest says, 'What I usually do is draw a big circle around me. Then I throw the collection-plate money up into the air. What lands in the circle is mine. What lands outside the circle is for God's good works.' The minister says —"

"Sam," I broke my promise. "I've heard —"

"Shush! You promised to let me finish, so let me finish. We got a deal."

"Okay."

"The minister says, 'I draw a big checkerboard on the floor. I toss all the money up into the air. What falls on red is mine. What falls on black is for God's good works.' The rabbi compliments his fellow holy men on their wisdom and says his method is not so different from theirs. 'I don't draw anything on the floor, because I have such faith in God's powers. I throw the money up as high as I can. What God catches, he keeps. What falls to the ground is mine.'"

"Bah *dum* dah," I imitated a rim shot. "I heard that joke in the womb, Sam."

"*Oy,* I guess I didn't make you —" Just

then, he stopped talking, grabbed his stomach, and let go a sonic boom of a fart. "Sorry, *toteleh.* By the way, do farts have lumps?"

"No."

"Then I'm in a shitload of trouble."

Now I was laughing.

On the way down to the lobby, I took my symbolic hat off to Sam for his rare talent. He said he learned to bomb onstage, so to speak, when he was bombing onstage.

"Gas by itself," he explained, "ain't so funny. But if you can do it and make believe you didn't notice it yourself, or if you can control it and point to people in the audience and go with it . . . Once, I did it by accident and I went with it. You gotta go with what works for you. So, whenever I was dying onstage, I added some sound effects and I was dying no more. Always gets a laugh, every time."

"I'll have to remember that."

"You want I should drive?" he asked, fishing for his keys.

"No. I'll drive. Hanrahan's, right?"

"Doesn't have to be, but okay." As we stepped outside, Sam asked: "You sure you don't wanna give the fat girl a ring?"

"I'm sure, Sam."

Walking around back, to where my car was

parked, I thought I smelled smoke.

"You smell something?" Sam spoke before me. "Smoke maybe?"

"You think?"

I ran. As I came around the edge of the main building, I spotted flickering light and shadows in the vicinity of my car. Great, I thought, another car up in flames. My car had been torched as a warning to me during my search for Katy's brother. I didn't think my insurance company was likely to renew me now. When I got close enough to get a good look, I was relieved to discover that it wasn't my whole car up in flames, just the hood. The flames were dying, but their presence was no less a message to me than if they had actually burned the whole car. I was being warned.

This time the word *KIKE,* not *JEW,* was spelled out in flame, not spray paint.

"Anti-Semitic bastards!" Sam hissed breathlessly, finally catching up to me. "I'll kick that little *pisher*'s ass myself, that son of a —"

"Take it easy, Sam. You're outta breath. I'll deal with that cocksucker in my own good time, on my own terms. We had some unfinished business to begin with. This is just one more item on the agenda, that's all."

Suddenly the idea of walking into Dick Hammerling's office and offering up Anton Harder as a likely suspect for the Fir Grove fire became very appealing — guilt or lack thereof notwithstanding. But Harder's type would probably enjoy the media circus. He could use it as a platform for his warped worldview. I could hear his voice in my head: "See how it is the Jews who persecute me. They control the media. They control the money. They . . ." Like I said to Sam, I'd deal with him in my own way.

Sam frowned. "I guess this means we ain't gonna have that drink."

"Bullshit! I'm not gonna let that asshole fuck up my life. But can we take your car?"

Sam said that we could, and that in the meantime he'd have one of his employees clean up the hood of my car as best he could.

"You sure you don't wanna report this to the police?" he wanted to know before having the hood cleaned.

"Nah. Besides, you don't need that kind of publicity for this place anyhow."

Sam drove exactly the kind of car I expected he would: an electric blue '59 Cadillac Coupe de Ville. It was all tailfins and flash and weighed more than a showroom full of Hondas. Other than the aroma of cigar smoke which oozed out of the white vinyl seats, the beast from Detroit was in immaculate condition. And given the speed and recklessness with which Sam drove it, its museum condition was more of a surprise.

"I'm not sure you call enough attention to yourself in this thing, Sam."

"Again with the smart remarks. Remember, you're the straight man. You want a stogie? It's top-shelf, from Cuba. I got a customer brings 'em down from Canada."

"Why not?"

"You know how to use one of these things?" Sam wondered, producing a diamond-studded gold cigar knife. "You make like a *mohel* and take a *bissel* off the top."

I took the fancy tool out of his hand and clipped off the tip of the big cigar. "Maybe I should go into circumcisions, I did that so skillfully. I hear there's money in it."

"With a cigar it's okay to clip a little too much. With a *petseleh,* you go too far and the mother will hunt you down like a dog."

"Good point."

"*Oy!* Now he's making puns."

I had to confess, the cigar was exceptionally smooth, though not quite so velvety as a chocolate shake. The burning tobacco was both earthy and sweet. As we rode into town enjoying our cigars, listening to Keely Smith and Louis Prima, I got to thinking about Sam. He didn't seem to spend a dime extra on his hotel — duct tape being its most prominent design feature — yet the car, the cigars, the bejeweled knife were not inexpensive items. Who was I to judge how a man spent his money?

"That old black magic . . ." Sam sang along. "I opened for Louis Prima, you know. Great musician and such a character. You know Louis Prima?"

"My folks."

He understood. "Such a character," he repeated.

Then we sat silently, just listening to the music, until we got to Hanrahan's. Luckily, the cigarette brigade wasn't out in force tonight, and a man could actually breathe and see his hand in front of his face. That said, it occurred to me that Sam and I were smoking cigars the size of small cannons. What fun would life be without hypocrisy?

The barmaid from Saturday night recognized Sam immediately, but took a second to place me: "You're Molly's friend, right?"

Without Molly around, I could confess to Sam that I thought the barmaid pretty damned attractive. She had long, thick black hair, dark skin, and pale blue eyes. My bet was she cleaned up in tips.

"See," Sam gloated, "I knew you weren't dead."

"I'm not bedding her down," I assured him.

"Good thing. Her husband's a professional wrestler."

"What'll you have?" I asked, pulling out my wallet.

"Sally knows. Don't you, Sally?"

Even before Sam finished his question, Sally the barmaid was reaching under the counter. The bottle she placed on the bar was an exquisite cut-glass decanter. For effect she let the deep-amber liquid inside settle before pouring two snifter-fulls.

Sam winked. "You like cognac?"

"It's okay."

"This," he said, raising his glass as I raised mine, "is more than okay, *totty. L'chaim!*"

He was right. It was more than okay. As with the car and the cigar, Sam had a taste for the finer things in life, very fine things.

"Mr. Roth tells me you were big once."

I thought I was paying him a compliment, but the cut-glass cognac turned to battery acid in his mouth.

"He did, Mr. Roth? I was big, but in a small way. Lenny Bruce with the foul

188

mouth, he was a big hero for free speech. Pity poor Lenny, the tragic, drug-crazed genius. Some genius, phooey! Didn't you know the great hero of the ACLU worked up here, telling the same stupid dirty jokes Cro-Magnon man told? Redd Foxx had the filthiest mouth I ever heard. He made me blush. He got a TV show and as many weeks in Vegas as he wanted. Me, I got the Swan Song. That sound big to you?"

"Depends, I guess."

"On what?" he hissed, beckoning Sally for a second glass. "If you're comparing me with some *nebish* from Minsk-Pinsk, then I was big."

"Sorry, Sam, I didn't mean to bring up a bad subject."

"You're forgiven. Now have another drink."

It wasn't presented as an option.

There was a premeditated shift in subject away from Sam Gutterman's past career. We talked a little about my years on the job in Coney Island. He asked me if it was tough being a Jewish cop. I told him I never really thought about it. I wasn't born to it like the Irish, but it had its moments. We talked about Katy and Sarah, I showed him their pictures. He thought Sarah was beautiful — "Thank God, she looks like your wife!" — and made lustful remarks about Katy. I would have expected nothing less. I told him about the wine shop, about Aaron.

"What, no doctors or lawyers? Your mother must be spinning."

"My sister Miriam's married to a doctor."

"Good, now I'm sure you're a real Jew. First, with the police work, I was beginning to have my doubts."

Eventually, we got around to talking about Arthur Rosen and my amorphous quest in the Catskill Mountains. I wondered if Sam remembered either Karen or Andrea.

"Not really, sorry," he apologized, not bothering to wait for Sally to pour himself another cognac. "I worked up here for so many years, saw so many girls pass through the hotels I worked at, I wouldn't remember them. If I knew they were going to die, maybe I would have made an effort to remember."

I accepted his apology on behalf of the Rosen and Cotter families and suggested we get back to the Swan Song. I was tired and a little light-headed, because of the cigar more than the brandy. Sam was amenable. He even paid the bill and the tip, a rather too generous tip at that. But, hey, like I said, who was I to judge what a man, especially an old man, did with his money?

"Nice tip," I said as we walked back to his Caddy.

"Yeah, she used to work for me, Sally, when she was a kid. She —" He cut himself off. "She's just a nice girl."

I took his word for it. We weren't two blocks away from Hanrahan's when I felt myself drifting into sleep. Maybe it was Louis Prima's lullaby, but the sleep was an unpleasant one. Something was nagging me, something I couldn't put my finger on. No big deal, I thought, wishing Sam good night. I figured to go straight upstairs and let the nagging begin again. But without Louis Prima to rock me to bed, sleep came peacefully.

CHAPTER NINE:
DECEMBER 1ST

Though it sounded like an air-raid siren, I knew it was only the phone, and, having once dropped the receiver on my forehead, I was very careful to get a firm grip before bringing it to my ear.

"Yeah."

It was Katy. "Moe, my dad's in the hospital." Talk about a surge of mixed emotions. But in spite of a strong desire to click my heels, I knew I had to be sympathetic for Katy's sake. Regardless of how I felt or what I knew, Katy loved her father very much. If anything, circumstances had brought them closer together.

"Okay, okay, what's wrong?"

"They think he had a stroke, but they're not sure yet."

"Where is he?"

"In intensive —"

"No, kiddo, what hospital?"

"Mary Immaculate Medical Center."

"Where are you?" I wondered, trying to shake off the last remnants of sleep.

"Home."

"All right. Ask Cindy or Miriam to watch Sarah. I'll head straight to the hospital from here and meet you there later. Take your time driving up. I'll look after your mom until you get there, understand? We don't want to get anybody else hurt."

"I understand. I . . ." She began sobbing.

"Okay, I love you. Everything will be fine. Somehow I don't see a little thing like a stroke doing your dad in. He's too fucking stubborn for that."

That stopped her crying, at least for the moment. "What about your case?"

"What about it? Family comes first. I love you. Remember, take your time."

I threw my clothes together, made myself as presentable as I could in five minutes, and set out to find Sam, Mr. Roth, and a pot of bad coffee. For once I got lucky and found all three in the dining room. I went for the coffee first. Sam invited himself to sit down at my table. I noticed Mr. Roth standing to come over, but when he spotted Sam he changed his mind.

"I had fun last night. We gotta do it again before you go," Sam said, patting me on the shoulder.

"Listen, Sam, I've got to leave for a few days. My father-in-law had a stroke."

"I'm sorry to hear that."

"Don't be. It couldn't happen to a nicer fellow. I'm just worried about my wife and my mother-in-law."

"I wouldn't wanna be on your shit list, *bubeleh*."

"You'd have to work pretty hard to take his spot on that list. He's a real piece of work."

"I can tell by the tone of your voice and the fact that you're drinking my coffee without gagging. Can I do anything?"

"Thanks, Sam. Do you think I could get my room back when things settle down?"

"The old farts are going back to Boca in two days. Don't worry, you'll have your pick of rooms. Take care of yourself." The old comic stood up to go. "And don't sweat your bill. We'll have time to settle our accounts when you come back."

As soon as Sam left, Mr. Roth appeared.

"Good morning to you, Mr. Moe. Is something wrong? You look a little out of kilter. Did Sam say something to —"

"No, Mr. Roth, it's got nothing to do with Sam."

I explained again about my father-in-law. He, like Sam before him, was taken aback by the strength of my distaste for Francis Maloney Sr. It was simply that I had to keep a lid on my feelings around Katy and the family. I guess, when I got the opportunity to express the way I truly felt, I just sort of boiled over. But something was bothering Mr. Roth beyond my lack of enthusiasm for my father-in-law's recovery.

"When are you gonna be back?" he wondered.

"I don't know."

"I'm leaving in two days. I'm fond of you, Mr. Moe," he confessed. "I would hate to not see you before I leave."

"I like you, too, Mr. Roth, very much. You remind me of my dad, only without the baggage."

He smiled, but rather sadly. "We all got baggage. You just haven't lifted mine. You've been toting your dad's around so long, you don't realize it's probably not as heavy as you think."

Mr. Roth was right, of course. I promised to try and get back before he left, if only to say goodbye. He liked that, but he had an expression on his face I recognized from before. The day he had knocked on my car window with his cane he had worn such a face. There was something he wanted to tell me, but he needed me to prompt him. If things were different, I might've spent the time playing twenty questions. If, if, if . . . A man, even a man in his thirties, could choke on all the ifs in his life. I wished Mr. Roth a safe trip home if we missed one another. There was that word again. Whoever Sam had work on the hood of my car was wasting his talents as a cook or porter. No sign remained of the impromptu campfire, and the flat black that covered the area was painted on far more skillfully than I'd managed. I'd have to lay a big tip on him when I got back.

Why did it always have to snow on travel day? Just when I hit the highway, the white stuff started falling in a thick, blinding sheet. But snow must have been in the forecast, because half the Department of Transportation fleet was already plowing and sanding. I tucked myself in among a squadron of their yellow-and-blue trucks and let them escort me halfway to the hospital. I worried that Katy would not have the same good fortune and that her ride was likely to be more dangerous.

Mary Immaculate was a busy medical center that had grown up around an old maternity hospital. Its architecture suffered from a lack of planning and too many hands in the pot. As the county grew, so had Mary

Immaculate. It sort of looked like a designer showcase of the ugliest possible contrasting architecture. I'm almost certain one section of the place was designed by the guy who was responsible for the Old Rotterdam Town Hall.

My mother-in-law was pacing a furrow in the green linoleum of the smoking lounge. She fell somewhat awkwardly into my arms, her lit cigarette breaking in half against my shoulder and tumbling to the floor. She wasn't really crying, and she wasn't really not crying. I can't do justice to the sound she was making. There was something feral about it, something that harkened back to the cave. It was equal parts anger and grief. Katy had lost two brothers, but her mom had lost two sons, one, at least, forever. I couldn't conceive of what she was feeling at the prospect of losing her husband.

"Moe, I . . . I . . ." She kept trying to speak.

"It's okay, Ma. I'm here, and Katy will be here soon. We'll make sure everything's taken care of. Tell me what happened."

We walked down to the cafeteria for a cup of coffee that neither of us drank.

Apparently, Francis had been having his usual glass of whiskey in the living room, watching the tube. "I thought I heard something fall," my mother-in-law explained. "I came running in, ready to rip Francis' head off for getting whiskey on the carpet. But when I came in, the glass was on the floor and Francis was struggling to get up out of his recliner. He was trying to say something, but . . . no words, he had no words. Then he collapsed and I couldn't wake him."

The doctors were running tests, she said, but they were pretty certain it was a stroke of some kind. I concurred, for all my opinion was worth. I tried telling her consoling stories of relatives who weren't half as stubborn or tough as Francis who'd come through this sort of thing without a hitch. She wasn't buying, not yet. This was all too new and frightening. She asked me if I would go speak to the doctor for her. I'd understand him better, ask smarter questions.

"His name is Dr. Cohen, Dr. David Cohen," my mother-in-law was quick to tell me.

"Half the kids on my block were named David Cohen, Ma." I laughed. "But don't worry, I'll get the information out of him."

Sitting there across from my mother-in-law, I was aware that Arthur Rosen had lately been sitting on my shoulder. Although the last week of my life had been about him,

I'd been able to push his presence away, to abstract him. I can't say why I should have been thinking of him at that moment, but I was, and I suddenly had an idea I wanted to try out if and when I got back up to Old Rotterdam.

Waiting at the nurses' station outside of ICU, I actually started wondering if I *would* know Dr. Cohen when he eventually answered his page. I had my answer soon enough. I'd never met the man.

"You're the son-in-law," Cohen said, after a perfunctory shake of my hand.

"Among other things, yes. I'm the son-in-law."

He wasn't in the mood for witty repartee and buried his face in the steel-jacketed chart.

"Your father-in-law's had a mild stroke. He's now fully conscious, and we're moving him out of ICU as soon as we can clear a bed for him on the floor. Will there be anything else?"

"How long has it been?" I asked.

That confused him. "How long has it been since what?"

"Since you had your bedside manner removed. Was it a painful operation?"

"Look, Mr. . . . Mr. Prager, I'm a —"

"No, Doc, *you* look. I'm not in the mood

for the 'I'm a busy man' speech you use on the *goyim*. I don't view doctors named Cohen as the Second Coming, understand? So now take a minute and explain what you mean by a mild stroke. What's his prognosis? Will there be any lingering effects? You know, minor stuff like that, that the family really wants to know but is too afraid to ask."

Dr. Cohen was not used to being addressed in such a manner and almost told me so before thinking it through. Though I never once raised my voice, he got that I was dead serious and was apt to make his life unpleasant if he wasn't forthcoming. So His Majesty deigned to give me five minutes of his time.

There wasn't that much to tell, really. He called what my father-in-law suffered a TIA, a transient ischemic attack. The brain scan didn't show any major damage. He would suffer some temporary weakness on his right side and aphasia, a loss of speech. Eventually, his strength and speech would return. Most of the time, he assured me, patients who suffered TIAs didn't even require therapy. I thanked him and apologized. He didn't exactly kiss me on the lips, but he seemed relieved to be done with me.

I relayed this information to my mother-in-law and explained that Dr. Cohen would probably be more cooperative in the future. She didn't ask why. Maybe she assumed Dr. Cohen and I had exchanged secret tribal handshakes. I told her to go home and get some sleep, that we didn't need her ending up in the hospital, too. She didn't argue the point. She was exhausted, but hadn't realized just how exhausted until she heard the positive prognosis. I promised to keep her informed if anything changed, and that either Katy or I would come pick her up later so she could visit Francis.

She gave me a strong Italian hug and held my face between her palms. "You're a good man, Moses, a good son-in-law. We're lucky to have you."

I was pretty certain her husband would have a dissenting opinion, but her love and approval were important to me. "Thanks, Ma. Now get outta here. Go!" I gave her a twenty to more than cover the five-minute ride back to her house. "There's a cab stand right out front."

I half hoped Katy had gotten frustrated by the traffic and snow and turned back home to Brooklyn. Hoping was all I could do. Actually, I knew better. She wouldn't let anything short of a roadblock stop her, and I guess that's what worried me. Until she arrived I had nothing better to do than go back to the cafeteria. I left word at the nurses' station as to where I'd be and asked to be paged when Francis was moved into his room.

Sitting alone at the orange Formica table, actually sipping my coffee this time, I tried piecing together the last week of my life in a way that made sense. What I concluded was that I'd been more bored with my life than I'd known. It took mad Arthur Rosen to jostle me enough so I could see it. It was like having your leg fall asleep while you're watching TV. You're sort of aware it's asleep, but you don't feel the pain until you stand up. My life was like that. Arthur Rosen had made me stand up, and when I did I realized more than just my leg was asleep.

Maybe R. B. Carter's trying to buy me off *had* rubbed me the wrong way, and maybe I did feel the slightest bit guilty over how I'd treated Arthur Rosen when he came to beg my help, but when I went looking for Arthur I wasn't looking to make amends, not really. I was looking for a purpose. If Rosen hadn't written my name on his wall and hanged himself, I might still be looking. I doubt he could have talked me into taking the case. What case? Who was I fooling? There was no case, just a disturbed man's grief and denial. I was making it up as I went along. Arthur's suicide had provided a cloak of guilt under which I could freely operate. Eventually, I'd have to go back to restocking Pinot Noir, but for now I was flying.

A pleasant-faced old woman in a candy-striper uniform tapped me on the shoulder. "Mr. Prager . . . That's who you are, isn't it?"

"The last time I checked."

"The ICU nurse asked me to come down and tell you that your father-in-law's been moved to Room 344."

"Thank you."

"No thanks necessary, that's what we're here for. Now, when you leave the cafeteria, walk past the chapel, turn left, and take the far elevator up to the third floor. Make a left out of the elevator and a left at the lounge, and you'll be on his hall. I hope everything turns out well."

There he was, his thick, short body laid out like a cadaver. Maybe that was just wishful thinking on my part. He didn't realize it was me, and his eyes lit up when I came into the room. The light went out soon enough. It wasn't pronounced, but the right side of his face drooped like a wax mask that had gotten a little too close to a hot lamp.

"You had a stroke," I said, pulling a chair around to face him. "The doctor says you'll probably have a full recovery. The weakness on your right side will go away, and you should regain your speech. I sent Ma home to get some rest, and Katy'll be here in a little while."

Oddly, I felt myself smiling at him. I don't know, maybe for the first time since I met him, I was the cat and not the prey. It didn't last. Droopy face and all, he smiled back. I went out to call my mother-in-law. When I got back he was still giving me the Mona Lisa. I think I was fantasizing about his funeral when he tried speaking.

" 'atch hout 'ut 'ou 'sh 'or," he gurgled, almost laughing. " 'atch hout 'ut 'ou 'sh 'or."

I tugged my ear. "Sounds like . . . Charades, what fun."

But instead of getting frustrated, he just kept repeating those six nonsense syllables over and over and getting quite a kick out of them. I went out into the hallway, for, as usual, my father-in-law had squeezed all the breathable air out of the room.

I got out to the hall just in time to see Katy coming my way. Corny as it was, she started running as soon as she spotted me.

We kissed long and hard, but we hugged longer and harder. Being apart had been hell for both of us. When I gave her the rundown on her dad's prognosis, she began crying with joy. I wanted to ask her about Sarah, about how her trip up had been, but first she needed to see her father.

"You go in and visit. I've been in there with him already. I'll be around when you need me. Go on. I might go down to the gift shop."

I strolled — hobbled was more like it — down to the newsstand in the gift shop. Not having read anything but the *Catskill Tribune* for the last several days, I was in dire need of a tabloid fix. The *Post* let me down. There were no catchy headlines, just the usual body counts, drug busts, and gloomy predictions of the impending Japanese conquest of the world economy. The *Daily News* wasn't much better. The body counts weren't as high, the street value of the drugs was a little less, and Japan would take a little longer to crush the sluggish Western economies under its mighty thumb.

When I walked out of the gift shop, a familiar and unwelcome voice called after me: "Katy told me you'd probably be here."

"Hello, Rico."

Rico Tripoli was the third member of the

60th Precinct's Three Stooges. He lived up here. His wife, Rose, was Katy's cousin on her mom's side. I hadn't laid eyes on Rico since 1978 and was better for it. We'd once been close as brothers, closer in some ways. Now, as far as I was concerned, we were still as close as brothers: Cain and Abel. It was Rico who'd gotten me mixed up with the Maloneys in the first place. But he hadn't done it out of the goodness of his heart. He'd tried to use me, to play me like a fool.

"I'm here with Rose to see the old man," he said.

"So go see him."

"After three years, that's all you got to say to me?"

"All right, how about 'fuck you'?"

He wagged an angry finger in my face. "I did what I had to do for me and mine."

"Who you trying to convince? If it's me, don't waste your breath."

Rico's once-lush black hair was turning decidedly gray, and even under the muted light of the hospital lobby I could see the young buds of gin blossoms creeping along the sides of his nose. He could always hold his liquor, but I wondered if it wasn't beginning to hold him.

"If it wasn't for me, you wouldn't'a met

your wife."

"Look back at things however you want, Rico. You're the one that's got to live with what you did."

"I thought after all this time you could gimme a break."

"You want forgiveness, the chapel's over that way."

"Fuck you, Moe."

"That's better. Now, if you'll excuse me . . ."

Walking away, I heard him call out to me. "Get your shield yet?" he taunted loudly enough for the entire lobby to hear. "That's right, you got a cane instead. How's the wine business and that asshole brother of yours?"

I kept walking, but he wasn't finished.

"I made my big case. I got my name in the papers. I got my gold shield."

I turned around. "Good. Now when you get to hell you and Judas will have something to compare. I told you three years ago, Rico, table scraps are table scraps."

When I got back upstairs, Rico's wife, Rose, was just coming out of Francis' room. Even before the falling out between her husband and me, Rose hadn't much use for me. I think she saw me as a threat. She was his second wife and viewed every aspect of

Rico's earlier life with suspicion.

"Did he find you?" she asked without bothering to say hello.

"He found me."

"I wish you two would kiss and make up already. He's driving me crazy."

"Till death do you part, Rose."

"Yeah, and if he keeps drinkin' the way he's been drinkin', that'll be about a year from now. What he do to you that's eatin' at him?"

"You'd have to ask him about that," I said. "Besides, the way I remember things, you never much cared for me, anyway."

"That was then."

"It's too late. If it means anything, I miss him, too, sometimes. But you can't go backward. You can't make yourself forget. And even if I could, he wouldn't forget. He would know. Have a good life, Rose."

She shook her head in disdain. "You're a cold-hearted son of a bitch, aren't you?"

"Yeah, maybe. Maybe."

I put a halt to further discussion by stepping into Francis' room. Katy was holding his hand, recounting how much she loved their trips to Coney Island when she was a kid. He was transfixed by her. He did love her so. When he caught sight of me, he screwed up his face into that waxy half-smile. I imagine if Katy wasn't there he would have started with the syllables again. I signaled for Katy to come talk with me outside.

"Did Rico find you?"

"No," I lied. "I must've missed him."

"That's too bad."

"I saw Rose, though, and gave her my best. Listen, I'm gonna go back to the house and get your mom. When we get back here, you and I can talk. Okay?"

"Okay, but first you've gotta pay the price."

We kissed, and the rest of the world fell away, if only for a few seconds.

Chapter Ten:
December 3rd

I had one more week to go tilting at windmills. That was it, Katy I and agreed. My wife was an intelligent, sometimes annoyingly perceptive woman. She noticed the damage to my car almost immediately and could see I was itching to get back to whatever it was I was playing at up in Old Rotterdam. She saved her questions, because she trusted me and, given her dad's stroke, probably didn't want to hear the answers.

Her dad was already improving, having regained most of his strength and some of his speech. He'd be coming home in a day or two, and she said I'd just get in the way. I didn't argue the point. Though she never broached the subject, Katy knew Francis and I weren't ever going to be fishing buddies.

She had already left for Brooklyn to fetch Sarah when I got out of the shower. I could have left last night, but I wasn't *that* anxious to get up to Old Rotterdam. Sam and Mr. Roth were entertaining enough, but my wife had it all over them. Besides, there was a stop I wanted to make on the way to the Catskills that wouldn't have been possible the previous evening. Too many people milling about.

"Hello, you son of a bitch," I whispered to my father-in-law as I walked into his room.

He was silent.

"What's the matter? Nothing to say? You were pretty talkative the other morning."

He gave me that cruel smile, though fuller, less waxy, now that he'd regained his strength. He pointed to his mouth and shrugged.

"Don't gimme that bullshit. I was here yesterday. I heard you talking to Ma and Katy. So what was it you wanted to say to me the other day?"

He shrugged his shoulders again. "I 'orget."

I just walked out. I thought I heard him laughing, but that might have been my imagination.

Sam fairly did a jig when I loped through the lobby of the Swan Song Hotel and Resort. Oddly, I nearly danced one myself.

I actually hugged the old bastard when he came around the counter.

"Thank God! My best full-price guest returns."

"Your only full-price guest, you mean. I'm happy to see you, too, Sam."

"Don't mince words. So — how's your father-in—"

"Still breathing, unfortunately."

"A real romance between you two, huh?" As was his habit, Sam wagged his finger at me. "Be careful, *boychik,* you should watch out what you wish for. You might get —"

I grabbed the old comic's shoulders. "What did you just say?"

"What?"

"What you just said."

"What?"

"*Oy,* Sam. No, what's on second. Who's on first."

"I don't know."

"Third base!" we exclaimed simultaneously.

"Good," I said, still laughing, "now that we got Abbott and Costello out of the way, what did you say about watching —"

"Watch out what you wish for —"

"— you might get it," I finished. "That's what he was saying. 'Watch out what you wish for.' But why would he say that to me?"

I mumbled.

"What?"

"Forget it, Sam, we've already been down that road. You got a room for me?"

He did, my same room. And, to make me feel right at home, he hadn't touched it since I left. My bet was he paid his cleaning staff per room.

"Is Mr. Roth —"

"That's their airport bus pulling up outside." Sam pointed over my shoulder. "He'll be down in a minute."

I didn't wait. Mr. Roth never seemed quite comfortable in front of Sam and me, so I headed up to his room. Unlike Sam, Mr. Roth wasn't dancing. He was rather melancholy.

"I thought you'd be happy to see me," I said.

"Oh, I am, believe me. But I'll miss you. A son like you, I could have been proud of."

Though tempted, I didn't ask him to explain. "That's a generous thing to say, Izzy. Thank you. I'll miss you, too."

My calling him Izzy made him smile. He handed me a sheet of paper with his address and phone number. I gave him a business card from the store and wrote my home number and address on the back.

"A pleasure," he said, extending his hand.

"A pleasure."

"Here." He reached for something on the bed. "I bought this for you to enjoy and remember our making friends. We're friends, right?"

"Friends."

The gift he gave me was clearly a gift-wrapped bottle of liquor of some sort. Shrewd, huh? Three years in the wine business and I could spot a bottle of liquor a mile away. The gift wrapping was the standard patterned foil, but the wrapping job itself was rather shoddy. I began to unwrap the bottle.

"Please, Mr. Moe, save it for when I'm gone," Mr. Roth implored, grabbing my wrist. "Maybe tomorrow or the next day, you'll open it up and think of our nice talks."

"For you, Mr. Roth, anything. Have a safe flight home."

"You'll call sometime?"

"I promise."

He finally let go of my wrist. "The best of luck to you with what you're working on. I'll be interested to know how it turns out."

I helped him on with his coat, handed him his cane, and carried his bags down to the bus. He carried my bottle. I didn't stay and wave as the bus pulled away. I hated long goodbyes.

The Swan Song was eerily quiet now that the Boca Raton contingent was gone. There were a few other guests besides myself, but we were easily outnumbered by Sam and the staff. I'd have to ask Sam how he managed to keep the place up and running with such a dearth of cash flow. I would have asked him right then and there if I could have found him, but he had gone, too, probably to the bank.

I went back up to my room. Sam was as good as his word: it was untouched. I slid Mr. Roth's gift under my bed, pulled the pictures of Arthur Rosen out of my bag, and considered when to begin trying out my new strategy. There was no time like the present, of course, but I was more than a little worn out by the last forty-eight hours and by the prospect of not seeing Sarah for several more days. I closed my eyes, remembering the feel of Katy's naked back against me. The warmth of the recollection was dampened, however, by the sound of Francis Maloney Sr.'s aphasic gibberish rattling around in my skull.

" 'atch hout 'ut 'ou 'sh 'or. 'atch hout 'ut 'ou 'sh 'or. 'atch hout 'ut 'ou 'sh 'or. . . ."

Why should I watch out what I wish for? That man could get under my skin like no one else. Now he had a new mantra to go along with his warnings about ghosts. Gee, I couldn't wait for what he had planned next. I grabbed the pictures of Arthur Rosen and got out of that room. There was no time like the present.

By the time I hit the lobby on my way out, Sam Gutterman had returned from parts unknown. I didn't waste any time before showing him the pictures.

"Sure, I've seen him before," Sam said, chortling. "In the dictionary, next to the word 'psycho.' A friend of yours?"

"An acquaintance, Arthur Rosen."

The name seemed to have about as much impact on him as the death of a blade of grass. I didn't want to spend a lot of time explaining myself. If Sam didn't know him, he didn't know him. *C'est la guerre!* But Sam was curious.

"Who is he, really?"

"Was," I corrected, producing one of the autopsy photos.

"I'll take a five-by-seven and two wallet-sized."

"You're a sick man, Sam."

"If you don't joke, you cry. So who was he?"

"The older brother of Karen Rosen, one of the girls who died in the fire."

There was a limit to Sam's curiosity and we'd reached it. Now it was my turn. I asked him about how he could afford to keep the Swan Song up and running.

"I can't. We're closing for the season next week. Everybody out! Even you, *toteleh.* And just between you, me, and the duct tape, I don't think I'm reopening."

"Why?"

"You mean besides the fact that when I have guests off-season they make the Ancient Mariner feel like a teenager? You mean besides the fact that every building on the estate is the perfect setting to reenact 'The Fall of the House of Usher'?"

"You're pretty well read." I noted, ignoring his hyperbole.

"What, just because I'm a nasty old prick you think I never picked a book up in my life? See Spot run. Run. Run. Run."

"Okay, sorry. So why are you thinking of closing up?"

"*Gelt.* There's a development company buying up every big piece of land they can get their hands on. For golf courses, I think. I know for a fact two of the other hotels are already under contract. Of course, the developer's offering *dreck mit dreck,* but when the ugliest girl in town is also the only girl in town, she don't look so bad."

"So this is the Swan Song's swan song."

"I bet you waited your whole life to make such a joke."

"No," I protested, "not my whole life."

"Some things, *boychik,* are better left unsaid."

Sam had to go. He had to oversee the mowing of the polo grounds and the polishing of the good silver.

Much to my surprise, Molly Treat had abandoned her desk at Town Hall. I figured Molly was a lock to know something about Arthur Rosen's movements in town over the last several years. I guess I could always wait for Saturday night and show up at Hanrahan's, though I think if I heard "Piano Man" again I couldn't be held accountable for my actions. Hammerling seemed to be missing in action as well. That was unfortunate, but not tragic — I wasn't sure what he could have told me.

So I was batting 0 for 3. My new approach, my brilliant idea to trace Arthur's footsteps — which were bound to be fresher than those of his dead sister had gotten me to the same place as my old approach. Then it occurred to me that I might have a good idea but I was going about it in the wrong way. Instead of seeking out people I was acquainted with, people who knew bits and pieces of the story, I'd try my hand with strangers.

After a few awkward attempts with passersby, I worked out a routine. I walked into all the shops along Main Street. In rapid succession, I'd flash my badge, then a mug shot of Arthur Rosen at the counterman and/or customers waiting in line. Several people were pretty certain they'd seen Arthur Rosen in town. A few knew his name.

"That crazy fella," the counterman at the hardware store said. "I remember him. All he wanted to talk about was the fire."

The more I showed his picture, the more I got that reaction. Some folks were less kindly than the guy at the hardware store. As Molly Treat, Hammerling, and the doctor had warned, the citizenry of Old Rotterdam was more than a little bit touchy about the fire.

"What'd he do now?" a persnickety old biddy at the library wanted to know. "He kill somebody?"

"He did," I answered plainly. "Himself."

"No surprise there." She walked away, quite satisfied with her powers of prognostication.

I didn't know whether to be simply discouraged or depressed. Clearly, Arthur

Rosen had made a general nuisance of himself. No wonder Hammerling had emphasized the detrimental effect of being associated with Arthur. He was about as popular as a case of crabs. I decided to try Doc Pepper and his wife. Maybe they could tell me something of interest about Arthur Rosen sans running negative commentary.

On my way over, I passed what used to be the local synagogue. The Hasidic sects would have their own, but this building had served the summer crowd; the Conservative and High Holy Day Jews up from the city. It wasn't quite a storefront, nor was it the Wailing Wall. Temple Beth Shalom was a converted — no pun intended — two-family, wood-frame house painted a somber blue, sandwiched between a vacated bakery and an empty Laundromat. Its old-fashioned black-felt-and-glass billboard was still affixed to one wall. Where once white plastic lettering had announced births, deaths, dances, and services, the following was the only word left: **CL SED.** There is something particularly sad about the death of any congregation. It's a symbol of atrophy, the death of community. And when I saw my reflection in the billboard glass, my nose where the **O** in **CL SED** should have been, I recognized my culpability and that of the other unobservant in the death of congregations everywhere.

As I turned away from my reflection, I sensed another presence.

"Come out, come out, wherever you are!" The words I hadn't uttered since I was a kid poured out of my mouth as if I'd said them only yesterday.

Out of the shadows near the alleyway of the abandoned bakery stepped the man in the threadbare suit I'd seen float by the hardware store. As Molly had said, he wore the infamous yellow star sewn to the chest of his coat. He was more frail, less ghoulish up close, and younger than I had thought.

"Are you a Jew?" he asked haltingly, swerving his head about.

"Why?"

"A proud man would answer yes or no, not why. Are you a proud man?"

When I did not answer immediately, he actually smiled at me. He handed me a small sheet of paper and walked silently away. I didn't chase after him. I read the flyer.

ARE YOU A PROUD JEW?
29 Short Mountain Road
Old Rotterdam, NY
7 PM

That was it. That was the entire text: no phone number, no directions, no overt message, just a question. I neatly folded the little paper and slipped it behind my license. But out of sight is not always out of mind. The question even drowned out my father-in-law's voice.

I decided to pass up my chat with Doc Pepper. I needed to sit and have a drink. I looked at my watch and considered heading back to the Swan Song. It was getting close to dinnertime, and the bottle Mr. Roth had given me was waiting eagerly under my bed, but Hanrahan's was a lot closer. I thought about smoking half a pack of cigarettes to get my lungs in shape before heading over. I decided to rough it.

The usual crowd of losers surrounded the bar. By this I don't mean to imply that the people of Old Rotterdam were necessarily losers, or that the patrons of Hanrahan's were any worse than the patrons of any other watering hole. Not at all. Like I said before, cops know bars. Bars, especially ones that serve food, are naturally crowded between noon and two o'clock. The same is true between the hours of five and seven. But at four or four-fifteen, when those who have jobs are at them, the denizens of most bars are losers.

No one's drinking piña coladas or munching on a delightful Cobb salad. At four in the afternoon, they're reading the *Racing Form,* smoking cigarettes or Tiparillos, drinking speed-rack scotch with a cheap beer chaser. "A bat and ball" is what the old-timers called it. Who was I to be a nonconformist? "A bat and ball," I ordered without bothering to look up.

"Hey, how are you?" It was Sally, Molly's friend and Sam's ex-employee.

"Hey, Sally, what's shakin'?"

"Nothing shakes in Old Rotterdam, not even the leaves."

She went to service one of the losers at the other end of the bar, but came right back when she was finished.

"Molly tells me you're a city cop."

"I was," I said, shoving a twenty at her. "Why don't you buy something for yourself on me." She did. Sally had a taste for Jack Daniel's on the rocks. "Sam tells me your husband's a professional wrestler."

"Sam's so full of shit I'm surprised he's got room in there for his internal organs. Cheers!" We hoisted our glasses. "I haven't had a husband in five years, and he was a professional all right, a professional asshole."

We both liked that. I told her to buy

herself another. She didn't exactly put up a fight. No matter what you might think, bartending is a hazardous occupation. It's a breeding ground for alcoholism. When I was on the job and we'd go unwind after a shift, it was always a toss-up whether the cops at the bar or the bartenders were the bigger drinkers. And it was doubly hard on an attractive, amiable woman like Sally. Men, even the lowliest bums, have rich fantasy lives. When they sit at the bar across from a pretty barmaid, they're not thinking of floral arrangements. They'll buy her two drinks for every one they drink, and then drop a ten or twenty on the bar to impress her.

"I hear you used to work for Sam," I said.

That didn't go over any too well. She kind of sneered, not so much at me as at herself. "I did, yeah. That was a long time ago. I'm not into that anymore."

I certainly wasn't going to press her on the subject. I offered to buy her another drink as a peace offering.

"No thanks," she said, pushing my twenty back across the bar at me. "Your drink's on me. Take care."

Sally walked to the other end of the bar, apparently more comfortable with her regular losers. I was all ready to leave when a big-bellied man of fifty in a brown uniform and trooper hat put his left hand on my right shoulder. He might've been fat, but he was strong. If I'd wanted to, I would have had a difficult time standing up.

"I'm Lieutenant Bailey," he said, "Old Rotterdam Police."

"I'm Moe —"

"I know who you are, Prager. Would you please step outside with me."

"If you take your hand off my shoulder, I'd be happy to."

I left the twenty on the bar for Sally and followed the lieutenant out the door. Darkness had descended in the time I'd spent unintentionally offending the barmaid. The lieutenant's cruiser was parked at a sloppy angle to the curb in front of Hanrahan's. It was comforting to know small-town cops had as little respect for traffic laws as their big-city counterparts.

"What can I do for you, Lieutenant?"

"You've been harassing people in town, and we'd like that to stop as of five minutes ago," he said plainly enough, in a nasty-cop tone. Cops tell, they don't ask.

"I'm a licensed investigator working a case. I didn't harass a soul."

"Walking up to complete strangers, asking questions about a subject no one wants to talk about — around here, we call that harassment," Bailey let me know.

"Well, then, we agree to disagree."

"Well, then," he mocked, "we'll just have to have somebody swear out a complaint."

"You do that. I wonder what Councilman Hammerling will think about you trumping up charges."

"What's he gonna do, get Old Rotterdam Rodney to bite my ankles? Hammerling's a local joke, Prager. I wouldn't want to count on him for getting your ass out of the frying pan."

"I'll take your advice under consideration," I mumbled, taking a step to leave.

"That wasn't advice, shithead," he said, pushing me off balance.

"Keep your fuckin' hands off me, fat boy," I warned.

He didn't like that. He grabbed my coat with his left hand and began to pull me toward him. I clapped my right palm over the back of his porky hand, pressed my thumb over the nail of his left thumb, and flexed my thumb hard. Lieutenant Bailey, all 250-odd pounds of him, shrank to his knees. An ounce more pressure and his thumb would have snapped like a pretzel stick. My instructor at the academy, a black belt in jiu-jitsu, called this a thumb crunch. I'm sure there was a mystical Japanese name for it, but the English term got the essence of the technique dead on.

"Listen, you fat fuck, I'm just doing my job. With any luck I'll be out of this town by the weekend. You wanna strong-arm somebody, try another candidate."

I released my grip and walked away into the fallen night. I turned back to see Bailey flexing the feeling back into his hand. Good thing he hadn't taken a swing at me. There's no doubt in my mind he could have kicked the living shit out of me, but for now I was the king of thumb wrestling. The thing about glory is that it is always short-lived. When I got back to my car, Lieutenant Bailey and three other uniforms were waiting.

"Moses Prager," one of the uniforms spoke, "you're under arrest for assaulting a police officer. Turn and face your car. Spread your legs far apart, and place your hands on the roof of your automobile."

"I know the drill. I'm licensed to carry a firearm," I shouted loudly enough for anyone in the general vicinity to hear. "My .38 is holstered on —"

Before I could finish my sentence, I was being patted down and my revolver was being removed. Looking over my shoulder, I could see Bailey smiling at me. He probably thought it a wonderfully evil smile, but compared with my father-in-law's it was purely amateur-hour material. I was cuffed, given my Miranda warning, shoved into the backseat of a cruiser, and driven to the station. I was inked, mug-shot, and put in a holding cell along with a twenty-something. Given the look of his eyes and the smell of sweat, my guess was he was in for DWI. When I entered, my cellmate retreated to a corner and curled up into a ball of himself.

I didn't start screaming for my phone call, nor did I demand to see a lawyer, the judge, or the chaplain. I needed time to think this through. I didn't know who I'd call, anyway. Sam? Maybe, eventually. The only lawyer I had lived in Forest Hills and was good at drawing up business documents but wouldn't know criminal procedure if it bit him in the ass. I could live without seeing the judge for now, and since the electric chair had been unplugged years ago, I was unlikely to need the chaplain. Besides, getting demanding with cops only gives them another way to torment you. I knew the game. You can't deny somebody something he doesn't want.

They served me dinner around seven: meat loaf, mashed potatoes, gravy, green beans, Coke, and Jell-O. When I got out I'd have to recommend the chef to Sam, though I suspect the food came from the local luncheonette. Somehow I didn't think there'd be much need to keep a full-time kitchen staff on duty at the Old Rotterdam jail. My cellmate wasn't hungry, nor was he very talkative. He did, however, stay rolled up in a ball longer than I thought humanly possible.

"Come on, Prager," the uniform who brought me in ordered. "Your arraignment won't be until the morning. We're moving you to more comfortable accommodations for the night. Do I have to cuff you?"

"Not unless you want the practice," I joked.

"That's fine. Come on."

He opened up the cell and marched me down a long corridor, through a steel security door, and into a tidy little cellblock. There were six empty cells, three on each side. They each came with two beds, and a stainless-steel sink and toilet. There was even a TV mounted so that it could be viewed from any of the cells.

"Take your pick," the cop gave me the option.

I chose the cell closest to the TV. My jailer made no bones about my selection. He let me in and handed me the remote control.

Once I was settled in, he turned the TV to face me more directly.

"You want your call now?" he asked.

"I'll save it for the morning, thanks." I made myself as comfortable as possible and got down to watching some serious TV. Though I enjoyed my buddies at the Swan Song, the Old Rotterdam jail was tough competition. The food was better, the TV worked, and the bedding was cleaner. Maybe it was a good thing Sam was selling. I guess I started drifting off a little past ten. I think I remember listening to the local news.

I was yanked up, a pillowcase pulled over my head. My hands were held behind me; my wrists were cuffed. Something that felt like a two-by-four whacked my right kidney so hard I nearly blacked out. I wasn't dreaming. Even in the fog of interrupted sleep, I knew this was payback time for treating Lieutenant Bailey with disrespect. I held my breath, waiting for the second blow. It never came. Instead, I was being pushed along by big strong hands — Bailey's, no doubt — guiding me, tugging my clamped wrists this way or that. Now I was worried. I'd been too smart for my own good. If I'd only taken the opportunity to make my call, someone would know where I was.

The big hands shoved me into a car. When I tried to sit up, I was shoved down. When I tried to right myself again, I was shoved back down. I didn't go for a third attempt. I tried talking, trying rather unsuccessfully not to sound desperate. No one answered. It was a very short ride, maybe two minutes at most. That was good. I wasn't being driven beyond the town limits into the vast woodlands and snowy terrain, where a stranger could easily disappear until the spring thaw.

I was being yanked out of the car. The air was cold, but I was sweating so intensely that I imagined steam must have risen off my body. Bang! I was slammed into a car. Then that second blow finally came. This time so hard I almost revisited my meatloaf dinner. My knees buckled like card-table hinges and I went down hard. I struggled to catch my breath without puking up my guts. I heard keys clink on the pavement. My hands were uncuffed. A car rode away, fast.

I just lay there trying to orient myself. Then I realized that if I was in the middle of the road it might not be such a good idea to lie there too long. I pulled the pillowcase off my head as I scrambled to my feet. Still unsteady, I braced myself against a car, my car. I'd recognize that black-painted hood anywhere. My keys lay in the street, not too far from where I must have fallen. I reached over to pick them up, and when I did my kidneys screamed for me to take it easy.

Strangely enough, my car door was open. There on the driver's seat were my personal effects, including the pictures of Arthur Rosen, and an old yellow police folder. I checked my wallet and license holder. All the cash was there. Everything seemed to be in order, even my .38. But the file had me curious. I flicked on my dome light. I was looking at a sixteen-year-old file on one Robert Higgins. The file was rather thorough. There were black-and-white pictures, detectives' handwritten notes, typed witness statements, crude maps of the Fir Grove, even a psychological evaluation of the young Mr. Higgins done by a state-appointed shrink. I didn't spend much time reading the contents, but one thing was as obvious as the nose on my face: somebody was trying very hard — too hard, maybe — to get me to finger Anton Harder née Robby Higgins for the Fir Grove fire.

When I dragged myself into the lobby of the Swan Song, Sam was pacing back and forth behind the front desk. He didn't even appear to be enjoying the fancy cigar hanging out of his mouth.

"You're all right!" he said, looking genuinely relieved. "I was worried when you missed dinner. I was gonna call the cops."

"That's rich."

"What?"

"Never mind, Sam. Never mind."

"I'd say you don't look so good," he said, coming to get a better view, "but that would be a lie, *toteleh*. You look a lot worse than not so good. You okay?"

"I've been worse."

Sam did his famous finger-wagging. "I may be dumb but I'm not stupid. You don't want to talk about it, right?"

"Right. I'm just gonna haul my ass upstairs and take a hot bath."

"Lukewarm," he corrected. "A hot bath hasn't been here since the war."

"Vietnam."

"French and Indian."

"Good night, Sam."

"Oh, I almost forgot. You got two messages." He ran back around the front desk and handed me two slips of paper. One call had been from Katy. I was more intrigued by the second. It was from someone named Joe, and he left a local number at which I could call him at any hour. I knew lots of

233

Joes. None, however, with a local number.

"Thanks, Sam. I'll see you at breakfast."

I called Katy back immediately upon getting upstairs. Her dad was improving almost by the minute, though the doctor wanted to keep him in the hospital for another day or two to run tests and for observation. The old man wasn't happy about it, but he wasn't about to piss Katy off. Her mother had calmed down considerably with the increasingly good news. Sarah missed her daddy, so I was told. No more, I assured my wife, than I missed the two of them. I just said I was beat and had to get some sleep. I promised to call every day until I got home.

"You sound awful," Katy pointed out.

"Dead tired, that's all. I have a feeling things are coming to a head. I love you. Kiss Sarah for me in the morning."

As Sam predicted, the water was lukewarm. That was all right. It seemed to ease the tenderness around my kidneys. Two wicked, fist-sized bruises had already begun to form before I got in the tub. I read the Robby Higgins file for relaxation. The lead detective had suspected Robby from the very first, but could find zero physical evidence and no witness to tie him to the crime scene. He had an alibi, though weak by most standards. He claimed to have spent the night with his father, who was up visiting, and his father backed him. Neither ever wavered from his story.

The fire investigation, such as it was, was laughable according to the cops. In the margin of one of his interview sheets, the detective wrote: "Fire department determined smoking in bed on way to fire!" The fire inspector never wavered from his story either.

In a desperate attempt to shake something loose, the detectives convinced a local judge to order a psychological examination of Robby Higgins. I read the report carefully and it added up to nothing. The shrink made sure to cover his behind by covering every base and some that hadn't been invented. Robby Higgins might have done it and he might not have done it. He might have wanted to do it and might not have wanted to do it. He was conflicted. He was clear-headed. The doctor's assessment was as easy to get a handle on as a suitcase full of fog. And what made it worse was trying to wade through all the Freudian mumbo-jumbo that persisted through the sixties.

Shortly after the report was filed with the court, Robby Higgins moved to Pennsylvania with his dad. Though the cops continued to suspect him, short of new evidence there was nothing they could do. The police department was not immune from the momentum to get beyond the fire. The file was classified as inactive within a few months of the fire.

Frankly, I was less intrigued by the file itself than by the arcane method used to put it in my possession. I'd already pretty much given up on Anton Harder as a suspect. Someone had a lot invested in getting me reinterested in him. Who? It had to be someone with money and/or influence, someone who had a lot to lose by my poking my nose around. Obviously this someone had some serious juice with the local police. I thought about R. B. Carter, but that didn't make any sense no matter how I kicked it about. I'd sleep on it.

I put the mysterious Joe's number on the nightstand next to the bed. I tried shutting my eyes, but I needed to get the phone call out of the way.

"Hello," a man's tentative voice answered.

"Joe there?"

There was a second's hesitation, as if the man on the other end had to try and remember who Joe was. "This is Joe."

"This is Moe Prager. You called me before at the Swan Song."

"I recognized him from the picture you showed me."

"Arthur Rosen?"

"That's him."

"Is there anything you can tell me or that you want to tell me?" I asked as kindly as I could manage.

"I couldn't talk before, when you saw me in town, you understand?"

"I'm beginning to," I said.

"That Rosen guy was one of them Yellow Stars. His prescriptions used to come into the pharmacy. Most of the time one of the others would pick them up for him, but once or twice he came in for them by himself."

"How long ago was this, would you say?"

"Two, maybe three years ago. Listen, I don't know anything else. I hope this helps you."

"Thank —"

He hung up before I could finish thanking him. Joe might have been an excellent pharmacist, but his espionage skills needed a little fine-tuning. He hadn't exactly done the best job of covering his identity. It was of little consequence, because for the first time I actually had a tangible place to start. And the less-than-mysterious Joe had confirmed something both R. B. Carter and

Hammerling had alluded to: something had happened two or three years ago to reinvigorate Arthur Rosen's search for the cause of his sister's death. Somehow I doubted his membership in the Yellow Stars was completely coincidental. I decided I had an appointment for 7:00 P.M. the following day at 29 Short Mountain Road.

Now there was only one thing preventing me from sleep. My bladder suddenly had a mind of its own, and I was going to pee whether I liked it or not. I didn't, because instead of the mundane yellow I'd grown accustomed to over the first three decades-plus of my life, a burning stream of pink and red poured out of me. Getting thumped in the kidneys will do that to you. I'd deal with Bailey in my own way on my own schedule. For the moment, that was third or fourth on my to-do list.

Chapter Eleven: December 4th

I kept my breakfast appointment with Sam. Unlike the last time we ate together, we sat in the dining room, completely unfettered by the presence of other guests. The silence was both peaceful and unsettling. We had spinach-and-cheddar omelets, home-fried potatoes, and copious amounts of bacon. It had all the trappings of a condemned man's last meal.

Sam was curious about why I'd walked into his hotel the night before looking like something the cat would be too afraid to drag in. He tried several indirect questions and a few direct ones, and, in the end, resorted to guessing. It got him nowhere, but I enjoyed watching him try. He was an entertaining fellow even offstage. With a promise to see him later, I excused myself and went back upstairs.

Earlier, I'd been afraid to took at my back. Now, with some bad coffee and enough cholesterol in me to clog a three-quarter-inch pipe, I peeled up my shirt, lowered my pants, and stood before the wardrobe mirror. What last night had been a couple of fist-sized bruises had spread into nearly convergent purple patches covering a good portion of my lower back. The damage appeared worse than it felt. There was pain, but it was duller, less urgent than when I was flat on the cold, damp pavement. The color of my urine was still unnaturally pink. Less so, however, than when I'd gotten up.

Last night's sleep had been exceedingly uncomfortable. I pulled the shades and settled into bed with a copy of yesterday's *Catskill Tribune*. I didn't have anywhere to be until the evening, so I tried letting the news of the day be my lullaby. As I read through the pages, I finally recognized one of the comforts of living outside New York City. Not all the world bordered on insanity. There were actually parts of the world that functioned without a constant stream of bodies and chaos to feed the machine. It was no wonder that the Fir Grove fire would have had such a profound impact on a place where the big stories of the day involved jackknifed tractor trailers carrying mixed poultry.

I had reached well into the paper, to the

pages with recipes for green-bean salads and charity bake-sales announcements, before I began drifting off. As I did, a voice inside my brain told me to snap out of it and pay more careful attention. My body shut down on its own even before I could decide to ignore the voice.

It was about 5:00 P.M. when, with paper clamped between my chin and chest, I opened my eyes. After washing the newsprint off my neck and dunking my head in a sinkful of chilly water, I felt a whole lot better than I had in the morning. Sleep, however, hadn't completely muffled that voice in my head. I went back and studied the green-bean page. Alas, my perspiration and drool had rendered some of the print unreadable, but there really was nothing to see. The little voice was finally quiet.

Before heading up to the Yellow Stars, I decided to try and organize what I knew or thought I knew into a scheme in which the pieces might hang loosely together. First, I drew a time line dating back to just before the fire. On that time line, I filled in names and events. Second, I wrote out the names of everyone even remotely connected to my so-called investigation. Even people on the periphery, like Molly and Sally, were included. I ripped out the names into little squares and tried making an organizational chart, matching names with other names. It was difficult to know if it did me any good. Some of the players knew almost none of the others, whereas some knew almost everyone else. And what I couldn't see at all was who had the most to gain by Anton Harder's being presented to the authorities on my silver platter. I guess the fault lay in me. I just didn't know any of the players well enough to see things any of them might have seen if they knew what I knew. I went downstairs for dinner.

There were maybe three or four people in the dining room besides myself, each of us at a separate table. None of us moved to join the others. No one wanted to pretend the scene was anything but sad. Although I knew he was gone, I found myself looking for Mr. Roth. I remembered his gift beneath my bed upstairs. The scotch would have to age a bit longer. Until my kidneys were running properly, I wasn't about to put any alcohol into my system. Sam was nowhere to be found. That was fine. I didn't want to evade any more of his questions.

I found 29 Short Mountain Road where Molly had said it would be: distressingly close to the grounds of the old Fir Grove and Anton Harder's band of angry misfits. The appearance of the old bungalow colony hadn't been much changed by its new proprietors. It looked about like every other bungalow colony I'd ever seen. There were fifteen or twenty small cabins in a semicircle around two larger buildings shaped like old Indian longhouses. There was nothing sinister or cultish about the place, not a vat of Kool-Aid or a machine gun to be seen. The worst I could say about it was that it was rather dark. But for a few bulbs outside one of the longhouses, there wasn't a light to be seen anywhere. I parked my car next to the four or five others in the communal lot. I checked my watch: six-fifty-seven. Tick, tick, tick . . .

Since there were no signs or arrows pointing the way, I followed the light. I let myself into the longhouse. The innards were rustic as all hell. There were hand-hewed beams and log walls, a stone fireplace — a crackling fire burning in its maw — and an icy-cold flagstone floor. It was fairly dark inside: the faux gas-lamp fixtures held low-wattage bulbs. Three rows of folding chairs, seven chairs to a row, were laid out facing the fireplace. A rostrum built of tree limbs and twigs stood between the seating and the fireplace. Six people, four men and two women, turned to face me as the door creaked shut at my back.

There were other people in the room, though their presence was purposefully less obvious. In the shadows of each corner stood one of the Yellow Stars, all of them dressed in thrift-shop clothes with the now familiar yellow star sewn onto their left breasts. Three were men of different ages, and one was a woman about my age. Suddenly it dawned on me that my experience of the Holocaust was black and white, that it was odorless, without taste, that my experience was dry like the pages of an old history book. Yes, I knew many survivors, but I knew them only as my friends' parents or, like Mr. Roth, as old men. At that moment it occurred to me I did not know them, not really, not at all.

The Holocaust, it struck me, was as real as the moment I was living in. There was no soundtrack, no velvety-voiced narrator to rationalize the insanity in a neat sixty-minute segment. The real Holocaust was in color. It smelled of gas and burning flesh and hair. Actual people died. Those lifeless skeletons stacked like bait fish had once been human beings with dreams and feelings and destinies. They would no longer be pieces of film for me, forgettable or dismissable, like a boring movie. I was very angry and very weak. My head and heart were both leaden and light. I dragged myself to a seat in the third row.

A dim spotlight shone on the rostrum, and a man dressed not unlike the other Yellow Stars stepped behind the podium. Backlit by the dancing flames of the fireplace, his face was difficult to focus on. Yet he made eye contact with each of us in the small audience. His eyes were a burning deep blue that seemed to look through mine into the mass of conflict raging in my heart and head.

"My name is Judas, Judas Wannsee. You do not know me, but I know you, all about you, every one of you. We, the people who met you on the street, those standing in the corners, the others and myself, have no name. People call us the Yellow Stars for obvious reasons, but we are nothing but Jews. This is not a cult. We don't want your money. We don't ask for loyalty. We don't even want your respect. All of us here come and go as we please. We exist for you, and if you decide to follow our teachings, you will be here for the others who find their way to us. You cannot save a people all at once. You must save them one at a time. We will talk of this later.

"First, let us begin with humor. Appropriate, don't you think, given our locale? There is an elderly Jewish man, frustrated by what he's had to endure in his life. He looks to the skies, throws up his hands, and says: 'Dear God, the next time You're searching for a chosen people, do me a favor. Choose somebody else.' "

The seven of us in the folding chairs seemed finally to exhale and laugh, looking at one another for the first time. Judas Wannsee paused, letting us enjoy the moment of release. As he did, he smiled. It was a strange smile — superior and sad all at once.

"Yes," he continued. "That man was exactly right, wasn't he? Who needs the burden, the baggage we all carry just for being born Jews? God, wouldn't the world have been an easier place to live in if every time there was an oil shortage we wouldn't have to deal with those witty bumper stickers that say 'Burn Jews Not Oil'? Can you imagine the relief of reading a newspaper or watching television without praying that the murderer or thief or assassin wasn't a Jew? Okay, if the victim is a Jew, we can live with that. But God forbid the perpetrator of a crime is a Jew. We are all tarred by his crime. Wouldn't it once be a joy to un-self-consciously wear a cross around your neck? Wouldn't it be wonderful to not have to worry about how others might react to a star or a *chai?* Sometimes, admit it, you think you'd almost float if you were relieved of the burden of your Jewishness. So — wasn't that old man exactly right?

"No! No! No!" Wannsee pounded his fist on the rostrum so fiercely I thought the twigs and branches might snap. "He was exactly wrong. You can never escape your fate, and the romance of the myth that you can is why you are sitting here this evening. It is the reason even if you are not yet fully aware of it. You have been tormented all your lives, mostly tormented by yourselves, by the dream of escape. But I am here to tell you that this torment can end, that it will end, and that you are not and have never been truly responsible for it."

Another spotlight came up. This one shone on an American flag hung on the wall over Judas Wannsee's left shoulder.

"There are a thousand things, a million things I love about this country. I fought for that flag in the rice paddies of Vietnam. I would do it again tomorrow. The Constitution, the Bill of Rights are both brilliant documents, maybe the most brilliant documents of their kind that will ever be produced. Yet they are not perfect. They promise what they cannot deliver. But for us, for Jews, there is one aspect of the Bill of Rights which has been our undoing.

"Yes, we are guaranteed freedom of religion, the right to practice our rites and rituals unfettered by the state. But this has been disastrous for us, for we have been misled into believing we can both assimilate and be true to our Jewishness. This is a straw man, a falsehood, a myth that has done more damage to our collective consciousness than the Holocaust or the Spanish Inquisition. Assimilation is more effective than any gas chamber, more deadly than a cloud of Zyklon B. If the Nazis had used their heads instead of their hatred, they would have shipped our families to America. Assimilation, in the end, is the Final Solution.

"Assimilation will be the death of our souls. That's why you're here, because for all of your lives you've had to struggle with a haunting self-hatred. And what is the root of this struggle, of this impulse to hide what you are, to run away from what you are, to reject what you are? Assimilation. Or, more accurately, it is the myth of assimilation that has tormented you so much it has driven you into our womb.

"No, you say." He pointed directly at me.

"You reject my words as demagoguery. They are not, and in your heart, though you are fighting now to reject it, you know it's true. Go, move to Alabama. Will you feel free, protected to practice your faith? Or will you look over your shoulder and dread the time your neighbor asks what church you attend? Admit this to yourselves even if you can't admit it to me. Now, I harbor no hatred for Christians or Southerners. I had basic training in the South and served proudly with Christian men from North and South Carolina, Georgia, Alabama, and Mississippi. Sure, I took teasing. Certainly I was the target of some deplorable hate-mongering, but I never took it personally.

"What I could never get over, however, was my jealousy of those men. They lived their lives proudly as Christians, never hiding or running or assimilating. Their un-self-consciousness haunted me. You've felt the same thing, haven't you? *Haven't you?*"

We, all seven, shook our heads yes.

"The Hasidim embarrass you, don't they? You wish they would dress like the rest of us. Well, like you, at least. They're too visible for your taste, aren't they? They give us a bad name. They make us all targets. I know. I know. Sometimes, when they're walking down a crowded street, you want to run up to the Christians and swear that we're not all like them. They're fools. They're fanatics. They're not like us. If I am wrong, if you've never had these thoughts or feelings, please take this opportunity to leave." He paused for the longest thirty seconds I think I ever experienced. No one left.

"Feeling as I did, as you do, I gave great thought to how to deal with the torment of my self-hatred.

"First, I came to the realization that the torment, embarrassment, and shame I often felt were largely not of my own doing. Though generally I espouse a philosophy which would have people take full responsibility for their feelings, I would make this one exception. Furthermore, I beg you to make this one exception. It's not your fault. It simply isn't. It's a product of the impossible expectations laid out before you. Relieving myself of the guilt and responsibility was the easy part.

"The more difficult part of the equation was to work out a way for me to become un-self-conscious of my Jewish soul. How could I become like the Christians I was so jealous of? How could I free myself? Then it dawned on me to stop and pay attention to what was going on around me. I studied the civil-rights movement and the evolution of the Black Pride movement. It dawned on me that black people have a huge advantage over us. They can't hide the way we can. They cannot pretend to be what they are not. Every mirror is a reminder to them of what they are. It is a blessing to them. So I needed a way to be Jewish in the way that a black man or woman is black.

"You have seen our people dressed as if they just walked out of the Warsaw Ghetto. Do you know that some of us have even tattooed numbers on our forearms? Some, not all. It is a personal choice. But this is not dress-up. It is our way of being conspicuously Jewish. Dressing as the ultimate victims of hatred serves a dual purpose. While on the one hand it proclaims our Jewishness to the world, it allows us to work through our own petty self-hatred. And make no mistake about it, if you take our way, there is no compromise. You will wear the yellow star on your clothing for the world to see. It is not for everyone. Many people leave us. Some don't. Those who don't can be set free. Don't you want finally to be free?

"To paraphrase the late John F. Kennedy, we choose to do this thing not because it is easy, but precisely because it is hard. In conclusion, I want to set you straight on some issues. We are not concerned with your religiousness. It is almost beside the point. We are not the Hasidim. We are not here to be rabbis or parents. We are driven by a very reductionist view. If there is another Holocaust, would they burn you? Did you know that at the beginning of World War II many assimilated Jews served in every branch of the German armed forces? These were men and women who had a Jewish relative, people who never considered themselves Jewish. Yet, by the end of the war, many, if not most, were quite dead. They were victims of their own sleeping Jewishness. So, if you've married out of the faith, neither you nor your spouse will be protected, nor will your children. There is no immunity from your own essence. You are either a Jew or not. You are either a proud Jew or a tormented Jew. When you decide these questions, we will be waiting here for you. Thank you. Good night."

The spotlights, all the lights, went off. When they came back up, only the seven of us in the audience were still in the longhouse. Judas and his apostles were gone. No one spoke. What was there to say, really? Much of what the man had said rang true

— not the stuff about assimilation, but the stuff about self-consciousness was exactly right. For me, anyway. I could not speak for anyone else. Eventually, the six others drifted slowly out. I stayed behind, because, in the end, I was here about Arthur Rosen, not to be saved.

I figured if I sat around long enough I'd get somebody's attention. Strangely, I felt I was being watched. I think I'd felt that way all throughout Judas Wannsee's lecture. My mother used to say it was the eyes of God. She would point at the ceiling: "You can feel His eyes on you sometimes. He sees what you are doing and hears the things you say." When I asked why I couldn't feel His eyes on me all the time, my mom would say God was too busy to waste His time on such a good boy like me. She was such a charmer.

Unless God was using closed-circuit TV cameras these days, it wasn't He who was watching. I found two surveillance cameras: one mounted in the corner to the right of the fireplace, one above the front door. I waited a few more minutes before flashing my badge at the camera above the door. Miraculously, the man who had met me outside the abandoned synagogue in town came through the door within several seconds.

"How may we help you, Officer?"

I produced two pictures of Arthur Rosen. One was a mug shot, the other an autopsy photo. "I need to speak to Mr. Wannsee."

"I'm afraid that won't be —"

"It's all right, Jeffrey," announced Wannsee's voice over a loudspeaker. "Show the officer to my bungalow."

Without hesitation, Jeffrey showed me the way. We walked to a bungalow hidden behind the two longhouses. It was about double the size of the other bungalows but in no better repair. My guide held the door open and did not follow me in. Wannsee sat behind a spare metal desk. On the desk were a microphone, a telephone, and several small TV monitors.

"Please, have a seat," he said, gesturing to a plain wooden chair facing the desk.

Wannsee was a handsome man in his late forties. He had a strong jaw, a full head of silver hair, and a smile like Burt Lancaster. He had the whiff of cheap charisma, the kind successful used-car salesmen possess.

I sat. Explained who I was, sort of. I guess I neglected to mention I no longer had any official standing. Even if I had, I was way out of my jurisdiction. Wannsee must have known that, but seemed disinclined to discuss it. Unfortunately, he seemed disinclined to discuss many things, one of them being Arthur's stint as a Yellow Star.

"I have a reliable source who will testify that Arthur Rosen, the man pictured here," I lied, pointing to the photos on his desk, "was a member of your group within the last several years."

"First, Officer Prager, why should anyone be testifying about anything? What crime was committed, and by whom? We have no interest or responsibility in any of this. Second, as I stated previously, we are not a group, per se. The only group we recognize belonging to is the same group, presumably, you belong to. We are all Jews. Some of us are proud of that fact. Some, like yourself, are tormented."

We went round and round like that for a few minutes. It seemed to me Wannsee was being intentionally confrontational. I just wasn't sure why. If he had simply let me ask my questions about Arthur, I would have been out of there in five minutes. No, apparently he wanted to do some probing of his own, but didn't want me to notice. He probably thought he was a real pro at it. Sometime I'd have to introduce him to my father-in-law. I decided to take the offensive.

"You chose your stage name quite carefully to elicit the maximum amount of

255

discomfort from your audience," I observed.

"Did I?"

"Judas, the Jew who betrayed Christ. Judas, the original scapegoat. Judas, who has served as the model for Jewish scapegoating throughout the centuries. I always thought it pretty interesting how the Romans escape culpability for the death of Christ, don't you? But it's the Wannsee I really admire," I complimented. "It was at the Wannsee Conference, outside Berlin, where the details of the Final Solution were arranged."

He stood and applauded. "Very, very good, Officer Prager. Bravo! You're a well-educated self-hater, the worst kind. All your life you thought that if you could understand why the Nazis hated us you'd understand your own hatred. I bet you are fluent in Nazi trivia and can sing 'Deutschland über Alles.' But this isn't a quiz show."

"Look," I said, "you want me outta here and I want to get outta here, so just give me some straight answers about Arthur Rosen and I'll be gone."

"Poor Arthur was with us a very short time a few years back," he relented. "We are the answer for some people, people like yourself, for instance. We were not, however, the answer for Arthur. He was so troubled by so many things, haunted by ghosts of his own making. We tried, but when he stopped taking his medication and became delusional, we were forced to ask him to leave."

"Delusional about what?"

"Oh, I don't know." Judas waved dismissively. "I think he was developing a Jesus complex."

He was almost too flippant about that. It was the first thing he'd said all night that rang like tin. His dismissive wave was also too Hollywood, a gesture not in his usual repertoire but one he'd aped from some B-movie actor. Class was out. He made excuses about being tired. I got the hint. When we shook hands goodbye, he stared into my eyes as he had earlier.

"I know your pain," he said. "When you're finished with whatever you're doing up here, please come back and see us. We can set you free."

"Sorry," I said, "I'm not in the market for a used car."

Outside now, I realized that last comment was too gratuitous and flippant by half. The truth was, he'd gotten to me, and there was no running away from it.

Back at the Swan Song, I noticed mine was now the only car in the guest parking lot.

Previously there had always been the same two or three other cars to keep mine company, but they were gone. I thought it very sad that I might be Sam's last guest. It would have been more appropriate if it had been someone like Mr. Roth, a man who had so enjoyed the Catskills over the decades.

Inside, Sam, standing a moot watch behind the front desk, was smoking one of his baseball-bat-sized cigars and enjoying cognac out of a crystal snifter. He had the newspaper, probably the *Tribune,* spread out on the counter. I watched from the doorway as he scanned the page. It was the only truly relaxed thing I'd ever seen Sam do. He was always "on" and always on the offensive, kibitzing, wisecracking, performing. He saw something in the paper he liked. He liked it a lot. A smile crossed his cigar-twisted lips, and he danced a little dance of celebration.

"Hey!" I shouted at him. "What, you just win the lottery or something?"

For just a brief second I thought I saw panic wash over his face, but when I looked more closely Sam had settled back into his world-weary comedian persona. He folded up the paper as if it were a linen napkin and unceremoniously dropped it into the wastepaper basket behind the desk.

"I bet a horse," he said. "Paid twelve to one. Maybe things are looking up."

"Watch out, Sam," I warned halfheartedly, "the ponies will get you in trouble."

"At my age, *boychik*, the only thing that'll get me in trouble is too much stool softener."

"Forget I brought it up."

"I already did."

Sam confirmed what I'd already guessed. I was, as fate would have it, his last guest. Unless some other detective or salesman showed up, I was it.

"I hope you like takeout," Sam said. "Because, other than breakfast, that's what we're eating for the next few days. I had to let the staff go."

"I'm a Jew from Brooklyn, Sam. Takeout is my middle name. Bacon and eggs for breakfast?"

"*Oy,* such a demanding guest, but bacon and eggs it is. I'll ring you around eight."

"Eight it is," I agreed. "Listen, I'm gonna need an outside line in a few minutes, okay?"

The old comic threw up his hands in mock disgust: "More demands! Get upstairs before I throw you out."

I actually made *two* calls. The first was to 212 area-code information. The second was to Sunshine Manor, Arthur Rosen's last earthly residence.

"Sunshine Manor."

"Dr. Prince, please."

"Speaking."

I gave him the pro-forma you-may-not-remember-me opening. In return he gave me the of-course-I-remember-you-how-can-I-help response. That was easy enough for me to answer. Without going into too much detail, I recounted to Dr. Prince what Judas Wannsee had said about Arthur Rosen becoming delusional.

"How long ago was this?" he wanted to know.

"Two or three years ago."

Now we returned to the same dance with which we had started. He gave me the old doctor-patient privilege routine. And I gave him the old but-he's-dead reply. I begged. I lied, telling him I was about to solve the crime of the century. I kept at it until he just gave in.

"This is off the record, right?"

"Very far off the record," I reassured.

"Okay, Mr. Prager, I'll dig the files out and call you tomorrow morning, before I leave."

"That'll be great, Doc."

"Not unless you enjoy watching the sun-rise."

Chapter Twelve:
December 5th

There were no hints in the blackness outside my window that the sun would rise again. The phone, however, demanded that I rise. It was a disgustingly chipper Dr. Prince on the other end of the line. He had the files. After several minutes of admonitions, caveats, qualifications, and cautions, we got down to business, sort of.

"What is it you want to know, Mr. Prager?"

"I'm not sure."

"But —"

"Was Arthur Rosen delusional?"

It was a pretty straightforward question. The answer, however, was not. First, Dr. Prince felt compelled to explain the difference between hallucination, delusion, and flight of ideas, giving practical examples for each. He went on to explain how laymen often used these terms interchangeably when they were in fact three very distinct psychological phenomena. So, when some-one like Judas Wannsee, for example, called Arthur delusional, he might have been describing one, two, three, or none of these things. Hey, I had several hours to kill before breakfast, and Prince was pretty entertaining.

"But was Arthur Rosen delusional?" I repeated about fifteen minutes into the lecture.

"Now, you must realize Arthur was with us less than eighteen months and we do not have a full psychiatric history," he equivocated.

"Doc, don't make me beg. Was Arthur —"

"No, as far as I can tell from his treating psychiatrist's notes and history of medication, Arthur was not delusional, not for his last eighteen months. And there's nothing in the data we have about his previous treatment history to indicate that he ever exhibited patterns of delusional thought or behavior."

"You mentioned medication. What medication?"

"Lithium."

"If he stopped taking his lithium, could that elicit delusional —"

"Lithium is prescribed to treat a chemical imbalance that contributes to the vast mood swings exhibited by many patients with Arthur's diagnosis. Going off his lithium might certainly affect his moods, yes, but if he wasn't exhibiting delusional thought or behavior beforehand, I doubt it would cause an onset of new symptoms."

"Was he ever on anything else?" I asked. "Any, what are they called, psycho . . ."

"Psychotropic drugs, antipsychotics. No, just lithium, as far as I can tell. Now, I want to be perfectly clear about this, Mr. Prager, I cannot say that Arthur never self-medicated. If he did, it would be impossible for me to give definitive answers."

"Understood. Thanks, Doc, I appreciate the information."

"Did any of this help?"

"It's like your business, Doc, it's hard to be sure right away. I'll let you know."

Talk about your basic dead end. How appropriate, I thought, that this was all about the aftermath of a fire. The whole of it was now smoke, because the flames had burned themselves out sixteen years ago. It dawned on me that I hadn't found anything new because there was nothing new to find. That the only flames that had burned these many years burned in the hearts of the Hammerlings and the Rosens.

Denial, like gravity, is a great unseen

energy of the universe, but, unlike gravity, denial can be created and destroyed. I was about to prove it. The power of Arthur Rosen's denial hadn't died with him, but I think I was on the verge of putting it to rest. I had had enough. Enough of the infection of sadness, of Anton Harder and Judas Wannsee, of smoky bars and small-town New York. I had a wife who loved me, the most beautiful, smart, and adoring daughter ever born, and a business to run. I had had my fill. What was it that Freud said? "Sometimes a cigar is just a cigar." Well, sometimes an idiot smoking in bed is just an idiot smoking in bed. Wouldn't the Rosens and the Hammerlings have been better off if they could have seen there was tragedy enough in that?

Bang! There was furious, insistent pounding at my door. It had to be Sam.

"What's the matter, Sam?"

"Hurry, there's a fire. Come quick, *boychik*."

I threw on yesterday's clothes and flew downstairs. Sam was waiting at the base of the grand staircase.

"Come!"

I followed him out the front door, onto a carpet of fresh snow, around the side of the main house toward the area between the

265

utility sheds and the old pool. Sure enough, one of the old sheds was aflame, and if the wind shifted, the main house might be next. We grabbed some fire extinguishers from the kitchen and doused the flames. The fire had actually looked a lot worse than it was. Sam seemed understandably shaken. When I tried to comfort him, he said it wasn't the fire that upset him so.

"If it was only the fire, so what? So I would have gotten maybe the insurance better than the money from selling. You know what they say, six in one hand . . . It reminds me of the old joke about the town veterinarian who also does taxidermy. His motto is: Either way, you get your dog back. Well, *toteleh,* either way I'm getting the money."

"If it's not the fire, what is it?"

He beckoned me to follow him. The words **DIE JEWS** had been spray-painted on the walls of another shed. They were painted in a familiar shade of yellow. I'd seen its like only a week before. There was something that didn't fit, but, as with everything else in this case, I couldn't quite put my finger on it. Then, when Sam started raging, I lost focus.

"I'm gonna go kill that disrespectful little *pisher,*" Sam threatened, throwing his extinguisher canister against the shed wall in disgust. "That hateful little bastard."

"No, Sam. I think it's about time for Anton Harder and me to have a pow-wow of sorts. Let's go inside and have breakfast. We'll talk it over over eggs and bacon. Firefighting gives me quite an appetite."

Sam and I discussed calling in the local constabulary. We each had our separate reasons for not sprinting to dial 911. I told Sam about my bizarre run-in with Lieutenant Bailey, carefully omitting the details about the police file. Sam said the Old Rotterdam Police Department made the Keystone Kops seem like the FBI. He recited a litany of complaints about the local force that practically reached back to the nineteenth century.

"And corrupt!" he hissed, waving his hands. "No offense to your former employers, but these guys make the bagmen on the NYPD seem like amateurs. The local cops take more under-the-table money than a cheap whore. They bleed all the hotel owners dry up here. But soon all the blood's gonna run out."

Now that we had clearly established that the cops weren't to be involved — not yet, anyhow — I asked Sam to give me as many details about the old Fir Grove property as he could remember. He had a remarkable memory. I guess he had room in that brain of his for something other than dirty jokes and cynicism. He knew every foot of the place, ways to access the property that Anton Harder's people would probably never discover. He drew me a fairly detailed map, based, of course, on the old layout of the place. Combining his encyclopedic memory with the intelligence I'd gained on my recent visit to the shantytown that had once been the Fir Grove resort, Sam and I figured I had a good shot at finding the little Harder before he found me.

My kidneys were feeling much better, and the blood in my urine, if any remained, was undetectable to the human eye. So, as I relaxed in preparation for my evening's appointment, I decided it was time to sample that bottle Mr. Roth had left me. When I reached under the bed, I grabbed nothing but air. The gift was gone. I thought about calling down to Sam, but realized one of his angry ex-employees had probably taken it. Revenge comes in many different forms, some of them quite silly and pointless. I needed my wits about me anyway, and as long as I still had Mr. Roth's address and phone number, I was fine. The bottle itself was unimportant. I owned a wine shop, for Christ's sakes.

For dinner, Sam and I ordered in a pizza from town. If you liked cardboard with red dye and flavorless cheese, Old Rotterdam was your kind of pizza town. Even eating the pepperoni, one had the sense it had been produced not at a Hormel processing plant but by Dow Chemical. We finished every last crumb, in spite of our better judgment. And, speaking of better judgment, Sam began voicing some doubts about our plan for the evening.

"You sure you wanna go through with this? I mean no offense, but you were a city cop, not a Green Beret. The woods at night can be pitch-black and dangerous."

"I owe that little prick. We owe him." I was rather too gung-ho. "Besides, they know I'm a cop. They wouldn't be stupid enough to kill me."

Sam shook his head. "I wouldn't be so sure. What you think their collective IQ is over there? You think Einstein winters with them? Besides, just to point out a minor detail or two, not so you should get upset with me, but you're not really a cop anymore, and you'll be trespassing. They could always claim they thought you were a raccoon or something. Hunting is a big thing up here. They'd probably get off."

"Sam, do me a favor. When you sell the

hotel, don't go into motivational speaking as a career. You've got no future in it."

"It's not *my* future I'm worried about."

I left it at that. He was correct, of course. What seemed like such a good idea this morning was no longer looking so wonderful. Our plan was full of holes. Sam hadn't been on the Fir Grove grounds for years, and I'd spent less than a half-hour there. I'd seen several hungry dogs who would have found an intruder more than a tasty treat. I knew they had at least one shotgun on the premises, and I was willing to bet the ranch it had a lot of company on the gun rack. Whether someone was willing actually to shoot me instead of just aim at me was a separate issue. Pulling a trigger is easy. Killing someone, even someone you don't especially care for, isn't. I'd just have to keep telling myself that, because, true or not, I was going.

Upstairs, I picked up the phone to call Katy, but put it down almost immediately. I didn't think I had it in me to lie to her tonight. Even if I'd been able to say the words, as accomplished a liar as I'd learned to be, I didn't think I could summon up the voice. She would have heard it, sensed it, and called me on it. Once that happened, I wouldn't be able to go through with it.

There was a good reason they always drafted eighteen-year-olds. No wives. No kids. No lies.

Sam picked the spot for my way onto the old Fir Grove grounds. It was right off the road, through some woods. He assured me there'd be no fencing to cut through or walls, just some tall, tangled hedges. Gee, what a surprise. Tangled hedges seemed to be a cash crop at the old Fir Grove. Once I was on the grounds, it would be only a short walk to the trailers through the shrine and cesspits.

The plan was simple. Sam was going to drop me off by the woods. Ten minutes later, after having given me enough time to get onto the Fir Grove grounds, he'd go down the road to a pay phone and make an anonymous call to the cops. He'd claim there were shots fired, or a fire, or something like that. When I heard the sirens, I'd start working my way up to the trailers. When the sirens were really loud, they would draw everyone's attention, dogs included. If Harder came out, I'd get into his trailer and wait for his return. If he didn't come out when the others did, that was okay, too. I knew which double-wide was his. When it was established that the call was a false alarm and everyone settled back down, I'd have already worked my way to Harder's cabin.

Besides the small .22 automatic and ankle holster I had purchased in an adjoining town that afternoon and my .38, Sam and I had taken a few other precautions. I carried a bag of ground black pepper and paprika to throw the dogs off my scent if necessary. Hey, it always worked in the movies. I also had a plastic bag full of Sam's private bacon stock in case I had to distract the dogs or buy a few seconds. I carried Sam's binoculars, a flashlight, and a road flare for signaling purposes. I think I was more prepared for a barbecue than for what I was about to do.

We didn't talk in the car until we reached the drop-off point.

"For any reason, you don't like how things are going, *boychik,* you turn your *tuches* right around. This isn't worth getting yourself . . ." Sam didn't finish his sentence.

I shook my friend's hand. "Don't worry about me, Sam. I'll be fine."

"Who you tryin' to convince?"

"Whoever it is, I'm not doing a real good job of it. Check your watch."

Sam patted the back of my neck. "Okay, you take care, you haven't paid your bill yet."

"Thanks for the sentiment."

I stepped out of his old Caddy and walked into the woods without looking back. Though the sky was clear, only a silver sickle of the moon lit the night. Fifty yards into the pines, that light was pretty much lost to me. Flashlight in one hand, .38 in the other, I slogged through the snow for about three minutes. Twenty or thirty yards ahead of me, I could just make out where the woods came to an end. There was a narrow clearing, and beyond it a tangle of overgrown hedges. Sam knew his shit. Then things started to go wrong.

Behind me in the distance, I thought I heard Sam's car pull away. I fumbled to check my watch, dropping the flashlight in the process. That was stupid of me. I didn't really need to check my watch. I was good with time. Sam had left a good four or five minutes early. He was supposed to give me ten minutes before going to call the cops. Maybe he had been spotted and was drawing attention away from me. Maybe it was simply a passing car which I'd mistaken for Sam's. It didn't matter now. Finding the flashlight mattered.

I must have been a sight there on my hands and knees, groping around in the blackness and snow. When my fingers wrapped around the barrel of the flashlight, how I looked was beside the point. I flicked the switch a few times, and its beam popped back on. I calmed myself, brushed the snow off my pants, and continued ahead. The clearing was just another few yards away.

Out of the corner of my eye, I saw the downward arc of the baseball bat. My hands went numb. Time stopped flowing smoothly. My eyes caught glimpses of things between seconds of nothingness. I could see the flashlight in the snow, its beam shining on the feet of my attackers. I saw one of those feet sweep my .38 back into the pines. Fists came at me, legs. I was deaf with panic, though a word would filter in between the kicks and punches. "Jew . . . blood . . . skull . . ." I was being dragged now. Then things got very still. I could hear again, but there was nothing to hear. Then there was nothing at all.

And in that split second before nothingness consumed me, I had a revelation. No, I didn't see God or a womb of light. I did not see Christ smiling down at me. I saw the boots of my attackers in my mind's eye. I never thought I had an eye for footwear, but apparently I was wrong. I actually thought I recognized one of my attackers' boots. Layered atop that flash, I had another vision: the burning shed at the Swan Song. I thought of the footprints in the snow, how they all ran between the hotel and the shed. There had been no tracks leading away from the grounds. And in that one lucid moment between clicks of the second hand, all the bothersome loose ends knitted themselves neatly together.

Suddenly I knew who had gone to so much trouble to try and hang the Fir Grove fire on Anton Harder. I still didn't know why. If I lived through the night, I'd worry about that. I was getting sleepy, the cold covering me like a shroud. I thought of Katy and Sarah, but I found I was worried more about Aaron. I didn't think he'd ever forgive me for missing my Christmas-New Year's shifts. It's crazy what you think about sometimes.

CHAPTER THIRTEEN:
DECEMBER ?

I woke up. That was something, at least.

I felt like a ripe floater that had been fished out of the East River by Harbor Patrol: swollen, stiff, broken. Even my hair was bruised. My left wrist was particularly stiff and painful. I raised my left arm to have a peek. It was in a neat white splint that ran from just below my elbow to my fingertips. I remembered the arc of the baseball bat and winced. Except for the wrist, I guess I was mostly just bruised. Well, my head did have someone in there trying to pound his way out with a dull hammer. When I rolled to one side, I became aware of the pulpy lump behind my right ear. I didn't think I'd lost consciousness for convenience's sake.

I was in a bed, but it was no hospital bed. The sheetless mattress was thin and soft as a Ritz cracker and smelled of last week's beer sweat. I'm not complaining, mind you. The pillows were fluffy, the quilt was warm, and, on the whole, it was better than being left to die in the dark and in the snow. The walls were covered in cheap wooden paneling, and the floors in worn-out blue carpeting. Grayish light shone through the Windex-starved glass over the bed. The flickering overhead light was a bare fluorescent tube.

Propping myself up on my right elbow, I took a better look around. From all appearances, I was alone. Beyond the end of the bed was a little den area, and beyond that was a tiny kitchen, tiny even by New York City apartment standards. You couldn't fit two cooks in there with a tub of Crisco and a shoehorn. I was in a camper or trailer of some sort. Who it belonged to was a mystery.

That little guy with the dull hammer told me to get off my elbow and lie back down. I paid careful attention to his instructions, but not quickly enough. The camper was spinning. Shutting my eyes helped a little to slow it down, but I just knew that when the spinning stopped I wouldn't be in Kansas anymore. Waves of nausea rolled over me. Eventually, the waves calmed and the spinning stopped. I think they did. They must have, because I fell hopelessly asleep.

When I reopened my eyes, there was no

appreciable light coming through the glass of the aluminum slider over the bed. It was nighttime wherever outside of Kansas the camper had come to rest. The fluorescent tube above my head still had its tic, the bed still reeked, the mattress was no more comfortable, I still felt like I'd been dropped out of a B-52 without a parachute, but something had changed. I was no longer alone. I heard a racket coming from the little kitchen. Maybe a fat chef had gotten himself wedged in between the sink and stove. Remembering the last time I elevated my head, I thought twice about trying to peer into the galley. My host saved me the trouble.

"You're up." It was Anton Harder.

"This is pretty ironic," I said, not realizing how sore my jaw was until I used it. "I was on my way to see you last night. Was it last night? What day is it?"

"It's today," he answered blankly. "If you're asking when we found your trespassing carcass bleeding on the property, then, yes, that was last night."

I repeated: "I was coming to have a little talk with you."

"Your soup's almost ready." He ignored me. "Your wrist is broken, but we have a former army medic here. He says it should be fine until you get to a hospital and have it set properly."

I raised my broken wrist. "You didn't do this to me?"

"To what end?" he wondered. "You think we would have kicked your stupid ass and then fixed you up because we felt guilty about it? We don't want the cops around here. Somebody might have shot you by accident. You would have deserved it, too, but no one from around here did this to you."

"Where did you find me?"

"By my mother's — By the grave," he mumbled.

"I know your mom was Missy Higgins. Sam Gutterman told me about her. She died in the fire."

"Yes, over there." He wasn't interested in talking about his mom.

"I was attacked on the other side of the hedges by two or three men," I explained. "They purposely dumped me over on — over there."

He was curious. "What for?"

"I think they thought if they were really lucky you'd finish the job for them and kill me. But mostly I think they wanted me to believe you did this to me. This way, when the cops showed up, I'd point the finger at you. Somebody's trying very hard to have me think the worst of you."

"Cops! How did you know about the cops if you were unconscious?" he demanded.

"The cops were part of the plan. They were supposed to be a diversion. When they showed up, I figured they would draw everyone's attention away from the rear of the property. I guess that part of the plan worked pretty well. Unfortunately, there were parts of the plan nobody bothered sharing with me."

He gave me a big bowl of canned soup. As I ate I studied my reluctant rescuer. Though he was a man by all measures, he seemed like such a boy. Maybe it was his diminutive stature. I think maybe it had more to do with the humanizing effect of Molly Treat's stories. He was cute once, she said. They'd kissed. And, having read his psych evaluation, I had trouble seeing him as anything but a wounded little boy. Wishing to be a monster doesn't make it so. Wishing never does.

"So," he asked when he thought I'd gotten enough soup down, "why did you want to talk to me?"

I told him about the other incidents. He did not shy away from taking responsibility for my car being vandalized at the Fir Grove. In fact, he seemed disturbingly pleased with himself. However, he vehemently denied having anything to do with the fires at the Swan Song. I told him that I already knew as much, but that someone was deeply invested in trying to pin the Fir Grove fire on him. Though Harder was curious, I played dumb about who that someone was. Until I knew the whys of what was going on, I was going to keep my own counsel.

"The cops thought you did it, you know?" I said just to see his reaction.

"Fuck what the cops thought. That was my mother who died out there in that fire. My mother." His thin chest heaved. "How could they think I would kill my own mother?" he whispered haltingly, choking back tears.

"Cops think stupid things sometimes. It's their job."

Hearing the sympathy in my voice made him furious. "Tomorrow morning I'll have someone drive you to the hospital." Harder sneered. "Then, if you should do me a favor and drop dead, it won't be my headache."

"Thank you."

"Don't ever come back here!" He slammed the trailer door behind him.

In spite of everything he represented, I could do nothing but feel terribly sorry for the pieces of Robby Higgins that lived inside the pint-sized man. He couldn't possibly loathe me as much as he loathed himself. That was very sad, very sad indeed.

I shut my eyes for a while, trying to fall back asleep. It didn't work. I was sore as hell, not tired. My eyelids were beginning to twitch synchronously with the fluorescent fixture. I leaned over the edge of the bed to see if I could find something to read. I hadn't perused *Mein Kampf* since college. Alas, the only things to read besides the soup can on the kitchen counter were two copies of old reliable, the *Catskill Tribune*. Unfortunately, both were days old.

I buzzed through the December 4 edition without getting the slightest bit drowsy; not that reading the Tribune was remotely like wading through the Sunday *New York Times.* It was more like reading your high-school newspaper, only with more advertisements for foundation garments. In desperation, I reread the December 3 edition, the one with the green-bean-salad recipes. It had put me to sleep once before. Maybe it would do the trick again. Sure enough, as I read down that same page my eyelids began to shut. But as I drifted into the world that existed between waking and unconsciousness, I heard an unsettling voice. I had heard it before, urging me to pay more attention.

This time I did.

I surrendered my hard-fought battle for sleep, forcing my eyes open. I reread the green-bean-salad recipes for the third time. I hated green beans in any form, but especially in a casserole with a can of condensed cream-of-broccoli soup, peanuts, and fried onion sticks. The key to my universe was not to be found in that recipe, so I scanned farther down the page. Mary Obenessor, eighty-one, of Old Rotterdam was dead of pancreatic cancer. Jim Moody and Eileen Barker were pleased to announce their engagement. There was going to be a Christmas festival at Town Hall on the 18th, and the Candle Commune on Beacon Road was having a charity sale.

At the bottom of the page, in the last column to the right, was a section called "Poetry from the Soul." I was getting nauseous again. There's nothing like bad poetry. Poetry, everyone thinks they can write it, and it's perhaps the hardest thing to write well. I considered rereading the green-bean-casserole recipes yet again. It was an impossibility to hate green beans as much as I hated haiku. The voice didn't let me go back. The first poem was a little ditty by that bard of the Catskills, Edith Cohen, called "I Love the Sunshine."

I Love the Sunshine

I love the sunshine in the air of blue.
I love the green grass and its mossy dew.
I love the truth because it is so true.
And I love my love because it is for you.
I love the sunshine.

The next poem had the catchy title "A Capella 132" and it was penned by anonymous. But it wasn't anonymous at all. I'd read poems just like it before, poems entitled "A Capella 77" and "A Capella 24". The same poet had written "Trio for Two and One" and "Coney Island Wheels." It had been a long long time ago, in high school, that I'd read them. I'd even heard "Coney Island Wheels" read aloud in our school auditorium.

My heart was beating so incredibly fast that I actually clutched my chest. Sweat gushed out of every piece of me with a pore. I stood for the first time, and in spite of the racking pain, I ran around the trailer in a panic. I didn't know what to do. I wanted to scream, but I had no words to give, no shape for my mouth. What could I do? What do you say when you read a poem written by a girl who's been dead for sixteen years? Arthur Rosen was right: one of the dead girls wasn't. And I knew exactly what to do. I fell down on my knees and cried like a fool. Suddenly things fit, the loose ends were knitting themselves more tightly by the moment. That voice inside my head fell finally silent.

I had to get out of there now. I couldn't wait for tomorrow. I couldn't wait five minutes. I fumbled to get my still-damp clothes on. Dressing is less complicated when you've got two good hands, but I managed nonetheless. I ran out the door of the trailer, forgetting I wasn't exactly a popular figure in these parts. None of that mattered. I just stood out in the snow screaming for Harder.

He didn't appreciate being summoned by the trespassing cop. Too fucking bad, I thought.

"Tomorrow," he repeated, trying to push me back into the trailer.

"Now!" I demanded in a whisper. "Right fucking now."

"Why?" he whispered so that the gathering crowd could not hear.

"Because I'm on the verge of answering a question that's plagued you for sixteen years. If you get me to a hospital or Doc Pepper's tonight, I'll be able to find out what really happened at the Fir Grove."

"Why should I trust you?"

I didn't like the crowd. I didn't think they'd do me any harm, but Harder was unlikely to allow himself to appear even remotely weak in front of his friends.

"Slap me in the face," I whispered, "and push me up the stairs into the trailer."

He didn't ask why. For a twig of a man he hit pretty good.

"You've got my attention," he said, slamming the door purposefully hard behind him. "Why should I trust you?"

"Because you've got nothing to lose. Just get me outta here so I can do my job. People besides yourself have been suffering for a long time, too. And whether you hate them or not, you know how they feel."

"When you find out, no matter what it is, I want to know."

I put my good hand out. He took it. "For what it's worth, you have my word."

When he let go of my hand, I gestured for him to start screaming at me. Again, he didn't need more prompting. He went into an invective-laced tirade, calling me things I'd never even heard of. During his performance I grabbed the fluorescent tube that had haunted me throughout the day and smashed it against the door. He liked that, but not nearly as much as I did. I hated that damn bulb. He opened the door and pushed me down the front stairs.

"Peter!" Harder screamed to the man who days earlier had held the shotgun on me. "Do me a favor and get this asshole out of here. Take him into town. Take him wherever he wants to go, but get him out of here."

"But —" Peter started to object.

"Now!"

"The wrist's not broken," Pepper explained, holding the X ray up to the light. "But you won't be swinging a golf club for a few weeks. That was a professionally done splint you had on there."

"Retired army medic."

The old doctor shook his head proudly. "Thought so. The rest of you is just banged up, and there's some blood in your urine. I think we can rule out bladder cancer. Somebody gave you a pretty good licking."

"Pretty good, yeah."

"Nothing a few days of bed rest and a bottle of aspirin won't cure. Here." He handed me some drug samples. "That's in case the pain gets bad. They'll either knock you out or make you forget about the pain."

I thanked him, asked him to bill me at my home address, and requested the use of his phone.

"Use the phone at my wife's desk."

Katy was frantic. Why hadn't I called? What was wrong? Was I okay? How could I do this to her? If someone hadn't killed me already, she was prepared to do it herself. I told her she had every right to be mad. When I told her where I was calling from and why, she really went nuts. I let her get it out of her system before I dropped the bomb.

"I think Andrea Cotter's still alive."

There was silence on the other end of the line. She didn't try arguing me out of it. Katy knew I would never say something like that for effect.

"Do you know where she is?"

"Not exactly," I said. "Somewhere up here, I think. I'm pretty sure I know someone who knows. But I've got to be careful about that."

"Who is —"

"I can't talk about it. I've got to go soon."

"I'm coming up there." Katy was adamant.

"No you're not. If things go the way I think they will, I'll be down in the city tomorrow. Can your mom spare you for a day? I'd like to sleep in my own bed for a night, if that's okay with you."

"My dad came home from the hospital

yesterday. I'll be back in Brooklyn whether they can spare me or not."

"Bring Sarah with you."

"I love you, Moses. Take care of yourself."

"I love you, too, kiddo. And tomorrow I'll let you take care of me."

The next call was the more difficult of the two to make.

"Is that you, *toteleh?*" Sam, the consummate performer, spoke before I could get two words out. "I was panicked already. Where are you?"

"The doctor's office in town. Can you come get me?"

"I'm on my way."

Fifteen minutes later, Sam pulled his Caddy up in front of Pepper's office. I'd spent the time rehearsing what to say. I had a pretty good idea of the sorts of questions Sam would ask. The problem would be to strike a believable balance between ignorance, suspicion, and knowledge. Playing dumb and playing dumb well are two very different things. If I didn't act somewhat wary of Sam, he wouldn't buy the act. On the other hand, if I let too much slip, he'd clam up and cover his tracks.

Doc Pepper locked the door behind me. Sam was out of the car, helping me into the front seat. I was careful not to thank him, not to get emotional one way or the other. I would wait him out, just like Katy and her dad did to me. A clever man like Sam would expect as much.

"Is it bad?" he asked as we neared the road out of town.

"The wrist? It's not broken, but it's not great. I just have to keep it wrapped and keep ice on it."

"And the rest of you?"

"I'm still breathing."

That was the extent of our conversation until we got back to the Swan Song. Then it was my turn to take the offensive. He was waiting for it. After pulling up to the old hotel, Sam made a show of trying to help me in, and I let him. He took his coat off and poured us some cognac.

"Some plan we had, me and you, huh? A broken-down cop and dirty-mouthed comic, what were we thinkin'?" I winced from laughing. "I just made it to the hedges and three guys jumped me. You know, Sam, I couldn't help noticing your car pulling away a little earlier than scheduled."

"I saw a state trooper coming my way. I didn't want him to pull over, so I moved up the road a little. I'm sorry, *boychik*. So," he puzzled, "what happened to you after you got whacked around? It's almost twenty-four hours already since I dropped you off."

If I blew this answer, the game was over. I was being tested.

"I woke up in this little cemetery they got in back of where the Fir Grove used to stand. I think it was when the cops showed up at the front gate — the commotion must've brought me around. I was hurtin' pretty bad. Between the knock on my noggin and my wrist, my balance wasn't great, and I was kinda disoriented. I wandered into some woods, but not the woods I'd come through. I found some old discarded shit like garbage bags and a ripped-up boat tarp. I used some sticks and pitched a little tent for myself, covering it with snow for insulation. Fucking thing collapsed on me. My part of Brooklyn doesn't produce too many Eagle Scouts, you know what I'm saying?"

His laugh came easily, and the upturn of his mouth was matched by the corners of his eyes. He was buying it — maybe not lock, stock, and barrel, but enough.

"At least the snow did my wrist some good. Around dawn I began trying to work my way through the woods. I had less luck with that than with the fucking tent. It took me hours, and a few times I wound up back near where I started. A few hours after noon, I found my way onto a road. By nightfall, I hitched my way into town, and I've been at Doc Pepper's ever since."

He didn't like that quite so well. It was too neat. I had the timing down too pat, like I'd sat at a desk with a calculator and worked backward.

"It took so long to hitchhike into town? Why didn't you get to a phone and call me?"

Good question.

"I wasn't thinking clearly, Sam." I sounded almost apologetic. "You're right. I shoulda called."

"Don't worry about it. You're mostly okay. That's what's important. To your health!"

We clinked glasses and took our cognacs in one swallow. I excused myself, saying I needed to get some sleep. He was back to believing me, I think, and asked if I needed help upstairs. I told him to take an anatomy class, that I didn't walk on my hands.

"Gay cockum af in yom," he yelled to me.

"You go shit in the ocean, old man," I shouted back.

"Good," he said, "at least your hearing works fine."

Upstairs, I didn't waste a second before retrieving the copies of the *Catskill Tribune* I'd taken from Arthur Rosen's room the night of his death. As I suspected, one of

Andrea's poems appeared in each edition. I wasn't the only one who'd noticed. When I checked the dates, they confirmed something else: the earliest of these papers dated back nearly three years. Now the time frame made sense.

I could only imagine how Arthur had stumbled onto the poems. He must have been up here on one of his little crusades to get the investigation reopened. Maybe he was sitting in the anteroom of Hammerling's office, or out in the hallway across from Molly's desk. Arthur, bored and frustrated, picks up the *Tribune* like he's done on many of his other visits to Old Rotterdam. Usually, he doesn't get through the whole paper. The stories are silly. Who really cares about the biggest pumpkin in county history, or whether they're going to zone Route 42 for strip malls? His sister is dead. That's what people should care about.

"Is Councilman Hammerling available yet?" he nags Molly.

But Hammerling, categorically prompt and respectful of Arthur's grief in the past, isn't in the mood for Rosen's badgering today. Today the bill to reopen the inquiry into the Fir Grove fire has once more been tabled in committee. The consensus he worked so hard to build has fallen apart yet again. So Arthur must wait a little longer. Arthur reads a bit deeper into the paper. And then he sees it, the poem, one of Andrea's. He doesn't believe it. He's grown so weary, too doubtful of his own judgment and sanity over the years to be sure.

Maybe it didn't happen like that at all. How it happened was beside the point. That it did happen was the thing. The big questions remained for me to answer. If Andrea was alive, where was she? And what did all this have to do with Sam? I thought I had a pretty good idea where Andrea might be. I didn't want to think about Sam. It would be hard enough to play out the string as it was. That he had arranged for my two most recent beatings and seemed perfectly willing to pin seventeen potential murders on another man would make it nearly impossible. The thing that haunted me, though, was that I couldn't bring myself to dislike him.

CHAPTER FOURTEEN:
DECEMBER 7TH

Sleep had come quickly, dreamlessly. There were no omens lurking around the bends in the dark corners of my night. I despised omens. Omens were what you made them. I showered, dressed, packed my bags, and left Room 221 without looking back. With any luck at all, the place would crash around Sam's head before I returned. But that would be luck at the expense of justice, and too many lives had been sacrificed to make that trade. There's an old quote by a British jurist about justice alone being insufficient. It's not enough for justice to be done, he said. Justice must be seen to be done. Could there ever be justice for the dead, I wondered, seen or unseen?

Sam couldn't control his shock and dismay when he caught sight of my bag. Then I reminded myself that just maybe he was controlling them perfectly.

"I've got to get down to the city for a day

or two."

He was decidedly suspicious. "Why? What besides everything they got in the city I don't got here?"

"I couldn't've said it better myself."

"So . . ."

"I'll admit I was beginning to have my doubts about Harder." I began with the truth before switching to my cover story. "But now I'm sure he did it. He's been acting guilty since I went up to the old Fir Grove that first time. That's what the vandalism and the fire in the shed were for. He tried to make me think that stuff was about his anger, but it's all about the Fir Grove fire. It was his clumsy attempt at changing the subject. He's probably had me followed around."

Though he liked what he was hearing, Sam couldn't reconcile my leaving. "Why go to the city if the arsonist is here?"

"For one thing, I can't trust the cops up here, especially Lieutenant Bailey. For another, I want to go have a talk with an old friend, an arson investigator with New York's Bravest. I want to know how some teenage kid could burn down a big building and fool everybody for sixteen years. And it's an anniversary I don't want my wife to spend alone."

"Mazel tov!" Sam beamed. "How many —"

"Sorry, Sam, it's not our anniversary. It's a sad anniversary."

"Pearl Harbor?" He was trying to be funny.

On December 7, 1977, I was alone in my apartment at 3000 Ocean Parkway. I was recuperating from knee surgery, quite probably out of my gourd with painkillers and Dewar's, and feeling sorry for myself. Several miles away, in TriBeCa, at an artsy-fartsy little bar with the best jukebox in lower Manhattan, a handsome young man was pouring drinks at a college fund-raiser. At around 1:00 A.M., he was swallowed up by the cobblestone streets of the city like a thousand men and women before him. His name was Patrick Michael Maloney. I was married to his sister. For Katy, today marked the anniversary of his disappearance. Of course, my father-in-law and I knew better. Maybe that's why I felt compelled to finish this job, not to speak for Arthur Rosen or to deliver justice to the dead. Maybe it was my way to atone for continuing to keep the truth about her brother's disappearance out of my wife's grasp.

"Pearl Harbor, yeah," I said. "An uncle I never met died on the *Arizona*."

He didn't know how to take that and I

didn't care. When I tried to pay my bill, Sam was wounded. "Your money's no good here, *toteleh.* Go buy your wife a gift or something."

My instinct was to fight back. This was no free ride. Sam was as genuinely magnanimous as the Grand Inquisitor. This was blood money: my blood, his money. But fighting back too hard would raise his suspicions. Friends accept gifts from friends, graciously.

"You sure, Sam?"

"Put your money away. Don't insult an old man."

I shook his hand. "Thanks."

"You coming back?"

I squeezed his hand tightly as reassurance. "Oh, I'll be back soon. That's a guarantee. Take care of yourself."

At the offices of the *Catskill Tribune* there was no need for a pack of lies, a badge, or an explanation. Maurice, a young black intern who was working on his journalism degree at Syracuse University, was happy to help. Actually, he confessed to being bored out of his skull and regretted taking this internship as opposed to the one in Buffalo. If nothing else, he said, at least the snow in Buffalo was dramatic. Nothing about the

Catskills was dramatic. Even the decline of the Borscht Belt had taken so long it elicited only yawns.

Maurice dug out the film files as far back as the fire. "The last big story in these parts," as he put it. He was right. For weeks the fire dominated the news. Though the fire itself was not what I was here about, I couldn't help skimming through many of the stories, as I had done previously at the library. But I think I spent at least fifteen minutes just staring at the pictures of the dead, three pictures in particular: Karen, Andrea, and Missy Higgins. My heart still beat fast at the sight of Andrea, but now it was for more than a long-dormant crush.

From the date of the fire, there was a four-year gap until one of Andrea's poems appeared on the green-bean page of the *Tribune.* Most years, poems by Anonymous appeared twice a year, at six-month intervals. Some years, as many as four poems made it into the paper. That was a little too regularly to suit me. Why always the *Tribune?* Why not some other rag? Surely there were a thousand local papers and small presses across the country that would have published her work under any cockamamie name she chose. I remembered Andrea as a bright girl. Would she risk having her secret discovered, as twice it had been, just to satisfy some egotistical whim? I didn't think so. There must have been some message component to her method. And I had a pretty good fucking idea who those messages were for.

I thanked Maurice and asked him to refer me to the editor in charge of the green-bean page.

"The green-bean page," he repeated, laughing. "I like that. Can I use that line in a book someday?"

"Be my guest."

Mary Heggarty was the editor of everything that went into the *Tribune* other than sports and international news. She was a frazzled chain-smoker with leathery skin, a take-no-prisoners demeanor, and a voice that was a cross between an umpire's and Lauren Bacall's. She would have been happier to have root canal than to give me five minutes. She had a paper to run.

"What?" she barked.

I showed her hard copies of all the poems Maurice had so graciously made for me. "What can you tell me about these?"

"They're poems." She coughed. "Didn't they teach you that in school?"

"Why do you publish them?"

"Because I like them," she said, turning

down the curmudgeonly editor routine a few notches. "Have you taken a look at the other poems I've had the pleasure of publishing over the years?"

" 'I love the sunshine in the air of blue. / I love the green grass and its mossy dew. / I love the truth because it is so true . . .' " I quoted from Edith Cohen's classic. "Yes, I've had the pleasure."

"*This* is poetry, mister," Heggarty said, waving the photocopies at me. "This girl's got talent. I suppose I publish them in the hope that the Edith Cohens of the world will catch on."

"You said, 'This girl's got talent.' How do you know Anonymous is a g—"

"Look, Prager, anyone with half a brain can tell these were written by a girl, and even after all these years of editing this be-shitting paper, I've still got half a brain."

"Do the envelopes come with a local postmark? Are they hand—"

That got her attention. "You're the third person in ten years to ask me that question about local postmarks. What gives?"

"Let me guess. One was a detective type who tried giving you some bullshit story about a runaway wife or daughter. That was about ten years ago, right? Then, three years ago, there was a crazy-eyed guy with a beard who wouldn't tell you why he wanted to know."

"Anytime you want a job as a reporter, you let me know," she said. "Even your timing is right. And, to answer your question, the postmarks are from all over the place."

"That figures," I said. "Thanks for your help, and thank Maurice for me."

"I was serious about that job offer," she wanted me to know. "How'd you hurt the wrist?"

"Sticking it where some people thought it didn't belong."

R. B. Carter wasn't an easy man to see. He might have been impossible to see if he had wanted it so. Men like Carter didn't see the neighborhood Fuller Brush man when he stopped by the old office tower to show his wares. Men like Carter had layers of security between them and the world they perceived as hungry for their attention. There were little blue men with square badges on their chests, ex-cops and ex-jocks in blue blazers, men in fancy suits with fancy titles and odd gun bulges. There were secretaries, assistants, vice presidents, unlisted phone numbers, seven different offices in New York City alone, and schedules to keep. Yet, in spite of it all, I was confident he'd eventually make room to see me.

It took more than a few phone calls. I got put on hold more times than the plan to build a bridge across Long Island Sound, but no one hung up on me. With every message, I left my phone number at the store and a cryptic message about my love of anonymous poetry. More than one person asked me to repeat the message. I'd tell them not to worry about it, that Mr. Carter would understand.

Waiting for the message to filter through to Carter, I reclaimed a part of my life I'd abandoned for Arthur Rosen. On Columbus Avenue, two blocks north of the American Museum of Natural History and the Hayden Planetarium, sat Irving Prager and Sons, Inc. We'd named the corporation in honor of our father, who knew less about wine than a tree stump did and hadn't lived to see our success. The shop itself was called City on the Vine. Aaron let me have the honor of naming it, but we both understood I could have called it Armpit. In Manhattan, names are important only for restaurants, bars, and designer boutiques. I can't remember the last time I went to see a play because of the theater in which it was being staged. It's not the way things work.

For about the first five weeks we were in

business, we stubbornly made a show of answering the phone with a chipper: "Good day, City on the Vine." We finally surrendered and went with the generic but succinct "Wine shop." Reality has a way of reshaping even a stubborn man's most modest dreams.

My guts were twisting themselves into unpleasant shapes as I put my hand on the door handle. I both dreaded and basked in the notion of my return. The wine business paid better and was decidedly better for a man's connective tissue and kidneys than ghost hunting, but even as I drew my first breath of the familiar dusty air inside the shop, I could feel a little of the life drain out of me. By any measure of my police career, I hadn't been much of a cop. With the exception of saving Marina Conseco's life, a recounting of my career read like a recipe for hot water. Nothing to it. But I guess I was as much a cop as any man who'd ever put on his blues. The shame of it was, it took a bum knee and other people's suffering to wake me up to the facts.

No one was at the front register. No surprise in that. We were doing well, but not so well we could afford to pay someone just to ring sales. We all had to do a little bit of everything. We all stocked the aisles, helped customers, suggested choices, unloaded orders, and made deliveries. I cleared my throat loudly enough to be heard in the dry cleaners' down the street.

"Be with you in a second," Klaus called from the sparkling-wine aisle. His chipperness quotient was always low. From the sound of his voice, it was in negative numbers today.

"Get your ass up here!" I ranted.

Klaus appeared in a getup that made me long for his Dead Kennedys tee shirt. He had makeup on his face that David Bowie wouldn't've worn on a bet. His hair had been bleached blond and was coiffed so that it looked like a wave crashing on the beach. He had on a chalk-striped charcoal suit with a ridiculously ruffled white shirt and frilly sleeves. And yet his face lit up in spite of himself. When Klaus dressed like this, it meant he and Aaron were at war. Aaron and I were yin and yang. When I was out, Aaron's overly anal tendencies came to the fore, which had the effect of alienating our more creative employees.

"Boss! You look awful, but wonderful."

"You should talk," I chided, pointing at his do with my bandaged wrist. "I know several poodles who committed suicide after getting coiffed like that."

"On me it's —"

"— fashion. Yeah, I've heard that line before. Where's my brother?"

"The Führer's making a big delivery. Splash in the Pan Caterers is doing a big corporate Christmas party. I think the company rented one of the Circle Line ships. Aaron's at the pier."

"Klaus," I said coldly, "you know I like you a lot and I put up with your shit because you're a good employee, but don't ever let me hear you refer to my brother that way again. Understood?"

I could see in his face that he was about to make a joke. My eyes screamed for him not to. He didn't. Klaus was a flake, but a smart flake, with a strong instinct for self-preservation.

"Sorry, boss."

"It's forgotten."

Without having to ask, Klaus went into full detail about what I'd missed. Business had been unbelievably good. Kosta was a real pro, and he and Klaus were getting along famously. It was that music-connection thing. Kosta would be in in a few hours. Aaron, a born worrier, was driving everyone nuts. I told Klaus that I wasn't in to work today, but that I'd be back in just a few days. I promised him a bonus if he could put up with Aaron until then. Klaus liked the word "bonus." He had visions of all the tasteless clothing a little extra money could buy.

"I'll be in the office waiting for a phone call."

I didn't have to wait very long. I thought I recognized Blue Suit's voice on the other end of the line. We didn't have a conversation. I got polite instructions that weren't up for negotiation.

"Please be out in front of your store in five minutes."

In Sheepshead Bay, Brooklyn, limos meant one of two things: a wedding or a funeral. It's not that uncomplicated in Manhattan. Limos are more conspicuous than you can imagine. In Manhattan, limos are not about function. They make a statement. They call attention. Hence the streets can be so full of them that no one notices: the Big Apple Paradox. It used to be that showing up outside the hottest club in a limo would guarantee you an in. But New Yorkers catch on to gimmicks fast. These days, showing up in a limo guarantees you nothing but a big bill. I know a Chinese restaurant on the East Side that uses an old limo for takeout deliveries.

Today I was lucky. There weren't more

than three or four limos on Columbus when I stepped outside the shop. A pity, I thought, I was in the mood for hot-and-sour soup. Gus, the old guy from the dry cleaners', gave me a careless wave. He'd sat behind that counter so long his body was probably shaped like a chair. I don't think I ever saw him stand up. When I turned back around from waving at Gus, Carter's limo was waiting.

Blue Suit was Gray Suit today. Again, his clothing fit him with that unnerving perfection. He was smiling at me, of course, as he pulled open the door and gestured for me to climb in. I thought about tipping him a buck just to see his reaction, but the door was closed behind me so quickly I didn't have a chance. Carter was there, waiting in the light. We weren't going to play shadow games today. Nor, apparently, were we going to shake hands. Just as well. We pulled away from the curb.

"Where is she, Mr. Carter?"

He did not answer, holding a tense right hand over his mouth, obscuring his expression. What I could see of his face looked troubled. I couldn't blame him. If he loved his sister, he had plenty to be troubled about.

I tried another approach. "Arthur Rosen

thought she was alive, but didn't trust himself enough or have the wherewithal to find her. I know she's alive, but I can't prove it, not yet. You, I suspect, know for a fact. You've had contact with her."

Again, he was silent. His hand began to tremble slightly; the trouble on his face became more pronounced.

"It bothered me that you tried to pay me off not to take the case," I continued the monologue. "But I didn't lose any sleep over it, because your story was reasonable enough. As soon as I read the poem, that all changed. Look, Carter, I think both of us have a pretty good idea who started that fire sixteen years ago. You're a smart man. There's no statute of limitation on murder, and even if there was, there's no moral limitation."

That got a rise out of him, but not the one I was hoping for. He took his hand away from his face and reached into his suit-jacket pocket. He produced a Mont Blanc pen and that fancy leather checkbook. The first time he tried to buy me off, it was his idea. This time, I could see how he thought I was trying to shake him down.

"Put that away. I still don't want your money. This isn't extortion, for Chrissakes! I want your help."

"Help?" he finally said. "Help with what? What's this nonsense about my sister? As far as my family and the rest of the world is concerned, Andrea died sixteen years ago. I'm afraid I don't know what you're talking about, Mr. Prager."

I guess he had to try that routine. Maybe if he could raise some doubt in me he could get me to take his blood money and go away, or stall me for a little while, until he could relocate Andrea. On the whole, however, it was a pretty halfhearted try. He was probably exhausted by it all.

"Let me lay it out for you. Unless you plan to kill me right here, right now — and I don't think you will — I'm gonna find Andrea. I'm not some certifiable loony with a dead sister and an ax to grind like Arthur Rosen. You can try to smear me, but it won't work for long. I have friends. Some of whom can't be bought off. Eventually, someone'll listen to me, and then you'll have the FBI, the State Police, and half the law-enforcement officials from Albany south on your ass. If you let me bring her in, I'll keep your end out of it. If it had been my little sister, I'm not sure I wouldn't've done the same thing. This way it'll look like she's turning herself in out of remorse. You can have the best lawyer on earth waiting and have a story prepared."

"I don't know where she is. I never have known, and I'm glad I don't know."

My first instinct was to laugh at him, but his body language, his intonation, his expression said he was telling the truth. I pushed him anyway, just to make sure.

"Come on, Carter. You expect me to believe that crock? I don't appreciate it when people piss on my head and tell me it's raining."

"I don't care what you believe. I don't know where she is. She's somewhere up there, I suppose, but she doesn't want to be found. Do you think Arthur Rosen was the only party involved in this mess to hire detectives? Over the years, I've employed an army of detectives. None of them has come up with a thing that's checked out. You'd think someone would have seen her, that she'd have gotten careless or would have to go to a doctor or something." He threw up his hands in exasperation. "Nothing."

"What are the poems about?" I prodded. "And don't tell me they're published for nothing. What's the message?"

"Money," he answered without hesitation. "The day after the poems appear, there's an ad in the personals column. 'Dear Mike, You've been gone these 10 days. If you want

me back, I'm at 1120 So-and-So Lane. . . .'
Something to that effect. I multiply the number of days by a thousand and ship the cash to the address she supplies in the ad."

"Why not just follow the —"

"Tried that, Prager," he sneered. "Do you think I'm a complete idiot?"

"What happened?"

"No one showed up, and I received a letter from a third party." Carter handed me a sheet of paper, unfolding it as he leaned forward. "Here, look for yourself."

It was a brief, typewritten note that made things painfully clear to Carter:

Big Brother —
I know what your sister did. She's under my protection, but if you try to follow the money again, her secret will be out. No second chances. Don't look for us. You won't like what you find.

Regards,
One of Seventeen

P.S. Remember the time your dad caught you playing doctor with your cousin Helen? Weren't you a little old for that? You wouldn't want to get caught with your pants down again.

"What's this last part about?" I asked.

"Only four people knew about me and Helen."

"You, Helen, your dad, and —"

"— my sister. So, you see, there was little doubt Andrea was alive. She knew how embarrassed I was about that incident. She would never have shared that with anyone else."

"You've been blackmailed all these years."

He waved his hand dismissively. "Pocket change. She's safe. She's alive. That's what matters."

Carter wasn't even looking at me any longer. Instead, he stared sadly out the tinted window at the streets of the city. It wasn't in me to berate him for what Aaron or I might have done given the same circumstances. Sometimes it's not the morality of a thing, it's a lack of resources. Who wouldn't pay people off to protect a loved one if they could?

"Drop me back at my store, please."

"Are you sure you won't accept the money?" Carter wondered, still unable to look me in the eye.

"I can't, sorry. But when I find Andrea, I'll let you know where I'm bringing her. You can have a lawyer waiting."

He had nothing to say to that. Five minutes later, we were pulling up to City on the

Vine. I opened the door before Gray Suit could get out from behind the wheel. Carter grabbed my forearm.

"Thank you, I would appreciate that call," he said, finally staring into my eyes. "Here is a number you can reach me at, regardless of the hour."

I took the card and got out, Gray Suit closing the door behind me. He smiled at me, but it wasn't that smile of perfect artifice. It had elegant cracks in it, like an old china cup, broken and glued back together. Gray Suit felt pain, other people's pain. I guess he wanted me to know that. For the first time I wondered if he had a life, what his name might be. The black Lincoln was gone before I could inquire. When I turned toward the shop, Gus the dry cleaner waved again. He hadn't moved from his chair.

Unlike the shock of mixed feelings I experienced walking into the shop, I was exhilarated stepping through the door to my house. In a city of seven million there are about 6,295,306 renters. I'd grown up a renter, lived as a renter, and would likely have died a renter if not for Katy. Katy gave me a sense of permanence, even if it was only an illusion. She made me see that life, by its very nature, thrust transitions upon us. Why add artificial insecurity to the mix if you could avoid it? And if I had needed any more convincing, watching Sarah's birth sealed the deal. She wouldn't have to worry year to year, as I had the whole time I was growing up, if we were going to lose our lease.

Though we never lost that lease and we never moved from that shitty four-and-a-half-room apartment, I had made the move ten thousand times in my head. My dad's financial circumstances always left us a phone call away from Allied Van Lines. I had said goodbye to my friends, thrown my last pitch, all in anticipation of what was never to come. I would not inflict that gnawing anxiety on my daughter. Nor would I find it impossible to utter the phrase: "Everything will be all right." Katy taught me to believe that.

Katy heard me come in. She tiptoed up to me, her index finger across her lips. Sarah was sleeping. It was just as well, I thought, noticing the tear streaks on my wife's face. There was no use in pretending about Patrick. He had been gone for four years now. I was convinced he had run, with good reason, as far away from his father as was humanly possible. Katy, without the advan-

tage of knowing what had transpired between her little brother and her father,
suspected Patrick had met a darker fate.
Neither of us believed we would ever see
Patrick again, though Katy tortured herself
with hope.

She pressed herself into me, and I let her
press as long and hard as she needed. I
stroked her hair, kissed her forehead. After
a few minutes, she noticed the Ace bandages
wound around my left wrist and the bottle
of Dom Perignon in my right hand. When
she started to ask about the wrist, I pressed
my index finger across her exquisitely thin
lips. I hoisted up the bottle.

"I'm gonna put this on ice, and we'll drink
to your brother, okay?"

She kissed my ear and whispered: "Thank
you."

"Meet me upstairs," I said. "We've got a
lot of catching up to do."

Katy hadn't gotten up one step when we
heard Sarah happily chatting away. We both
sort of shrugged.

"Don't think you're getting off so easy,
mister," Katy chided playfully. "You owe
me."

She was right, of course, I owed her
everything. I told myself that, later, if the
moment was just right, if we'd had just

enough champagne, if we'd tired ourselves out properly, I'd tell her the truth about Patrick's disappearance. I knew I wouldn't. I owed her everything, but there would always be one debt I'd be afraid to pay.

CHAPTER FIFTEEN:
DECEMBER 8TH

I let Katy sleep while I changed and fed Sarah. It had been too long a time since I just sat and played with my little girl. We got a kick out of *Sesame Street,* especially since Sarah had overcome her Big Bird-phobia. For her first birthday party/family barbecue, I had the brilliant idea of hiring a guy in a Big Bird suit. Unfortunately, the lovingly klutzy, unthreatening character on TV is only several inches tall. In person, his seven-foot-plus, yellow-feathered torso scared the hell out of all the kids. And since it was ninety-six degrees and humid, Big Bird fainted from dehydration and heat exhaustion. Aaron videotaped me pulling off Big Bird's head in front of twenty freaked-out kids and giving CPR to the out-of-work actor inside the suit. All in all it was a fiasco, but the kind of fiasco that made me smile. I knew it would be a story we'd all laugh about for the rest of our lives.

Eventually, Katy wandered on downstairs. It's my guess she had lounged about upstairs to give Sarah and me some extra time together. We put Sarah in her swing and had breakfast together. Katy didn't understand and I wasn't ready to explain exactly why I wasn't in the mood for eggs, bacon, and potatoes. We settled on toast and coffee. It was pleasant to once again taste coffee that tasted like coffee. I had to go. I was about to turn many people's worlds upside down. For most of them, the next twenty-four hours would probably not be the kind of day to look back upon and smile. Some fiascos are only several days in the making, some several years.

"Thanks for last night," Katy whispered in my ear, trying to fight back tears. "Try not to get beat up for a few days, okay? It's harder on me than you think."

"I'll be all right. Everything will be all right." I kissed her lightly, but held her for a few minutes.

"I don't know why," Katy confessed, "but I almost feel sorry for Andrea."

I was taken aback. "She probably murdered sixteen people, hid it for as many years, and helped blackmail her brother. With her brother's money and influence behind her, I doubt she'll spend more than a few years behind bars. She'll cop a plea and the world will forget. It always does."

"I guess you're right," she said without much conviction. "I'm just being silly. What are you going to do about Sam?"

"One life at a time, kiddo. One life at a time. Andrea's, first of all."

Last summer's hit was playing on WNEW as I hit the Bronx, and I couldn't shake it. It was stuck in my head, doing a fierce pas de deux with the lines I was rehearsing to say to all the other players. Doomed by its infectious hook to the annals of one-hit-wonder-land, I thought the song ironically apropos. I was a one-hit wonder myself. I tried to focus. ". . . Jenny, don't change your number, I need to make you mine . . ." It was hopeless. ". . . 867-5309, 867-5309, 867-5309 . . ."

By the time I hit old Route 17, I knew what I would say to Andrea almost as well as the lyrics of that stupid song. Parts of me still considered dealing with the ancillary players first: Sam, Lieutenant Bailey, et al. But, like I had told Katy, Andrea was necessarily top of the pops. Her debts were biggest, and by choosing to trust R. B. Carter, I might have already given her opportunity enough to slip away. It wouldn't be the first time. And Sam was the wild card. I hoped he'd bought my act and hadn't spent the time I was away covering his ass and discarding evidence. I'd know soon enough. The old bungalow colony was just ahead.

Walking from the car to the longhouse, I flashed back to the last time I'd seen Andrea Cotter. I could smell the dirty salt water off Coney Island Beach. I felt her touch on my shoulder, a touch I had dreamed about since our days at Cunningham Junior High School. I turned around to see her hair blowing across her pale face in the afternoon breeze. I heard her politely asking if I was Moses Prager. I remembered that I suddenly believed in God. I felt the pen in my hand, the pen I'd used to sign her magazine. I could still see her walking down the boardwalk away from me, never turning to look back.

My heart was racing again, as it had that spring day sixteen years before. Even now, after all these years, in spite of Katy and Sarah, sixteen bodies, and the treachery, the fantasy endured. I remembered what Katy had said about Romeo and Juliet. Juliet was awakening after sixteen years, but this time the blood on her hands would not be hers.

Judas Wannsee was waiting for me alone in the big room. I recalled the feeling of being watched during my first visit here, remembered the video cameras.

"You've considered my words," he said.

"As a matter of fact, I have. A lot of what you said made sense. Maybe assimilation is the curse you say it is, and maybe I'll get gassed in the next Holocaust no matter what I do or who I know. Anyway, you know that's not why I'm here. Where is she?"

"Bungalow Eight," he answered. "Just knock and enter. The door will be open. She's been waiting for this day a long time. She's been with us long enough to know you cannot escape your destiny."

"It doesn't stop people from trying, does it?" I mumbled.

"Who would know that better than you?"

"What's that supposed to mean?"

He smiled at me. "You were at a meeting. I think you know exactly what it means."

"Well, thanks anyway."

"Don't thank me," he warned. "Even when we think we know the gifts we're about to receive, we can be surprised."

"Is it the mountain air or what? Can't anybody up here just say what they have to say?"

He laughed. "I suspect your answer to that question is in Bungalow Eight. No matter the answer, remember to ask yourself if you're a proud Jew."

Finding Bungalow 8 required no map, only elementary math skills. Hence, Aaron would have argued, I was at a disadvantage — arithmetic was never my forte — but I managed to find the cabin nonetheless. My palms were sweaty. My heart . . . Forget my heart. From the moment I put my directional on to turn into the old bungalow colony, my pulse rate was revving higher than my engine. I tried imagining what Andrea would look like after all these years, what toll the years of deception had taken on her. It was already abundantly clear what toll her deception had taken on everyone else. I raised my hand and knocked. The door fell back without my even having to turn the handle.

It was dark and musty inside the little shack, shafts of light slicing through the shadows like steel sabers through a magician's trick box. I sensed her presence. I could hear her breathing, I thought I could smell her breath. Like her brother, Andrea felt comfortable hiding in the shadows. She must have gotten very used to it.

"Come on, Andrea, let's get this over with. It's been a long time coming."

She didn't say anything, but I could hear her move. A frail arm flashed in the light and out again. Her breathing was labored. And the smell of the atmosphere, which I had taken for mustiness, was something different altogether. The air was sour and antiseptic all at once, like the poor wards at the old municipal hospitals.

"Please," I appealed, "let's make this easy."

A light snapped on. An unshaded lamp made out of a tree branch sat on a similarly constructed nightstand. My hostess stood just beyond the footprint of the bare bulb, in the corner of the room. Her face was difficult to make out, but her plain clothes and yellow star were unmistakable. She took a step forward.

Now my heart simply stopped.

"You look like you've seen a ghost," she said, laughing sardonically, grabbing her side in pain.

I couldn't speak. I felt a thousand things in one impossible jolt: rage, fear, confusion, disappointment, panic.

"I have seen a ghost," I mumbled at last, "just not the one I expected to see. Where's Andrea?"

"Dead. She's been dead for sixteen years."

"But the poems . . . I don't understand."

An object flew out of the shadows. I flinched reflexively, though I was in no real danger of being hit. Something thumped on the floor at my feet.

Karen Rosen said: "Pick it up."

It was a girl's journal. The spine had been taped and retaped over the years. The entries on the delicate yellowed pages dated back to the early sixties. There were poems on some of the pages, Andrea's poems. I bet there was also an entry about her brother playing doctor with Cousin Helen.

"I took it the night of the fire," Karen volunteered. "Talk about an albatross. . . . But it contains everything an aspiring extortionist needs." She laughed that laugh again, wincing as she did. "I never wanted any part of that — the blackmail, I mean."

"You had a long time to stop," I admonished. "And you didn't."

"I had only one chance to stop," she said, "sixteen summers ago. After that, what did any of it matter?"

"What really happened that night?"

"What really happened is that I murdered sixteen people." She hesitated, as if to gather strength. "Listen, I will tell you everything, and I will abide by whatever decision you make about how to handle things."

"There's a 'but' here somewhere, right?" I wondered skeptically.

"You have to hear me out, completely. You won't like a lot of it."

"I haven't liked most of it to this point. Nothing you say's gonna change that."

"Will you hear me out?" she shouted breathlessly.

"Agreed."

For the first time, Karen stepped fully into the light and sat down on the bed in front of me. She was thin like some of the other Yellow Stars, but her skin was terribly jaundiced. Initially I thought it was just the light from the cheap bulb that gave her skin that sickly tone, but no bulb was that cheap, and only those fancy new streetlights were that yellow.

"It had been a horribly rainy summer," Karen began. "It was bad all around. Just before Andrea and I came up here, my boyfriend . . . Do you remember Steven Glickman?"

I raised my hand over my head. "Tall kid, black hair, good-looking, played on the baseball team — yeah, I remember him."

"He broke it off with me, and when Arthur found out he went apeshit and threatened Steven that he'd kill him if he hurt me again. That pretty much ruined any hope for the two of us getting back together. He really fucked that up, my big brother."

I wondered how much she knew about Arthur's extraordinary efforts to find out what had happened to his little sister, or if she knew what had become of him. I wasn't going to tell her — not yet, anyway.

"My first week up here, I found out my dad lost his job and that he probably wasn't going to have the money to send me to Brandeis. Brooklyn College, here I come. Then I got the worst possible station in the dining room. My tables drove me crazy and didn't tip for shit. I thought about going back home. I was lonely and depressed and . . . God, I wished I'd gone home."

"So do seventeen families," I said tersely.

So far Karen wasn't exactly scoring a lot of points on the empathy meter. Kids break up. Kids go to work. Kids get lonely. Kids don't usually murder anybody.

"But I noticed that Andrea was always flush with cash, and her station wasn't a whole lot better than mine. I asked her about it. She said there were a lot of ways to make money up here besides waiting tables."

"You were curious?"

"I was real curious," she admitted. "Like I said, waitressing sucked and I needed money."

"There's no such thing as easy money, Karen,"

"I was a kid. I didn't know that. All money

looks easy to a kid."

"What's the catch?"

For the first time, she hesitated. "We had to a . . . we had to date guys that worked at other hotels in the area and find stuff out."

"Stuff! What kind of stuff?"

"When we were out with the guys from the other hotels, all we had to do was find out if there were any guests at those hotels throwing a lot of cash around or flashing lots of jewelry. That's all. We got twenty-five bucks a date, and sometimes we'd get an extra fifty. What's the matter? You look disappointed."

Karen found something about what she'd said very funny and began to make a sort of suffocated giggle. Then she grabbed her side and sat quickly down on the bed.

"Did you ever ask why?"

"Just give me a second. . . . Yes, Andrea asked. Someone was running a big-stakes card game and was interested in recruiting high rollers. They couldn't exactly advertise it in the local paper."

"And you believed that, this story about the high-stakes card game?"

"I believed the money. Yeah, I believed it. Why not? It made sense, and I didn't see the harm in it."

"You said you believed at first," I repeated.

"Something must've changed your mind."

"Something did."

A siren went off in my head. "The burglaries!"

"Very good." Karen applauded weakly. "Judas said you were some kind of cop."

"How'd you figure it out, about it not being for a card game?"

"Andrea did. I think she was a little more suspicious than me, but we sort of enjoyed the illicit nature of what we were doing. It *was* kind of exciting." The years seemed to disappear from Karen's face, an innocently mischievous smile spreading across her yellowy skin. For the first time she almost resembled the girl with the Siamese cat in her lap. "The money was great, and as long as we couldn't see anybody getting hurt, we figured, What the hell. Then . . ."

"Then what?"

"Then," Karen said, the years returning to her face, "the stories about the burglaries started appearing in the local paper and on the radio. It didn't take us long to match the names of the victims to the names we'd gotten out of some pimply-faced pool boy or horny bellhop."

"Did Andrea want to stop?"

"That's rich! No, Moe, she didn't want to stop. She didn't want to get caught. Those are two different things, just in case you're keeping score. I wanted to stop, but Her Royal Highness had developed a taste for danger. Andrea told me that as long as I kept my mouth shut she'd still throw some more money my way."

"You took the money."

"Why not?" Karen stood, pushing herself off the bed with quite a bit of effort. "No one was getting hurt, not really. So what if some old ladies were getting their rings stolen? The hotels were insured. We were kids having a lark. And now I was getting paid for doing nothing."

Then it occurred to me what went wrong. "This was all working out great for you, I guess, until that guy got beaten unconscious, huh?"

"How'd you know about that?"

"I'm some kinda cop, remember? But," I confessed, "I still don't see what this had to do with the fire."

"When that guy got knocked unconscious, Andrea panicked. She said she was going to the cops, but that she'd leave my name out of it."

"You didn't believe her."

Karen bowed her head. "The funny part is, I did. I suppose I was always a little jealous of Andrea. I think every girl in Lincoln was jealous of her, and maybe getting involved with her the way I did back then made me see her in a different light. I guess I grew to not like her so much, but she could keep a secret. I trusted her."

"But Sam didn't. He couldn't afford to. The stakes were bigger for him."

Her jaw nearly hit the top of my shoes. "Sam! You know about Sam?"

"Yeah, I know about him, good old Sudden Sam. But why don't you tell me about him anyway?"

"I told Sam about Andrea," she confessed. "It was stupid, I know. Even though I trusted Andrea, I was afraid. I mean, I had stopped doing this shit for him weeks before, but . . ." Tears began rolling down Karen's cheeks. "He told me to talk Andrea out of going to the cops. He told me that if he was going down he'd take me and Andrea with him. He held a razor to me and threatened to carve up my face if I didn't get Andrea to change her mind. He said he had a friend on the cops who would know if Andrea turned herself in. 'I might not be able to get to her, my *shaineh maideleh,* but I'll get to you,' " Karen imitated Sam's lilt perfectly, dragging a skeletally thin finger across her wet face. "He sliced open my cheek."

"You went to talk to Andrea."

"I waited until everyone was asleep, but she wouldn't listen to me. I showed her where Sam had cut me, but Andrea had made up her mind. When she wouldn't listen, I guess I just lost it. I was crying and shaking with fear of what Sam would do to me. I guess Andrea was coming to put her arm around me and . . . I . . . I pushed her away." Karen doubled over, again grabbing her side.

"So you pushed her," I prompted. "So what?"

"But she tripped. She fell back against her cot. I was still so furious with her. I started taunting her, telling her about what Sam was going to do to us, but she didn't move. Andrea never moved. She wasn't breathing. She had no pulse. She must have fallen awkwardly and snapped her neck."

"You panicked."

"I panicked. I didn't know what to do. I was a stupid seventeen-year-old girl."

I hung my head, knowing finally how the fire had started. "You lit her bed on fire to cover it up. How stupid could you be?"

"No! I mean I did, but not then, not right away. First, I ran to the only other person I thought I could go to."

"Sam." It all made a kind of horrible sense

now, I thought, balling my good hand into a fist. "What happened when you went to him?"

"He helped me. He told me to stay outside while he went to make sure Andrea was dead. When he was sure, he brought me back into the workers' quarters and told me to light her bed on fire to cover up the evidence. He'd put her back on the bed. He told me to use a cigarette to light up the bed and spray a little lighter fluid onto the fire once it started. I told him I couldn't do it. I knew she was dead, but I just couldn't do it."

"But you did do it, didn't you?"

Her tears came in waves now. "Yes, yes, I did it. Sam smacked me in the mouth so hard he knocked my front teeth out. He told me he'd kill me if I didn't do as he said. After I was done, I was to meet him in the employee parking lot."

"The fire spread so fast, though, Karen. What really happened?"

"I was too frightened to wait until the cigarette caught on the mattress, so I . . . I doused her with lighter fluid and threw a match on her. I couldn't believe how fast it spread. So I grabbed Andrea's journal and ran. That stupid journal, it meant so much to her. By the time I got out, it . . . the . . .

it was an inferno." Karen clapped her hands over her ears. "They were screaming, screaming. When I shut my eyes I can still hear them screaming."

"How'd you get away?"

"Before the fire trucks came, we were already on our way."

"To where?" I asked.

"Sam kept a little cabin not too far away from Monticello Raceway. When things quieted down, he got my teeth fixed and smuggled me over the border to Canada. He was happy to be rid of me."

"Until . . ."

Karen explained that she had drifted around Canada for a few years, working as a waitress mostly, but the fire and her victims were never far from her thoughts. Though she tried to stay away, the guilt over what she'd done kept pulling her back east. She said she felt compelled to find a way to deal with what she'd done. Then, in Toronto, outside an old synagogue, a man approached her and asked her the same question I'd been asked: Are you a proud Jew? It was an epiphany of sorts. From the second she heard Judas Wannsee speak that night, Karen Rosen knew what she would do with the rest of her life. Eventually, Wannsee bought the old bungalow colony. To Karen's way of thinking, it was meant to be.

"It was perfect." Karen seemed almost joyful. "I didn't have to run anymore, and I could deal with what I'd done where I'd done it. The world thought I was dead. No one knew me up here, and I thought Sam had probably gone."

"But he hadn't gone," I reminded her.

"No, he was still here. I got really sick one winter and I had to go see the doctor in town."

"Sam spotted you."

"Just my luck," she said sadly. "But he didn't confront me, not then. He came to a meeting like you did, and he handed me a note giving me a time and place to meet him."

"Knowing Sam," I said, "he probably tried to blackmail you first."

"He was down on his luck." She seemed to defend him out of habit. "He hadn't worked in a long time. Anyway, I didn't have any money to give him, and he was smart enough to know my parents' pockets weren't very deep. And what would turning me in to the cops do except make more trouble for himself in the end? He'd have to explain his part in all of it."

"But you had the diary."

"I had the diary. It didn't take Sam long

to figure what to do from there. Like I said, Sam's a smart man — he's been blackmailing Andrea's brother for years — but I'm no fool either. I never actually gave the book to Sam. I kept it as a kind of insurance. I just give him a poem every now and then, when he needs money. Now," she said, gesturing up at me, "you have the book. It would have ended soon enough anyway."

"Why?"

"Do you think I'm this lovely shade of yellow just to match the star on my blouse?" she snickered. "My oncologist tells me I've got a few weeks at most to get things in order. It's my liver. It's spread into my spine, and soon my brain. What shall you do with me, Moe?" she asked, seeming to enjoy my predicament. "It's a dilemma, no?"

There was no dilemma, not really. I just didn't see any point in hauling her in to die in the midst of a media circus. And the media would have made her out to be the victim here. I couldn't have stomached that. I couldn't dishonor the dead. This wouldn't be the first time innocent people had paid someone else's guilty debt with their lives. It wouldn't be the last. In any case, I got the sense that the closer she got to death the less serene Karen would be. Her bill was coming due.

"You can stay here and die in peace. Your secrets and Andrea's are safe with me."

She stood and made a move as if to hug me. "Thank you. You can't imagine how relieved I am."

"Just out of curiosity," I began, turning away from her approach, "when Arthur came looking for Andrea and joined your group, where did you —"

She answered my question with a question. "Where do you think?"

"The Swan Song."

"Yes, Sam was very accommodating to his cash cow."

"Arthur's dead. He killed himself. I'd thought you'd want to know."

I might just have told her I'd run over a squirrel. "He was never at peace, so horribly depressed, even when we were kids. If he hadn't latched on to me as a cause, he would have found something else."

I hadn't known her well in high school, but I couldn't imagine she had been so cruel, not the girl with the pajamas and Siamese cat. Murder changes you. I decided to leave before I let it change me.

"Thank you again, but don't go just yet."

I was terse: "What is it?"

"Can't you say you forgive me, just a little bit? Please? I get a lot of support around

337

here, but forgiveness isn't on the menu."

"I'll keep your secret, but I'm not in the forgiveness business. As far as I can see, there are no vacancies for you on Redemption Street. Maybe you can find what you're looking for in hell."

"We don't believe in hell, Moe. You know that."

"It's not really important if you believe in hell, if hell believes in you."

I quickly closed the door behind me and walked into the daylight. The air outside was cold and fresh, but the stink of her decay stayed with me. It wasn't necessarily the smell of the cancer eating away at her flesh that I couldn't escape. It was the rotting of her soul, I think.

A cop buddy of mine, Ferguson May, was our precinct philosopher. Every precinct's got one. With a few beers in him, Fergy fancied himself the black Aristotle. It was funny that I would think of Ferguson now. I hadn't thought of him in years. His favorite bit of wisdom had to do with falling from high places. You don't realize how fast you're going, he'd say, until you get close to the ground. That's when you realize it's a little too late to start praying. Ferguson May got stabbed through the eye trying to break up a domestic dispute. I wondered how comforting his own philosophy had been in the seconds before they pronounced him dead at the scene. I wondered if Karen realized just how profoundly fast she was traveling in relationship to the ground.

I sat in the lot outside Town Hall trying to compose myself. I had been hard on Karen — too hard, I thought. All those years ago, she was a kid, a sad, lonely kid who got in so far over her head that the heat of a match felt like the sun. What if it had been Katy or, worse still, Sarah? What was I like at seventeen? I was an irresponsible jerk who thought he knew everything about everything, but knew nothing about anything. Still, she hadn't batted an eye when I told her about her brother's suicide. I guess I hadn't had enough time to distinguish between what Karen was then and what she was now.

I was angry. I was angry that I'd gotten it wrong and disappointed that Andrea wasn't alive. I looked at her diary on the seat next to me and wondered if I would have been more charitable if it had been her waiting to die in Bungalow 8. Teenage crushes, I realized, can survive almost anything, arson and murder notwithstanding. God, how petty and stupid. I was tired enough of the

339

lies and secrets surrounding Patrick's disappearance. There were times, especially around Katy's family, they weighed me down so that I felt myself being crushed. My legs weren't strong enough to carry the weight of sixteen innocent bodies. I could already feel them pressing down on me.

Good old dependable Molly, sitting at her table, looked like salvation to me just then. I kissed her hello on the cheek and she blushed. It was a small thing, her blushing like that, but I don't suppose I'll ever forget it. Did people blush anymore?

"Is he in?" I asked, nodding my head toward Hammerling's office.

"Sure," she said, brushing her hair with her fingertips. "You're not leaving, are you?"

"Soon, but not yet. There's still some unfinished business to take care of. Maybe you can help. How would you like to play Mata Hari for a night?" Molly was all ears, eagerly leaning forward. "After I talk to Hammerling, I'll fill you in."

Dick Hammerling was seated behind his mission-style aircraft carrier, head buried in a book, when I walked into his office. His face said he was happy, but wary to see me. I imagine anything having to do with the fire produced extraordinarily mixed feelings in him. If things played out the way I hoped they would, those mixed feelings would become even more jumbled.

"Mr. Prager." He turned on the politician's charm as he stood. "Good to see you. Have a seat."

"Call me Moe," I said, closing the door behind me. "I'll sit in a minute. First, I've got something to ask you."

"Ask."

"I'm sorry to have to bring this up, but I know about what happened to your father."

Hammerling's face soured. "That's not a question."

"I'm getting to it," I promised. "And I think I understand how much solving the Fir Grove fire means to you, but I've gotta be sure. If I were to explain what happened that night, how it happened, and why, could you leave it alone? Would that be enough for you?"

He didn't answer right away. I liked that. He sat down quietly in his chair and spun it slowly about so that he faced the window. The sun was high and strong today, and he tilted his face upward to stare directly at it.

His back still to me, he wondered: "How can I be sure you're telling me the truth?"

"Because I'll give you my word, just like you'll give me yours that what I say in this office goes no farther."

"Further." He laughed sadly. "Goes no further. 'Further' is more correct."

He turned the chair back around, stood up, and held out his big right hand to me. In the end he realized this was about his dad and not about him. Only the truth mattered.

I took his hand. "I give you my word that what I'm going to tell you is the truth."

"I know," he said somberly. "Nothing you say to me in this room will ever be repeated."

I told him the story — the essentials, at least, but for obvious reasons there were details I was forced to omit or fudge over. I admitted as much. The only thing I actually lied about was the status of Karen Rosen's health. The way I explained it, the girl who set the fire was already dead. And, I rationalized, that would soon enough be true.

"So you see," I said, "your dad was right. It wasn't some idiot smoking in bed. The fire was intentionally set, and an accelerant was used. Not a lot was used, but that bunkhouse was just such a shithole it went up like kindling."

"This girl, the one who set the fire, is dead?" he asked.

I skillfully avoided answering. "Whatever price there is to pay, Councilman, she's paid it in full."

He spun his chair back around to the window and hung his head. "Thank you, Moe," he whispered, choking back years' worth of uncried tears.

"I'll wait in the outer office," I said.

Even through the closed door I could feel his anguish. I had a strange thought. I recalled that just recently an old Imperial Japanese soldier had been found on some isolated Philippine outpost. What, I wondered, would his life stand for now that his war was finally over? What would Dick Hammerling's life stand for now that he had his answers? Maybe that fierce energy he'd used to fight the good fight in the name of his father could be put to better use. I hoped it would. I hoped some good might come of this. Then, as I sat there trying not to listen to Hammerling's sobs, I thought of Arthur Rosen. Selfishly, I was relieved not to have to tell him. I don't know that I would have been able to tell him if he were still alive. That was one less secret, thank God, I wasn't forced to keep.

When Hammerling opened the door to invite me back in, he looked more upright, less constricted. One of us had had a load lifted off his shoulders.

He leaned over a liquor cabinet. "Drink?"

"Sure."

"My dad loved vodka," Hammerling said, waving a dusty old bottle at me. "But if that's not —"

"Vodka's fine," I said. "Let's drink to your dad, and mine, too."

We had two shots apiece and got back down to business. I did most of the talking. He was slightly suspect of my motives and confused by what I asked of him, but I was unwilling to share any more information. Sam and his accomplices were my responsibility, mine alone.

"So let me get this straight. All you want me to do is go down to the police station with you and stand outside the door while you have a conversation with Lieutenant Bailey."

"That's right. That's all you have to do."

"Okay, I owe you more than that, but if that's all you want . . ."

While Hammerling waited in my car, I had that little talk with Molly. She was also a bit reluctant, but couldn't resist a shot of intrigue into her mundane life.

"All I have to do is have a drink with him?" she asked warily.

"It wouldn't hurt to flirt with him a teeny-tiny bit, but that's it!" I wagged my finger at her. "I just need some time to set up a little surprise for him."

She agreed.

You'd have thought Lieutenant Bailey would shit his pants at the sight of me, fearing I was walking into his station house to swear out a complaint against him for false arrest and police brutality. I knew better. It was the same with cops and perps. When your hands have been dirty for so long that no one ever tells you to wash them, you start thinking you're Superman. No one can touch you. You're above it, beyond it, you're invincible. There are plenty of corrupt old-timers on the job with that aura about them. But it's that hubris that always brings them down. After the Knapp Commission, finger pointing and gun eating became popular pastimes among the old guard.

Bailey almost relished the chance to rub what he'd done in my face, and was glad to have a little chat with me in his office.

"What can I do for you, Mr. Prager?" He smiled smugly. "I see you've hurt your wrist. How that happen?"

"Sorta like how I hurt my kidneys."

"What's that you say?" He cupped his ear. "I'm not getting you."

"You're not? Okay. Maybe this'll help your hearing."

I sunk my left foot so deeply into Bailey's groin that you could see the imprint of my shoelaces on the skin of his ass. He went down like a sack of potatoes. Even as he struggled for air he called me a cocksucker.

"No," I corrected, pulling him up to his knees by the hair, "I'm a ball buster."

"Fuck you!"

"You won't be fucking anything but yourself for quite some time. So listen carefully. You're gonna put your papers in today, right now!"

"Get the fuck outta here," he said, a bit more strength returning to his voice. "No one's going to buy your stories. I'm a respected man in this town."

"Oh yeah? How respected you gonna be after Sam rolls over on you, asshole?"

He didn't like that. If it were possible for him to get any paler than he already was, he got paler. I had little doubt Bailey was a Grade A schmuck to begin with, but I didn't think he'd gotten in bed with Sam of his own accord. No, Sam had something on him.

"Whatever he's got on you, Bailey, he won't hesitate to use it to save his own skin. Think about it — you know that old fuck better than me. He'll roll over on you like that! They won't have to ask him twice. I was a cop, Bailey. Cops don't fare too well in prison, especially dipshit, small-town assholes like yourself. What's he got on you?"

I had him worried, but he tried stonewalling. "Eat shit!"

"You think I'm kidding, huh? You think maybe I'm bluffing. Councilman Hammerling," I called out, "will you stick your head in here a second?"

Dutifully, Hammerling complied. He was taken aback some by Bailey's disheveled state, but said nothing.

"Thank you, Councilman," I said. "Can you give us a few more minutes?"

"Does he have stuff on you?" I repeated when the door closed.

"Yes," Bailey admitted, "enough to put me away for a long fuckin' time."

"Now, if you want to save your shitass pension and any self-respect, this is what you're gonna do. You're putting in your retirement papers today. You're not gonna say word one to Sam. You're gonna write down the names and addresses of the other two clowns who helped kick the shit out of me in the woods that night. If they're cops, you make sure they put in their papers today, too, or you'll all fry. And I want my guns back that you took from me that night, especially the .38. If not, Councilman Hammerling will introduce a bill to bring in the State Police Internal Affairs Division to investigate your department. The higher-ups will offer your ass up faster than Sam, and you know it."

"The .38's in the bottom drawer over there," he said, pointing at a medal desk. "The .22's still out in the woods somewhere."

I checked out my old .38 while he wrote down the names of the men who'd helped him attack me in the woods that night. I folded up the paper and put it in my back pocket.

"Remember," I said, "put your papers in today, and not a word to Sam."

"What about the shit Sam's got on me?" he asked.

"You let me worry about that."

It was about 9:00 P.M. as I watched Sam's Cadillac pull out of the Swan Song parking lot and onto the main road out in front of the hotel. Good thing he was prompt. It was freezing in the damned bushes. Given his apparent affection for women of Molly's build, it was no wonder that he wanted to be on time for their tête-à-tête. He probably had the first erection he'd had since the Battle of Bull Run. Who knows, maybe he was letting it steer the car while he was lighting up one of those ridiculous cigars of his. I'd learned to take my time, and waited another fifteen minutes before heading inside. Once inside, I'd wait for Molly's signal before beginning my search.

At 9:27, the front-desk phone rang three times. Then it stopped. Then it rang twice again. It was Molly letting me know Sam had arrived at Hanrahan's.

Though Sam was a smarter man than Bailey, I was hoping Sam was as susceptible to the foibles of success as the corrupt cop. Success breeds complacency, and complacency leads to carelessness. I had little doubt that at one time Sam had made certain to stash his blackmail leverage safely away where only he could have access to it, but that sort of thing can get expensive. Access can be problematic if the goods are in your lawyer's office or in a safe-deposit box in a bank that closes at 3:00 P.M. Eventually, your victims get so whipped, you barely need to threaten them if they don't comply. Compliance can become as habitual as anything else.

That was all well and good. Now the problem was finding the goods, if they were here to be found. The Swan Song wasn't exactly the size of Windsor Castle, but it was a lot bigger than your standard suburban ranch. I came up empty at the front desk. Sam had even removed the big bell. My search of the office was equally unproductive. It's a shame I wasn't looking for ten years of hotel bill receipts. There were plenty of those. The kitchen was a waste of time, as were the dining rooms. I checked my watch; almost an hour had passed, and unless Molly succumbed to Sam's charms, which was not altogether impossible, I didn't have that much time left.

Then something Karen Rosen had said earlier rushed through my head. I had to get to Sam's room. I raced up to the sixth and top floor. Sam had a suite of rooms with a roof deck and views of the entire area. Once upon a time, this had probably been the bridal or presidential suite. The walls, not unlike those of Dick Hammerling's office, were covered with autographed pictures of the once-, near-, and no-longer famous. Though pressed for time, I just had to look. Sam had known them all: Crosby and Hope, Al Jolson, Eddie Cantor, Abbott & Costello, Sammy Davis Jr., Berle, Youngman, Myron Cohen, Jackie Gleason, Steve and Eydie, Redd Foxx, Mort Sahl, Woody Allen, Barbra Streisand, Goulet, Dean Martin, Bill Cosby, Lenny Bruce, Joey Bishop,

Frank Sinatra. The list was endless. It was like the roll call for the old *Ed Sullivan Show.* I had to stop myself.

It was nearly eleven when I found what I hoped I was looking for: a piece of junk mail with Sam's name on it, but sent to a Monticello, New York, address. Sam still owned the cabin he had hidden Karen in those sixteen summers before.

I was more concerned about finding the cabin in the dark than about how I was going to get in. The butt end of a .38 is great for breaking glass. The map I picked up at the Shell station in Ellenville was a nightmare. Folding maps must have been invented by the Marquis de Sade. I was just about to stop and ask directions when I stumbled upon the road leading to Sam's cabin.

Rolling carefully down the dirt-and-gravel lane, I could barely make out the shape of a cabin here and there. But as I came around the curves, my brights illuminated several of the tiny wooden houses. They were all boarded up for the winter. Some looked as if they were boarded up till the end of days. Even in the mid-sixties, when the Catskills was still a somewhat happening place, these cabins would have been fairly isolated. It would have been easy for Sam to hide Karen away here without fear of being found out.

As I approached the area of Sam's cabin, I got a sick feeling in the pit of my stomach. It didn't seem quite as dark as it should have been, as the rest of the road had been. The glow of house lights rose out of the darkness. I tried unsuccessfully to convince myself that Sam kept the porch light on, but it was just too bright for that. The silhouette of Sam's antique Caddy stuck the knife into any fleeting hopes I might have had left. I was expected. I didn't keep my host waiting.

Even though Sam had the TV playing rather loudly, the gravel beneath my feet rendered moot any chance I might have at achieving some level of surprise. The front door was slightly ajar, and I pushed it open with the nose of my .38. I didn't, however, walk right in. I guess I was going to dance this dance with Sam whether I was in the mood to dance or not, but that didn't mean I couldn't try to step on his feet every now and then.

"All right, Sam, come on out," I yelled from behind the wall outside his door.

"What," he called back, "you're not gonna tell me I should put my hands up? You disappoint me, *toteleh*."

"That makes us even, old man. Come on, Sam, let's go."

"I'm not going anywhere, *boychik,* it would be rude to my date."

Now that sick feeling got a whole lot worse.

"Cut the bullshit, Sam, and get your ass out —"

"I don't think I like your tone. Do you like his tone?" The question wasn't meant for me. "Unfortunately, my guest is in no condition to answer. I think maybe she had a little too much to drink, but you know what lushes these upstate *shiksas* are, especially the fat ones."

I walked in. Oddly, the first thing I noticed was the overly bright TV. Like a magnet, the screen pulled my eyes to the distorted freeze-frame image it held prisoner. The black-and-white image was of a man — that much I could make out, in spite of the warped and grainy quality of the picture his mouth agape, suspended in time between words.

"That's Jackie Jackson on the TV." Sam chortled. "He was the host on the old *Palais, Palais* show. I was on this show, February 23, 1952. It was my one shot at the big time."

The trance was broken, and I turned to

look at Sam. He was seated facing the TV, in an overstuffed recliner. It was all distressed brown leather and brass tacks. In his right hand he held a remote controller. In the left, he held a double-barreled shotgun. The business end of the shotgun pointed toward the couch. Molly Treat, her arm dangling so that her fingertips touched the floor, lay sprawled across the couch, unconscious. The dismay on my face was not lost on Sam.

"Don't worry, the fat girl's not dead," he reassured me. "I slipped her a Mickey Finn. You know what is a Mickey Finn?"

"You put something in her drink."

"When she got a little drowsy, I walked her to my car. That was easy. Getting her out of the car, *oy gevalt!* A man could get a hernia, for Chrissakes."

"Come on, Sam, this is stupid. There's nowhere to go with this that's good for any of us."

"You'll pardon me, *toteleh,* if I disagree. While we wait, have a seat and watch. And by the way, open up the gun and empty the cartridges on the floor. Don't think about being a hero. I may be an old fuck, but my finger works plenty good enough to blow the fat girl's head off."

I did as he said. The bullets bounced off

the hardwood floor. What, I wondered, were we waiting for? Whatever it was, I was glad to have some time to try and talk Sam down or get to the shotgun. I sat in the chair Sam had readied for me. At the foot of the chair was the gift-wrapped bottle Mr. Roth had given me. Only it looked a little worse for wear, as if it had been unwrapped and rewrapped several times.

"Open it up," Sam urged. "Go on."

It was, as I had anticipated, an expensive bottle of single-malt scotch, but there was something else in the box, a handwritten note:

Dear Mr. Moe,
I like you very much. You remind me, if such a thing is possible, of what I hoped my son would turn out like. He is not a bad boy. I was a bad father, and as you will soon see, an unfaithful husband. I won't blame it on my time in the camps. You can blame the Nazis for a lot of terrible things, but my weakness is not among them. I was always too much interested in the store, in the money and the pride of ownership. I neglected many things, my wife first among them. We lived together for over 40 years, but we had no life together. When I was in the

mountains, I oftentimes turned to girls to look for in them what my neglect had killed in my wife. Your friend Sam provided these girls to me. I suppose he is no worse a man than me, but I thought you should know. Don't trust him. For me already it's too late. Sam and me, we made our pact with the devil together a long time ago. For you, there's time. I am shamed that I was too embarrassed to just tell you. You're a good man, a better man than me. If you can forgive an old foolish man his past, I would like very much to hear from you.

Israel Roth

I put the letter down. Sam was watching me very intently.

Sam shook his head. "What a hypocrite, that pathetic old prick. I got him more pussy than almost anyone up here, and now he tries to cut my legs out. Fuck him!"

I was silent.

"Whatsa matter, *toteleh,* nothing to say? You think that little burglary scam I ran was my only outside source of income? I did a little bit of everything in those days. If you wanted pot or a little pussy on the side, Sam could get it for you. I was, after all, the entertainment director. You know that bar girl, Sally? Cute, right? She didn't start out her career mixing drinks." He smiled cruelly. "Speaking of drinks, go ahead, have one. Maybe the booze'll make you better company."

I twisted open the still-sealed bottle and had a sip. I liked blended scotch better, but even Dewar's wouldn't have held much appeal for me now.

"Good," Sam smiled. "Now close the bottle and roll it across the floor to me, slowly. I wouldn't want you should get any ideas of cracking me over the head with it."

I rolled the bottle by his feet.

"These new VCR things are great," he said, pointing at a big machine atop the TV. "This one's a Betamax, the Sony model. The picture's much better than those other ones, even with old kinescopes like this. Here, watch."

With that, Sam pressed a button on the remote, and the frozen image sprang to life: "And here now is an act we've all been waiting for. He's opened for the likes of Sammy Davis Jr., and the late, great Al Jolson. Let's have a warm *Palais, Palais* hand for Sudden Sam Gutterman. . . ."

Even before Sam appeared on camera, I had the sense that this was not going to be a triumphant debut. How could a man like

Sam succeed on TV in an era when you couldn't say "hell" or "brassiere" without being labeled a communist? I was not far wrong. Unable to resort to his usual blue shtick, Sam was lost. You could see he had impeccable comic timing, but his jokes were weak and unconvincing. They might've worked coming out of the mouth of Myron Cohen or Red Buttons. It was painful to watch. The audience was thunderously silent, and two minutes into the routine, Sam was bathed in flop sweat. Mercifully, the orchestra broke in.

"I sucked," he said, hitting the pause switch. "I was a one-trick pony, *boychik*. If I couldn't work blue, I couldn't work. I had great timing, maybe the best. Berle used to think so. I had a snappy delivery. The crowds liked me, but . . ."

"So being a thief and a pimp seemed like a good second career."

"*You* used the fat girl tonight, not me. Just because she wasn't getting paid for it, that doesn't make you a pimp? That was ham-handed on your part, by the way. I had my suspicions that you might be catching on, but getting a call out of the blue from Molly — then I knew for sure. If you hadn't gotten her involved, maybe nobody was gonna get hurt. Now . . . You shoulda thought things through, my friend. You set up such a perfect scenario to let me get out from under that I couldn't pass it by."

"What scenario is that?" I asked.

"You and Molly were fucking around up here. Christ, half the town's seen you two together at Hanrahan's. What, you think Molly didn't talk to her girlfriends about being smitten by your manly charms? Men aren't the only people who embellish, *toteleh.* The fat girl talked plenty. You think Sally won't back up my story? I got tapes of her doing some rather unpleasant things with some bored wives and husbands. You'd be amazed what a godsend cocaine dependency can be. Somehow I get the feeling Sally would do just about anything to not have those tapes surface. You wanna see the tapes? They were originally eight-millimeter, but I got them transferred to video. I'm telling you, it's a wonderful thing, this new video stuff."

"I'll pass."

"You sure? For a thin girl, Sally can really fuck."

"Some other time."

"I'm afraid not, *boychik.* You see, Molly's going to murder you in a little while, and then she's gonna kill herself. She found out you were going back home to your wife and

359

couldn't bear the thought of losing you. Tragic, don't you think?"

"No one will buy that."

Sam held up a piece of paper. "They will when they read this suicide note. One of my many talents. It's not perfect, but no one will question it when things play out. And, unfortunately for you, you don't know our fat little Molly as well as the rest of the people in Old Rotterdam. Stand up and take a close look at her wrists. Go ahead, it's okay, but do it slow."

I did as he suggested. There were faint, barely noticeable scars across the undersides of both wrists.

"High school," Sam said. "Her boyfriend dumped her on prom night. Word spreads in a small town. Even the dogcatcher knows."

"Come on, those are cry-for-help scars. She barely broke the skin, and the scarring is almost imperceptible."

"You must be kidding, *toteleh*. You're whistling in the boneyard here. Those scars will look like the Himalayas when the cops look into her history."

We both knew he was right.

"How are you going to explain you and Molly being together at the bar tonight?"

"That's easy," Sam said. "It even helps

the credibility of the story. She called *me*, remember? There are phone records of such things, no? I'll tell the cops she asked me to set up this little rendezvous with you. Being your friend, how could I refuse? I asked you to meet me here. You agreed. I dropped her off. I drove away and . . . *Voilà!* All of Sam's problems are gone."

"Not Karen," I pointed out. "She's still around."

"I don't give her two weeks with that liver of hers. And, what, you think she's gonna lose a liver and grow a conscience all of a sudden? The joke's on her, anyway."

I was confused. "What's that supposed to mean?"

"Oh, whatsa matter, the big-shot private detective didn't figure everything out? I guess there's no harm in telling you now. Karen didn't kill the other girl. What's her name . . . Andrea, right? Andrea Cotter. She knocked her a little unconscious, maybe, but she didn't kill her."

"You cocksu—" I started for him.

He swung the barrel of the shotgun around. "Sit down, *boychik*, right now! I wasn't planning on killing you myself, because I like you, but I will if you force my hand. I've killed before."

I went over Karen's story in my head.

361

"You son of a bitch! Karen told me you went back to their room to make sure Andrea was dead."

"So — I kept my word, no? I made sure she was dead. It was easy, with her being unconscious already. When Karen came to me and told me she'd killed Andrea, I almost came in my pants. You can believe it. That bitch was gonna rat me out. It was like my prayers were answered. Ah, but, just my luck, she wasn't dead."

"You sick fuck. You've let Karen live her life with sixteen deaths on her head."

"Hey, mister, if she had just listened to what I told her, the fire wouldn't have gone so crazy. Stupid little girl!"

"Hammerling knows," I blurted out.

"Hammerling knows *gotz!* That *nebisheh* thyroid case couldn't find his own *shvontz* with a roadmap. Besides, what's he got in the way of proof, some cockamamie story from a guy he barely knew? So, if you don't mind me asking, how'd you catch on?"

"It was a lot of little things, but," I admitted, "I barely noticed them at first. That fire on my car hood at the hotel, that was a nice touch. You were very matter-of-fact about the young Robby Higgins and his broken family, very sympathetic, almost affectionate. That was very good. If I had thought

362

about it, I suppose you were a little too anxious to get your hands on my faxes from the city. You read them, of course."

"Of course."

"Then you started pressing too hard. You shouldn't have taken me to Hanrahan's that night. For one thing, it hurt your image as poor old Sam the hotel keeper. The fancy car, the cigars, the expensive brandy. Showing off like that was a mistake. It made me question who you really were. Which, by itself, wouldn't have raised my suspicions, but when other things started happening . . . Then you slipped by telling me that Sally had worked for you. First you were almost boastful, and then you cut yourself off mid-sentence. I thought that was odd?"

"That was stupid," Sam agreed. "But what satisfaction is there in things if you can't brag about them?"

"When I later mentioned it to Sally, she fairly spit in my face. I didn't realize it then, but she must have assumed you told me about her past and thought I was soliciting her."

Sam shook his head. "You wouldn't want to hear the phone call I got from her that night. What else?"

"Your biggest mistake was bringing Bailey into it. He was about as subtle as an avalanche. First with all the strong-arm tactics, and then Robby Higgins' old police file magically appearing. I mean, come on! It showed me someone was pushing way too hard to hang Anton Harder for the Fir Grove fire. I think you probably realized as much, which is why you staged the fire at your utility shed. 'Die Jews!' Very nice. But something about that bothered me. It was too convenient. And then there were the footprints."

"Footprints? What you talkin', footprints?"

"In the snow, Sam. When I was helping you put out the fire, I noticed there were no footprints leading away from your hotel. All the footprints ran between the shed and the hotel."

I heard a car coming down the gravel road. A door slammed shut. I turned in the direction of the sound, and when I looked back at Sam a sort of a wistful smile washed across his face. Then I heard footfalls. Sam's help had arrived. Up to now we'd been killing time before killing time. I had to think fast.

"I've got the diary. It's hidden in —"

"This diary?" Lieutenant Bailey asked, Andrea's journal in his hand, as he strode in the door. "Hiding it on your front seat wasn't smart. You stupid fuckup. I'm going

364

to enjoy this."

"Give me the book, idiot," Sam ordered. "You know, if you had listened to me in the first place, this wouldn't have been necessary." Then Sam turned to me. "It's his fault you and Sleeping Beauty are going to die, you know. I told him not to rough you up when he gave you the file, but because you hurt his pride and his little fingers he had to hurt you. Then I told him to make the beating in the woods seem authentic, but no. He couldn't be bothered." Turning back to Bailey: "You fat putz!"

"Shut up, old man," Bailey sneered, and grabbed me by the throat.

"Don't! Schmuck!" Sam barked. "No marks on the bodies. It will ruin everything."

Bailey let me go. Molly stirred slightly. There wasn't much time now.

"Where's the box?" Bailey groused at Sam. "It better all be in there."

"It seems you underestimated Lieutenant Bailey, *boychik*," Sam said. "I guess he liked his career a little more than you thought. You gave us both an out."

Molly moved again, this time raising her arm off the floor.

Sam handed a small cardboard box to Bailey. "Here, you prick. It will be a relief to not have to deal with such an idiot any-more."

"Is this all of it?" Bailey demanded of the old comedian.

"All of it. Look for yourself."

Bailey opened the box and rummaged through it. Obviously, whatever Sam had been holding over the corrupt cop's head was supposed to be in there. I didn't like the smile on Bailey's face when he was done.

"Satisfied?" Sam asked.

Molly's eyes fluttered. If I was going to make a move it would have to be now.

Bailey put the box on the recliner and took the shotgun from Sam. He moved toward me. He *was* going to enjoy this.

"Enough stalling, moron!" Sam egged him on. "Do it!"

Bailey raised the shotgun, but swung it around and buried the butt end in my solar plexus. I collapsed, unable to breathe, chok-ing for air.

"You really are a fucking idiot," Sam yelled. "Now you're gonna have to blow a hole in him there to cover the bruise."

Bailey ignored Sam, talking to me instead. "That's for the kick in my nuts. Now we're even."

I could barely breathe, but managed to get to my knees. When Sam opened up his mouth to say something, Bailey pointed the shotgun at him.

"Shut up, you old cocksucker. Just shut up!"

"He set the fire at the Fir Grove!" I whispered, desperate to buy time.

"No he didn't," Bailey said. "But I can't blame you for trying that."

"Will you shoot him and let's get this over with already?" Sam coaxed. "The fat girl's coming around. I don't want her to know what's happening to her."

At least Sam was consistent: he only killed women in their sleep. Molly rolled over on the couch.

"I told you to shut up. I've taken fucking orders from you for years, and I'm through listening. Get Molly out of here," Bailey said to me. "And don't say a word about this to anyone. I'll handle it."

"What are you doing?" Sam screamed. "You're going to screw it up again!"

"I've done a lot of shit for you, old man, but I never killed nobody. What did Molly ever do to me?"

Sweating and looking very unnerved, Sam suddenly very much resembled the young comedian whom I'd just watched flop on national TV.

"Bailey, Bailey, okay, you're right." Sam

put up his hands. "Don't kill the fat girl. We'll figure something out, you and me. We always have before, right? But him we gotta get rid of."

"Get her out of here!" Bailey prodded me with the shotgun. "Go!"

I got to my feet and gathered up Molly as best I could. She was still out of it, and it was a struggle getting her to the car. I laid her across my backseat. I got behind the wheel and started up the engine, but I couldn't just let Bailey kill Sam in cold blood, though Sam seemed perfectly eager to have Bailey do the same to Molly and me.

"Don't do it!" I shouted, coming back through the door.

Sam looked puzzled, but relieved.

Bailey was angry. "I told you to get the luck outta here."

"It's murder, Bailey. You said it yourself, you never killed —"

The lieutenant turned to face me. "Get the fuck outta here!"

Sam, seeing Bailey was distracted, reached for something under his jacket. It was a big army-issue.45. Bailey wasn't that distracted, and he let Sam have it. The old comedian's head exploded, spraying blood and bone on the cabin walls and the TV screen, which still held the young Sam frozen in time. Sam's body, blown back by the force of the buckshot, crumpled in a heap. Even twisted and headless, Sam's body seemed to exude a kind of evil energy. Then, as if on cue, the pause function clicked off, and there was Sam retreating from the stage in defeat.

Bailey turned the shotgun on me. "This is the last time I'm telling you. Get out!"

I did, grabbing Andrea's journal and my empty .38 as I went. I could not afford to leave any record of my having been there. I pulled away, driving way too fast down the unlit mountain road. Almost to the main turnoff, I checked my rearview mirror. In it, I could see flames snapping at the black night. Sam's cabin was afire. Given the cabin's isolated locale, it was unlikely anyone would notice for quite some time. I thought of Karen, half out of her mind with panic, setting light to Andrea's lifeless body. It occurred to me that the Fir Grove fire had never been put out, that it had burned quietly for sixteen years, the embers smoldering in the hearts of the evil and the innocent alike. I realized that the final body count was much higher than the papers had reported, and that grief has a very long shelf life. As I turned onto the deserted main road, the flames disappearing from view, I wondered if it would all end now, here, finally, whether there would be some measure of peace and redemption found in the cold ashes of Sam's cabin, or if the Fir Grove fire would continue to burn forever.

Epilogue:
Ashes

When you look at the light of the stars, you are looking into the past. When you look at a fresh grave, you are looking into the future. Life is the thirty seconds between starlight and the first shovelful falling.

Andrea Cotter, April 14, 1965

Not everything Andrea wrote was brilliant or original. Though you probably couldn't have convinced me of that until I spent a lifetime at the Swan Song Hotel and Resort. The bit about looking into the past was a paraphrase of something our old high-school science teacher used to say. The rest was pure Andrea. Her journal was crammed with her woman-child philosophy, her poetry and pain. I was both guilt-stricken and exhilarated reading her words. It was a feeling not at all unfamiliar to me.

There is a certain voyeuristic quality to

371

police work. Even the lowliest uniform is thrust into the midst of people's lives — usually very low points in those lives. There were times when I went from buying a cup of coffee one minute, to standing by the crushed and bloodied remains of a woman who'd just thrown herself off the roof of the projects. You are once removed. You watch the curious eyes in the gathering crowd. You listen to their gossiping. A relative of the dead woman arrives. She breaks down. The detectives come. You move on. You buy another cup of coffee. After your shift you drink a beer and tell yourself you are untouched by the desperation of the woman who jumped off the roof. You know it's a lie.

For a time I considered not reading the book at all. An albatross, Karen Rosen had called it. I would weigh it down, I thought, and toss it off the footbridge at Ocean Avenue in Sheepshead Bay. I would burn it, as it should have perished in the first place. I would put it in the safe at the store, or in a box in the attic, leave the pain for someone else to deal with. But what to do with the book was my de-facto responsibility. How would I know what to do with the journal without first reading it?

The night of the fire at Sam's cabin, I drove straight into Old Rotterdam. I called Hanrahan's from a corner pay phone and asked for Sally. She sounded as thrilled to hear from me as she would have been at the prospect of doing shots of Liquid Plumr, but I was determined that none of the grime and ash that had washed off on me should touch Molly. At first Sally resisted my request that she take a break and meet me around the corner from the bar. She resisted until I told her Sam was dead and that the tapes of her were gone.

She took her break and helped me get Molly home and in bed. We worked out our story. If the cops asked, I told Sally to say Molly ran into Sam at the bar. That they had a few drinks together, but Molly wasn't feeling well. Too many drinks too fast. Sam mentioned as much to Sally. Sally asked Sam to take Molly home. As far as Sally knew, Sam had done just that. Molly had been in bed ever since.

"If they want confirmation," I instructed, "you were so concerned, you came over here to check during your break. Molly was passed out in bed, sleeping it off. I don't think she'll remember anything."

Sally was curious to know what really happened. I did not tell her. It wasn't a matter of trust. People cannot repeat what they don't know. If the cops ever worked their way back to Sally, it would be a dead end. At worst, she could point the finger at me, but Molly would be out of it.

I dropped the barmaid back around the corner from Hanrahan's. I promised Sally that her past was her own, that no one would hear about it from me. "The other night," I said, "when I mentioned your having worked for Sam — I didn't know then, but I'm sorry."

"I'm sorry, too, for a lot of things."

The cops did speak to Sally, but only to establish the time Molly and Sam had left the bar. When they talked to Molly, she could barely remember anything. She had passed out in Sam's car, and she woke up in her bed the next morning with a deluxe-sized hangover. The cops never bothered getting in touch with me.

They didn't find a body or any identifiable remains in Sam's cabin. He just seemed to have disappeared. They found his abandoned Caddy in the Bronx on Christmas Day, propped up on cinder blocks, stripped down to the frame. Again there was no sign of Sam. I had no idea what became of Sam's body. What did it matter? That was Bailey's business.

I try not to think too much about Bailey, though I wonder about him sometimes. Would he have been so noble about the act of murder if Molly wasn't there that night? Would he have really killed Sam if the old man hadn't stupidly gone for his .45? I'd like to think that Bailey was just going to throw a scare into Sam. Who can say? I hear that Bailey's still on the job in Old Rotterdam and that he's up for captain. I guess he's not worried about me exposing his past deeds. He's right not to worry. I'm a lot of things, but ungrateful's not one of them.

I hung around Old Rotterdam for another two days just to see how things played themselves out. Besides, I didn't want to call attention to myself by leaving town so close to Sam's sudden and unexplained disappearance. I stayed at a roadside motel. I'd had my fill of old Borscht Belt palaces.

When Molly recovered from her hangover, I took her to dinner as promised. She picked some chop house up near Cooperstown. The place had a huge fiberglass steer out front. When you passed by, the steer pawed the ground with a robotic hoof and steam came out of its nostrils. We stood outside while we waited for our table, and watched two little girls run back and forth in the snow in front of the steer. They got a kick out of the steam. We got a kick out of the kids.

Inside, the tables were all red-and-white gingham and the waitresses wore cowboy boots and big straw hats. Whenever the wait staff got a big tip, they played a tape of some guy screaming "Yahoo!" at the top of his lungs, and of a bullet ricocheting off a cow bell. After a while, you barely noticed. The food was okay and the beer was cheap. We laughed a lot, too much maybe. I could see in Molly's eyes that she wanted to ask about that night. She never did, and I didn't volunteer any information.

When I dropped her home, I thanked her.

"For what?" she wanted to know.

"For saving my life, Molly."

I kissed her as I had done that Saturday night at Hanrahan's and left it there.

The next morning, I went to say goodbye to Dick Hammerling. Hammerling was no fool. He could read the papers and put two and two together. He asked if I had anything to do with the fire at Sam's cabin, or with the old comedian's apparent disappearance. He believed my denials about as much as I believed in the tooth fairy. He told me he was getting out of politics and going back to college.

"Maybe I'll get back into politics again someday, but for the right reasons."

I wished him luck.

Molly was waiting outside in the hall, just as she had that first day. I thanked her once again for all her help and for dinner. I saw that question in her eyes. This time she got up the nerve to ask it.

"What really hap—"

I put my finger across her lips. "Shhh! Did you ever have a dream, Molly, where you tell yourself you've just got to remember, but when you wake up it's gone? What really happened was like that, like one of those dreams. It's gone."

I turned north out of town, toward the old Fir Grove and what had once been Koppelman's Bungalow Colony. Karen Rosen, I thought, for all her sins, had a right to know she hadn't really killed Andrea. I actually turned into the parking lot before reconsidering. In that moment I realized there was nothing I could say to set things right. Telling her she hadn't killed Andrea would only make it worse. At least she believed that part of the nightmare was an accident. Maybe she had taken some measure of comfort in that over the years. Did she really need one more torment so close to her own death? Then again, I could afford to be generous. There were sixteen souls counting off the remaining seconds of Karen Rosen's life who would be far less magnanimous.

I met Anton Harder at the Red Apple Rest on old Route 17. No one knew us there. We were just two men having a conversation. It was uncomfortable and awkward for both of us, but, I think, especially for me. He had helped me, and I had given him my word. Any way I handled it, however, would only serve to feed his anti-Semitism. If I had left town without fulfilling my end of the deal, I would have been the perfect example of the lying, scheming Jew. And if I told him the whole story, the gory details included, I could only imagine what effect that might have. No matter how I might try to dress it up, Harder would hear: This old, scheming, money-grubbing, two-faced Jew pimp and two Jewess whores conspired to burn your poor, innocent mother to death. . . .

I told him the truth. I didn't identify Karen or Andrea by name. He had already guessed at Sam's involvement. He had read the papers. His reaction surprised me.

"I always liked Sam," he said. "He had a way of making me feel special, like him and me were the only two people in the world."

"I know exactly how that is."

We shook hands without having to see who was watching, but I was not so much a fool as to imagine Harder would be magically transformed. Hate isn't immutable, but it isn't clay either.

Aaron was just glad to have me back at work in time for the holiday rush. Katy would be less easily satisfied. It was a delicate balance for the both of us. There were things she knew she shouldn't ask, and there were things I'd promised not to tell. I saved her the trouble of asking and gave an even vaguer version of events than I'd given to Dick Hammerling. Katy would put the pieces together for herself. She didn't say a word about it again until the drive up to her parents' house on Christmas Eve. Sarah was asleep in the backseat.

"You did it, Moses, didn't you?" she said, great pride in her voice. "You put the dead to rest."

"I guess."

With that, Katy took a small gift-wrapped box out of her coat pocket. "Pull over and open it. It's a special gift that can't wait until tomorrow."

I pulled over, unwrapped, and opened the box. Inside was a gold-and-blue enamel shield, a detective's shield. It bore my old badge number.

Katy leaned over and kissed my cheek. "You've earned it, whether or not the world knows it."

She was right. I had earned it.

After dinner, after Katy and Sarah had gone up to bed, I was sitting on the couch admiring the shield my wife had awarded me. I guess there were tears in my eyes. I was being watched. Francis Maloney Sr, whiskey in hand, stood snickering at me. He didn't say anything. He never had to say anything. I put the shield back in my pocket.

I threw him off balance. "How are you feeling?"

"Sorry to disappoint you, but I'm fine."

"I guess I'm responsible for that," I said.

"How's that?"

"I took your advice, Francis. I watched what I wished for. Good night."

On New Year's Day, I called Israel Roth. He was glad to hear from me, but there was a tension in his voice.

"Did you like the scotch?" he wondered.

"You know, Mr, Roth, I wanted to apologize about that. I lost the bottle."

"You did! So you didn't read the note?"

"Note, what note? Oh, before I forget, Sam Gutterman's missing. Did you know?"

The relief in his voice was palpable. "Missing! No, I didn't know."

"Yeah, they found his cabin burned to the ground, and his car turned up in the Bronx on Christmas Day. You said something about a note?"

"It was nothing. Forget it. Happy New Year to you and your family, Mr. Moe."

"The same to you and yours, Mr. Roth."

Did he know I was lying about the note? Maybe. That wasn't the point. Either way, I'd made an old man happy, and that was worth it. Like I told Karen Rosen, I wasn't in the forgiveness business. The funny thing about forgiveness is that it comes from the inside out, not the other way around. All I did was to let Mr. Roth forgive himself. I hoped someday I'd be able to forgive myself for the growing list of my lies of omission.

Everything we do changes us. Some things more than others. My time in Old Rotterdam had gotten me thinking. Old Rotterdam was as much about me as it was about Karen, Andrea, and Sam. I had seen bits of myself reflected in the faces of Hasidic men, in the words of Judas Wannsee, in the shame of Israel Roth, and, yes, even in Anton Harder's hate. Old Rotterdam had made it impossible for me to ignore my Judaism. No longer would I be able to trot it out like a tuxedo when, like with Sam Gutterman, I needed to speak a little Yiddish or cozy up to a customer. I wouldn't be able to put it back in its suit bag when I hung out with my old cop buddies. I was what I was. Now I was going to have to deal with it.

Katy, Sarah, and I started attending Saturday services at a local Reform temple. Katy was thrilled to go. Paradoxically, it seems, converted Jews are less conflicted. For years she had gone to Mass every Sunday, and though she had parted ways with the church even before we met, I think Katy missed the sense of ritual and tradition. I met with the rabbi once a week, on Tuesday nights.

"Who better than a man named Moses should be welcomed back?" he asked at our first meeting.

I reminded him: "Moses never made it to the Promised Land."

"Such is the nature of Jewishness. But will it be you or God that blocks the way?"

It took me a few years to figure out what to do with Andrea's journal. Karen Rosen was right: the journal was an albatross, but not in the way I expected. Like her life, Andrea's journal wasn't any one thing. It was her poems, her thoughts, her observations. It was growing pains painted in words. In some ways I had hoped to find something deep and ugly about her, something to make her death seem less horrific and tragic. No, she had her faults and foibles, her petty jealousies and grudges, but Andrea was very much the girl I had dreamed she was.

I had gone to see R. B. Carter to tell him that his sister was neither a blackmailer nor a murderer and that she had in fact been dead these many years. Like Hammerling and Harder before him, he just seemed relieved. I could not bring myself to give him the ugly details. But R. B. Carter was no innocent, for, in a subversively fitting way, he had been involved in the matter for quite some time.

If it hadn't been a particularly lazy Sunday, if Katy and Sarah hadn't been up visiting the Maloneys, I might have missed it. It was an article in the Sunday *New York Times* detailing the efforts by Albany lobbyists to push a legalized-gambling bill through the state legislature.

CATSKILLS REGION GAMBLING BILL VOTED DOWN

was the headline. Major real-estate concerns, it seemed, had been buying up vast amounts of property for years in anticipation of the bill's passage. The largest of those concerns was a company owned by R. B. Carter. The reporters also cited several less-than-savory tactics the companies had employed to depress the already depressed real-estate prices in the region. Guess who owned the old Fir Grove property? That's right, R. B. Carter. Carter had leased the land to the likes of Anton Harder in an attempt to drive down the prices of the surrounding real estate. There was enough irony in that to make me puke.

Andrea's journal wasn't always an albatross. Funny things happened in her life. She had a dog named Sweetie that used to pee on her mother's spider plant. She loved her big brother. She was jealous of the beautiful girls in school and thought Mr. Cantor, her social-studies teacher, was the handsomest man on the planet. She loved the Mets even though they were terrible. She thought George Harrison was the cute Beatle, but was hypnotized by John Lennon.

I thought back to the time Lennon was in my shop and we joked about Paul. That's one of my favorite memories. My favorite passage in Andrea's journal, though, is this:

Got my copies of the literary magazine. There was a great poem in it. It wasn't great like Ginsberg great. It was just that the poet was so in love with the girl he was writing about. I want someone to love me like that someday. I ran into him on the boardwalk . . . on purpose. His name is Moses. I had him autograph his poem. That was weird, I guess. He's pretty cute. Looked up his phone number. 332-8594. Maybe I'll call him when I get back from the Fir Grove.

I still have the journal. It's just hard to let some things go.

AFTERWORD
BY REED FARREL COLEMAN

In many ways, *Redemption Street* was a star-crossed project. As its author, the novel is, for me, an exercise in mixed feelings. While it no doubt represents some of the best of what the series has to offer, its lack of commercial and critical success has been my most bitter pill. I used to joke — maybe half-joke is the more appropriate phrase — that it was the first book in history to go direct from the printer to the remainder bin. For a long time, my friends and colleagues would whisper the words *Redemption Street* like my mom would whisper the word *cancer* and spit. But it is my nature to keep moving forward and my next Moe Prager Mystery, *The James Deans*, won the Shamus, Barry, and Anthony Awards. It was also nominated for the Edgar, Macavity, and Gumshoe Awards.

In the intervening years since the publication of *Redemption Street*, however, I've found that the book had many devoted fans, including numerous booksellers and fellow writers. While I have received more comments and fan mail for *Walking the Perfect Square, The James Deans, Soul Patch* and even some of my Dylan Klein novels, the comments and letters for *Redemption Street* are by far the most passionate. I've also found a real interest, almost a hunger, in fans of the later Moe books for a re-issue of *Redemption Street.*

I would like to say that when David Thompson and McKenna Jordan of Busted Flush Press and Murder by the Book in Houston first approached me with the idea of issuing a new, quality paperback edition of the novel that I immediately jumped at the idea, but I can't. For while I was of course curious about their interest and the devotion of *Redemption Street*'s fans, I wasn't anxious to revisit the events surrounding its initial release. That you've just read the new paperback edition the three of us discussed a few years back is both a testament to David and McKenna's persistence and my re-examination of the novel.

Moe may be a big believer in fate, but I'm not. Yet it would be less than truthful of me not to confess that something resembling my understanding of fate had a hand in the publication of the book you're holding in your hand. In late 2006 and in early 2007, I was approached to write essays on the persistent nature of the private detective novel and on the growth of the ethnic detective in mystery fiction. While examining my own work and that of my colleagues in order to write these essays, I found that I was drawn not to the obvious choice, *The James Deans*, but to *Redemption Street*.

In rereading *Redemption Street* for the first time in four years, I rediscovered for myself what it was about the novel that made me so enjoy writing it and, perhaps, came to understand the chemistry that makes the novel so engaging to its devotees. First and most evidently, *Redemption Street* is, if I do say so myself, a kickass title. But the appeal of the novel is obviously much much deeper than the title page.

What I noticed as I read was that the Moe I presented in *Redemption Street* was willing to bare different aspects of himself than the Moe of *Walking the Perfect Square*. In *Walking . . .* the reader is introduced to Moe the person. In *Redemption Street,* the reader is introduced to Moe's soul, particularly his Jewish soul. For Moe, that internal tug of war between his mixed and contradictory feelings about his own "Jewish-ness" is an essential struggle that continues to playout during the course of the series. And what, if not a protagonist's struggles, is it that gets a reader to invest his or her real feelings in the life of a fictional character?

That I then externalized that tug of war by placing Auschwitz survivor Israel Roth on one end of the rope and leader of the Yellow Stars, Judas Wannsee, on the other, was not anticipated. Amazingly, neither of these characters was part of a master plan. Neither Mr. Roth nor Wannsee came into my head until I actually wrote the Catskill sections of the book. Mr. Roth, maybe second only to Moe, is the most beloved character in the Prager novels. He is such a powerful presence in my own life that even I think of him as a living breathing human being. I also represented Moe's struggles by having Moe bounce between characters who represented the Freudian constructs of Moe's self: Sudden Sam Gutterman (id), Israel Roth (ego), and Judas Wannsee (super ego). I think some people enjoy the novel because I took on serious topics like cultural assimilation, Jewish self-hatred, and anti-Semitism.

But at its core, *Redemption Street* is the work that lays out the pattern of Moe's obsession with the past and his dread of its implications for the future. *Walking the Perfect Square* lays out the arc of the series, not its emotional underpinnings. Moe Prager is a sometimes reluctant, sometimes eager slave to the past and nowhere is that clearer than in this novel. Because for Moe, the past is never really past, and it's always personal. Always. Until I wrote *Empty Ever After,* the fifth installment in the series and in some sense a companion piece to *Redemption Street,* none of Moe's cases was as personal as the long delayed investigation into the death of his high school crush, Andrea Cotter.

Oddly enough, after going through all this soul searching and analysis, I've come to the conclusion that it doesn't in fact matter why people have a soft spot for *Redemption Street.* I am just gratified that they do. For my own self, I've come to the realization that writing *Redemption Street* was crucial to the series, that without it, *The James Deans, Soul Patch,* and *Empty Ever After* would not have been what they are. For in *Redemption Street,* Moe Prager reveals the depth of his soul and establishes many of the central characters and themes integral to the series. So while other titles in the series have received critical acclaim, garnered nominations and awards, had greater commercial success, none is more essentially a Moe novel than *Redemption Street.*

Reed Farrel Coleman
October 2007

ABOUT THE AUTHOR

Reed Farrel Coleman was Brooklyn born and raised. He is the former Executive Vice President of Mystery Writers of America. His sixth novel, *The James Deans,* won the Shamus, Barry and Anthony Awards for Best Paperback Original. The book was further nominated for the Edgar, Macavity, and Gumshoe Awards. He was the editor of the short story anthology *Hardboiled Brooklyn* and his short stories and essays appear in *Wall Street Noir, Damn Near Dead* and several other publications. Reed lives with his family on New York's Long Island. Visit him online at www.reedcoleman.com.

The employees of Thorndike Press hope you have enjoyed this Large Print book. All our Thorndike and Wheeler Large Print titles are designed for easy reading, and all our books are made to last. Other Thorndike Press Large Print books are available at your library, through selected bookstores, or directly from us.

For information about titles, please call:
    (800) 223-1244

or visit our Web site at:
    http://gale.cengage.com/thorndike

To share your comments, please write:
    Publisher
    Thorndike Press
    295 Kennedy Memorial Drive
    Waterville, ME 04901